About the Author

Maryka Biaggio is a psychology professor turned novelist who specializes in historical fiction based on real people. She loves unearthing the stories of people overlooked by history and bringing them back to life—portraying their challenges and foibles and rekindling their emotional world. She prides herself on carefully researching the period, place, and people and providing readers with an immersive experience. Her fiction has won several accolades, including the Willamette Writers Award, an Oregon Writers Colony Award, the *Historical Novel Society Review* Editors' Choice, La Belle Lettre Award, the Upper Peninsula of Michigan Notable Books Award, and a Regional Arts and Culture Council grant. She served on the Board of the Historical Novel Society North America Conference from 2015–2025. She's an avid opera fan and enjoys gardening, art films, and, of course, great fiction. She lives in Portland, Oregon. You can learn more at her website: www.marykabiaggio.com

By the Same Author

The Model Spy
The Point of Vanishing
Eden Waits
Parlor Games

Gun Girl and the Tall Guy

Maryka Biaggio

Gun Girl and the Tall Guy

Pegasus

PEGASUS PAPERBACK

A CIP catalogue record for this title is
available from the British Library.

ISBN-978-1-80468-092-6

Pegasus is an imprint of
Pegasus Elliot MacKenzie Publishers Ltd.
www.pegasuspublishers.com

First Published in 2025

Pegasus
Sheraton House Castle Park
Cambridge CB3 0AX England

Dedication

To my wonderful chosen family of friends.

Prologue
Tampa, Florida, May 1990

The police had picked up Ed's mother about a mile and a half from the nursing home. She wasn't difficult to track down: a wizened, round-faced woman barely five feet tall, her silver hair recently permed, her step spry. She was wearing her favorite dress, the one with a bold floral pattern and lacy white collar, and hurrying along as if she had a destination in mind. But when the police asked her where she was going, she told them, "Mind your own business, buster."

Apparently, she'd made her escape sometime after breakfast. When the staff noticed she was missing, they'd phoned him and the police. Now that she had been returned safely to the home, Ed intended to have a serious talk with her.

"What were you thinking, Mom, roaming the streets like that?" She sat on her bed smiling impishly, dangling her legs like a youngster perched proudly on a fence.

"I didn't want them to catch up with me."

"Who, the staff? Why were you running away?"

"If they find out who I am, they'll take me to New York."

"Nobody's going to take you to New York."

She tilted her head and gave him one of her waggish

smiles. "How do you know, Eddie?"

"Because this is where you live now."

She pursed her lips, and the wrinkles around her mouth puckered. With a sigh, she said, "If that's what you say."

"Now, I want you to promise me you won't try to leave again."

"I'll promise if you take me to Dairy Queen for a curly-top cone."

Good God, she could be difficult. This was probably the best he could hope for. "Okay, after lunch, I'll take you out."

His mother looked at the photographs on her dresser. She pointed at the one of him, his older brother, Patrick, and their father sitting on the porch steps of their white cottage on Long Island. "I like that one of you and Patrick with your father the best. Look how happy you all are."

That picture was a favorite of his, too. He hardly remembered his father, but when he looked at that photograph, he could almost pretend he recalled the day it was taken. He was only two years old at the time. He straddled his father's knee, and his father's good arm was wrapped around his waist. Patrick, who was five, stood beside them. Even with their father sitting down, Ed could tell he was a big man, probably a little over six feet tall.

Both boys must have inherited their body type from their father, because they were tall and husky, too. Sometimes when he walked beside his mother, he noticed people smiling or chuckling. They made a comical pair, his diminutive mother, all smiles, strolling along with her hand tucked under his arm, and him hunched over so he could hear her chattering away.

"Yeah," he said. "I like that one, too. Whatever happened to that house on Long Island?"

His mother had been given to reminiscing lately, and he liked drawing her out because he knew little about her early life. The doctor at the nursing home said that looking to the past was common in the advanced years. And his mother had recently turned eighty-six, so she certainly qualified as being in her dotage. Still, she got confused from time to time, and sometimes he couldn't make sense of her conversation. He'd just wait her out when that happened or steer her back to a more sensible topic.

"Those were happy days, when we lived in that house," she said. "But it took some doing getting there."

In the Pink
Brooklyn, January 4–5, 1924

She smiled sweetly, showing off the dimples her Eddie so admired, and said, "Please, sir, I'd like a dozen eggs."

Celia Cooney wore the sleek sealskin coat her husband, Ed, had bought for her, and she'd angled her tam-o'-shanter across her brow. Reaching into her pocket she grabbed the compact pistol, which fit snugly in her palm. *Gosh,* she thought, *won't the fellas be flabbergasted when I point my stubby twenty-five at them?*

When Ed, acting his part, turned and slid the imaginary carton toward her, she pulled out her gun. "Stick 'em up."

His arms shot up like one of those monkeys attached to a pair of sticks. She burst out laughing.

Ed scowled, pretending he was angry. "No, Celia, you can't laugh at the man. That'll only goad him. And we don't want them eggs scrambled."

"I know, Eddie." She tamped down a chuckle. "I'll do it right next time."

"Okay, let's take it from the top."

They practiced the whole routine again. Ed had come up with the idea for the stick-up business. They'd been married for four months when Celia told him she was pregnant and didn't want to raise their baby in a crummy one-room joint. He said that they should start saving up for a better place. But every time they put a few dollars aside they thought of something else they needed—like a winter coat for her or wool socks for Ed. And with Ed not wanting her to work at the laundry while she was pregnant, it got more and more difficult to save money.

"Something's got to give, Eddie. I won't have our kid grubbing around the streets."

That's when he said they could consider pulling off a holdup.

Celia had her doubts. "So, buster, how are we supposed to get away with this big-time holdup?"

He rubbed his chin and thought a minute. "We pick a place not too far away and get in and out lickety-split. And I make up fake license plates for the getaway car."

"You really think that could work?"

"Sure, we just plan it all real careful."
Maybe he was right. They sure weren't getting anywhere on his thirty dollars a week. "Let me think about it. I'll tell you tomorrow."

***

Celia certainly didn't want to make a habit of stealing. Even when she was a hungry kid she rarely thieved. She must have been eight or nine when she figured out how to scrounge up a few pennies for herself. She'd grown up in a tenement in lower Manhattan and knew every phone booth for blocks around. Late mornings, after she'd turned the take from her beggings over to her mother, she'd go around and check for left-behind pennies. She didn't always find any, but when she did, she went to the market on Fourth Street and Lafayette to show them off.

"Hello, Mr. Lehrman," she'd say. "Business hopping today?"

He always laughed when she talked to him like she was one of his cronies. Then she asked him if he had any fruit for her.

"Well, let me see, Cecilia." He called her that even though her name was Celia, and she thought if she ever took to the stage that's the name she'd use. Anyway, Mr. Lehrman would pick out an apple or two or maybe a few plums, whatever beat-up pieces nobody else would settle for.

"Thanks. You want me to buy a newspaper for you?"

Sometimes he'd say yes and give her two cents for the daily, and she'd fetch it from the corner newsstand. Then she'd ask the newsie if he wanted to buy one of her apples or plums for a penny. If he did, she'd come out ahead.

If she hadn't found any pennies in the phone booths that day, she'd go around the back of Mr. Lehrman's grocery and check on what he'd thrown out. He was always nice to her, and she never stole from him. If he hadn't put anything in the garbage she might go to another grocery stand. She was a scrawny half-pint so it was easy to hide behind a customer and grab a little something. But she only did that if hunger got the better of her, and she always played it safe and got away clean.

***

After thinking it over, Celia figured if she and Ed were careful, they could probably pull off a holdup. The following day, she told him, "All right, but we have to plan every little step. And dress up nice, like we're a couple of upper-crust types. Then they won't suspect us."

They worked out all their moves, from casing the store to making their getaway, even the neighborhood they'd target. Celia said Saturday was the biggest shopping day so they decided on late Saturday night when stores were preparing to close.

"There ought to be plenty of dough in the cash registers then," Ed said.

But come Saturday, she was as nervous as a mouse cornered by a cat. Being pregnant made her moody, and she kept bouncing between being happy as a song and touchy and sentimental. "Are you sure we won't get caught, Eddie?"

"No, doll, as long as we stick to the routine we'll be fine."

After Ed left to borrow his boss's car from the automobile shop, Celia dressed in her nicest outfit: a beaded pearl-gray dress, new nylon stockings, and a smart felt cloche. She only wore her one nice outfit when she and Ed went out for chop suey or to the movie house. And since she was petite and baby-faced, whenever she dolled up a few guys would always wink or whistle.

She plunked down at the table by the radiator to keep warm and looked around their shabby room. It cost them seven dollars a week, and that was no deal. The wallpaper was peeling in the corner by their bed, and the table tottered at the slightest touch. She hated sharing the bathroom down the hall with everybody else on the floor. The guys never cleaned up after themselves, except for her Eddie, and it always stank of pee and mildew. She was daydreaming about how nice it'd be to have a place with a regular kitchen, not just a hot plate, and even a bedroom when Ed walked in.

"Okay, sweets. Let's get us some dough."

Seeing Ed's sunny Irish smile always cheered her up. He was tall and beefy and looked downright dapper in his navy-and-gray-striped tie and wool overcoat. She slipped on her sealskin, and they waltzed out of there like they were headed for the Ziegfeld Follies.

Ed opened the car door for her and held out his hand. "Here you go, princess."

She smiled. He was always coming up with new names for her.

He hopped in and pulled the car onto the street. Celia smoothed her hand over the Oldsmobile's ribbed seat. "This sure is a nice jalopy."

"Nothing but the best for my baby. It's the newest model, an Oldsmobile Six." He glanced at her. "How are you feeling?"

"Not so nervous anymore. I know just what to do."

Ed reached over and curled his big paw around her hand. "That's my girl."

He was a good driver—since he worked in an auto repair shop and knew all about cars—and Celia relaxed and took in the scenery: the brick apartment buildings lining Atlantic Avenue and the few people out on the sidewalks bundled against the wind. It was a cold night and she could see her breath inside the car—and Ed's too. She could tell that he was excited because his breath steamed out in big puffy funnels.

They cruised down Seventh Avenue looking for a quiet business.

"Hey," Ed said, "what do you think about this place?" He pulled over in front of a Thomas Roulston Grocery Store.

She looked through the windows of the brightly lit store. "I don't see any customers."

Roulston's was a new store, part of a big chain, and popular with Brooklynites. She'd heard Mr. Gualazzi, the grocer on their street, complain the chain was putting the squeeze on him and other neighborhood stores. She figured it was as good a place as any to rob.

Ed kept the car running and leaned forward so he could look around her. "I just see three clerks. We ought to be able to handle them."

Her heart started ticking fast, and her mouth turned cottony. She nodded at Ed and said, "Okay, buster, it's showtime."

He thumped a hand on the steering wheel. "Time to make your entrance."

She shoved the car door open and stepped out. She bent over and gave Ed a big smile to show him she wasn't afraid. "Break a leg, partner."

She slammed the car door shut and headed into the store. The man behind the counter was arranging cigarette packs, while the two clerks in the aisles tidied up the canned goods. There were three more clerks she hadn't spotted from the street mingling at the back of the store. A couple of them were brawny, maybe even as tall as her Eddie. They looked all proper and threatening in their white coats. *Oh no,* she thought, *that's six clerks in all. And I'm such a simpleton, they'll laugh at me and throw me out on my neck.*

Now what? She and Ed hadn't bargained on having to handle more than two or three clerks. Should she go ahead with the plan? She figured if she backed out Ed would be disappointed. And they needed the money something terrible, what with still owing on her fur coat, the rent coming due every Friday, and a baby on the way. And Ed said the gun would talk for itself if she let it. So she told herself to buck up and marched to the counter.

"Yes, miss?" the clerk asked, nice as pie.

"Please, sir, I'd like a dozen eggs."

"Of course." He was about thirty with a pale complexion and small ears that stuck out like handles on fancy teacups. He turned on his heel and grabbed a carton of eggs from behind the counter.

While he was wrapping up the eggs, Ed walked in and nodded at her. She reached into her coat pocket and pulled out the gun. "Stick 'em up. Quick."

What little pink the guy had in his face drained away, and he threw up his arms.

"Look back there," she said to Ed, bouncing her head toward the aisles.

Ed was no dummy. He pulled out his two pistols.

"You, mister, join those others."

He looked at her. "Cover 'em."

Celia aimed her pistol at the clerk and motioned for him to move it along. "And keep your hands up."

When the other clerks saw their pal heading their way with his hands up, they froze and put their hands up, too. The clerk turned to face her. "We don't want any trouble."

"Then play it smart, genius, and don't make any," she said, giving her gun a bounce. "This ain't no parlor game."

She heard Ed rummaging around. Coins clattered; he must have dropped some change. But she kept her eyes latched on the clerks. They looked silly—six big guys in matching white coats kowtowing to five-foot-one Celia Cooney.

After a minute or two Ed hollered, "Don't make a move."

That was her signal to get going, and she headed for the door. Ed called out, "Okay, if you want your head blown off, just try and follow us."

Celia pushed the door open and held it for Ed. He backed out, keeping his guns aimed at the clerks.

The car was still purring. They hopped in and slammed the doors shut. Ed eased the car onto the street, and they hightailed it out of there without a hitch.

"Don't be speeding now, Eddie. We're not at the races."

"Don't worry, sugar."

Ed swung around the corner and drove the car smooth as silk. They were home in less than ten minutes. They'd only passed a single copper, who was strolling down the sidewalk as if he hadn't a care in the world.

"You go on in, doll. I'll just park the car and fix the plates."

Celia paced around their room like a caged cat waiting for Ed, hoping nobody would see him before he got to his shop and changed the license plates. She pinned the old shawl they used for a curtain over the window so gawkers wouldn't see them with their guns and loot.

Finally, he burst through the door with a big grin plastered on his face. "We did it, Celia. You were a peach."

"Oh, Eddie, you sure we got away clean?"

"Squeaky clean."

He emptied his pockets onto the table, slapping down the coins and smoothing out the scrunched-up bills. Taking out an envelope, he peeked inside. "Well, lookie here. Nothing but tens and twenties. And a few checks."

Ed lit a Chesterfield, took a big puff, and swept his arm through the air like he was in the movies.

She chuckled and said, "Yeah, you're a regular crackerjack."

They sat down and counted their loot. It came to six-hundred-seventy-two bucks and a heap of change, some of the pennies shiny new. She'd never seen so much money. They were in the pink!

But when she turned out the lights and crawled into bed, gloom and fright washed over her. What if the cops came banging on their door? Ed had wrapped the guns in a shirt and hidden them in the bureau, but it wouldn't take the cops any time at all to find them and the money. She hated to think of her and Ed locked up in jail like riffraff.

She started crying.

Ed wrapped his arm around her. "What's the matter, kid?"

She didn't want to admit she was scared to the bone, not when Ed was flying high. She said, "It's the baby. Thinking about the baby makes me all flibberty."

On the Case
Brooklyn, January 5, 1924

Captain William Casey sat down on the bed and sloughed off his shoes. He looked up at his wife, who stood over him with crossed arms, and said, "I'm just asking you to be patient."

The phone jangled from the kitchen. He grimaced and said, "Jeez, can't they leave me alone one Saturday night a month?"

But he was relieved the phone had interrupted the argument he and Fiona were having. Quarreling with her always discombobulated him. "Come on, Bill," she'd been saying. "All you have to do is ask for a month off. How hard can that be?"

She didn't understand all the pressure he was under. Casey had recently been promoted to captain and head of investigations in Brooklyn and Queens, and the commissioner was leaning hard on him to shut down the speakeasies and clean up the streets. Fiona complained about the long hours but not about the pay raise. They were putting their son through the military academy in Virginia, and Fiona had been angling to take an honest-to-goodness vacation to Ireland on a pricey ocean liner. They'd been saving up for it for four years, after she'd inherited three-hundred dollars when her parents died in an ugly car crash.

They were supposed to take the trip this summer. But he doubted he could get permission to take an entire month off so soon after his promotion. And now she was threatening to visit their daughter in Boston if he didn't ask for the time off. He resented the threat. Not only did he hate bumping around the house by himself, but he'd miss seeing their sweetheart of a daughter.

He trudged to the kitchen and lifted the receiver off its cradle. "Casey here."

"Bill, you need to get over to Roulston's on Seventh and Seventh. They just called in a robbery."

"Anybody hurt?"

"No, but I got a *Daily Eagle* reporter breathing down my neck. Can I give him the address?"

"He'll sniff it out sooner or later. Tell him to make himself scarce when I get there."

"I'll call Frank and send him over, too."

Frank Gray was his second-in-command, the detective who usually accompanied him to crime scenes, but this weekend was his wife's birthday. He hated to bother him. "No, just send a few officers."

"There are already two on the scene."

"Okay, I'm on my way."

Fiona had followed him to the kitchen. "What is it this time?"

"A grocery store robbery. Shouldn't take me long. We can talk about the trip tomorrow."

Casey slipped on his shoes and donned his overcoat. Fiona walked up to him and straightened his coat collar. She was two inches taller than him, which hadn't bothered him most of their twenty-seven years of marriage. But lately he'd put on weight around the middle, and standing beside her willowy frame made him feel like a fire plug. When they were out in public, he often wondered if people were thinking: How'd a block-headed slouch like him land this beauty?

He eased behind the wheel of his Ford and headed for Roulston's. He hated these night-time interruptions. It was bad enough traipsing around Brooklyn all day hunting lawbreakers, but Commissioner Enright and Mayor Hylan were pressing precincts across New York to do something about the uptick in crime.

He hadn't caught up on his sleep since the New Year's Eve fiasco. Prohibition Enforcement Chief Merrick had bragged he'd make this New Year's the driest in history, dispatching a hundred and fifty agents to confiscate booze. Instead, half of Brooklyn turned out to celebrate in the streets, firing off guns, boldly swigging rum, and generally creating a fracas banging pots and pans and tooting horns. The newspapers had a heyday, taunting Merrick as a showboater and claiming liquor had flooded the city with headlines like FATHER TIME REELS OUT ON A JAG and STORK'S GAIT UNSTEADY AS HE DROPS NEW YEAR BABY.

Casey pulled up in front of Roulston's Grocery and trotted into the store. The lighting was good, and he spied a spray of coins on the floor by the cash register. Two police officers were surveying the scene, and a couple of reporters with their pencils working overtime listened to one of the clerks jabber away. "It was a dame, all right, and she meant business. Sure knew how to handle a pistol."

"Okay, fellas." Casey inserted himself into the circle. "Let me do my job, and then you can get back to your questions." He asked the clerks, "Can we go somewhere private?"

One of them said, "Sure, the back room."

Casey and the two cops followed the six clerks to the back of the store, got their names, and interviewed them about the robbery. It was the damnedest thing—a pretty slip of a girl, maybe eighteen years old dressed up in a fancy dress and fur coat with a man of about six feet, wielding three guns between them. All the clerks had gotten a good look at the thieves and figured they could pick them out of a lineup. The girl had a bobbed hairstyle, but so did a million other flappers in New York. Still, the two had scored about six hundred eighty dollars, a big haul. Casey knew that once robbers got a taste of that kind of money they'd likely strike again. He'd put out their description to precincts across Brooklyn. It shouldn't be too hard to capture such a unique twosome.

As he headed out, one of the reporters hollered to him, "Hey, detective, you got any leads on the dame? Is she on your wanted list?"

No, he didn't have any idea who the woman bandit was, and he wasn't about to divulge this to the papers. These damn reporters were always trying to make the department look bad. "We're working on it. Maybe you guys can tell the story straight for a change and help us catch these hoodlums."

The Brooklyn Daily Eagle, Page 1
January 6, 1924

Woman with Gun Holds up
Six Men as Pal Robs Store

An order for eggs acted as a prelude to a startling holdup in the Thomas Roulston store at Seventh Ave. and Seventh St. late last night. The order was given by a woman richly dressed and, as John Hogan, 372 Eighth St., sought to comply with it, he was confronted with an automatic gun held in the hand of a man accomplice, who sneaked in behind the woman.

The woman whipped out another automatic and ordered Hogan into the back room, where there were five other clerks about to leave for the night, and she held them all at bay while the accomplice went behind the counter and emptied the cash register of $680, the receipts of the day. The pair escaped in a motorcar.

The woman is described as good looking, about five feet five inches in height, of dark complexion, with bobbed hair. She wore a dark fur coat. The man is about six feet, with a solid build, and was attired in a brown overcoat.

Going Shopping
Brooklyn, January 6–9, 1924

On Sunday, Celia and Ed attended nine o'clock Mass at St. Augustine's. They sat in the same pew as Eddie's mother and two brothers and afterwards visited with them on the church steps. But it was biting cold so they only chatted a few minutes before saying their see-you-laters. On the way home, they bought two newspapers and, surprise of surprises, they were on the front page of *The Brooklyn Daily Eagle*.

They read the column about their stick-up aloud to each other at least twenty times. It got funnier every time they read it, especially how they made Celia four inches taller, claimed she whipped out two guns, and didn't say a word about how Ed looked like Jack Dempsey, only with blue eyes and ginger hair. After they'd laughed themselves out, they got serious about planning their new life.

On Monday morning, Ed got up early, as usual, to start his workday at the auto shop. He planned on knocking off after lunch to look at an apartment they'd spotted in the Sunday newspaper. It was around the corner from the garage, on Pacific Street, only one block from his mother's place. They had their fingers crossed no one else would beat them to it.

After Celia cleaned up the breakfast dishes and swept

the floor, she went to Gualazzi's Grocery and picked up two boxes for packing up their belongings. She stopped at McCrory's and bought a Sherlock Holmes novel, *Valley of Fear*, which cost more than the dime novels she usually purchased. She settled down to read, but she couldn't concentrate. She was too juiced up about their stash of coins in the coffee tin and bills folded into the Sears and Roebuck Catalog.

So she browsed through the catalog and admired goods for babies: soft-soled shoes, cribs and carriages, bottles and teething rings, snuggly gowns, Baby Sunshine dolls, and things she'd never heard of, like a book to keep track of baby's new teeth, first step, and such. When she was a kid she didn't even know there were so many things people could buy. She figured everybody in the city lived in a crowded room with laundry lines strung across the alleys. But she supposed all kids thought the world was just what they knew, at least until they went to school and learned some geography.

Ed came home earlier than usual. "Hey, doll, we got the place. The landlady lives upstairs and keeps it up real nice."

Celia popped out of her chair and gave him a peck on the cheek. "Tell me all about it."

"It's roomy, with a parlor and a cellar. You're gonna love it."

"Is it furnished?"

"No, none of the good places are. But it's got a refrigerator and a stove."

"That's swell." Celia's family had never owned an

icebox or a stove. It'd be great fun stocking up on all kinds of food and cooking fancy meals for Ed.

Ed asked, "What do you say we go furniture shopping tomorrow?"

She clapped her hands together. "Is the sky high?"

He took Tuesday afternoon off and got cleaned up, even scrubbed his fingernails. That was one thing Celia liked about Ed—how he kept washed and tidy, just like her. Growing up, it seemed like she and her brothers and sisters were always grimy. She supposed the last thing her mother wanted to do after slaving over laundry all day was scrub a bunch of squirmy kids.

They strolled to John A. Schwartz's furniture store on Broadway, holding hands the whole way. Of course, Celia was wearing her fur coat, and she felt as cheery as one of those housewives in the advertisements.

The owner even waited on them. He was a pleasant man, dressed in a pinstripe suit and silk tie. Walking right up to them, he offered his hand. "Hello, folks, I'm Mr. Schwartz, how can I help you today?"

Ed shook his hand. "I'm Ed, and this is my wife-to-be, Celia. We're pretty much in need of a full set of furniture to get us off to a good start."

"Well, let me congratulate you. I'm sure we can accommodate your every need. Shall we start with the kitchen?"

That sounded swell to Celia, and she liked feeling like they were somebodies, real Americans who could waltz into a store full of thousands of dollars' worth of goods and pick out whatever they wanted. They could even ask

Ed's mother and brothers over for supper sometime. Her serving pot roast to Mrs. Cooney, Owen, and Willy—wouldn't that be dandy!

"Oh, yes, Mr. Schwartz," she said. "I'd like a nice dining table. So I can entertain six people." She winked at Ed. What fun it was pretending she was a high-society dame.

Mr. Schwartz led the way to the back of the store, weaving past sofas and bedroom sets and even desks. Right away Celia spotted a shiny, dark-colored table; she could practically see her reflection in it. She ran her hand over the polished top.

"That's mahogany. Comes with six chairs and that sideboard." Mr. Schwartz flapped a hand at the cabinet against the wall.

"Hey, how about this one?" Ed asked.

"That's fumed oak, very sturdy."

She looked at Ed. "I really like this one."

Ed came up beside her and smoothed his hand over it. The price tag read 'Mahogany Dining Room Set, $189.' *Gosh,* she thought, *that's an awful lot of money. Maybe I ought to pick out something less expensive.*

Ed looked at the table, then looked at her. "Well, what do you know, it's the same color as your eyes—real dark chocolate."

He slapped his hand on the table and smiled at Mr. Schwartz. "We'll take it."

"You won't be disappointed. That's a fine set." Mr. Schwartz gave them a sure-headed nod. He slipped his hand inside his suit jacket, pulled out a pen, and wrote

'Sold' on the sales tag.

Next they meandered over to the bedroom sets. Celia could hardly believe her eyes—there were beds in maple, oak, and other kinds of wood, with matching dressers and bedside tables.

She remembered a night when she was sleeping on the floor between her two sisters and waking to rough thumps and thuds in the hallway. It was her earliest recollection, and she must have been about four years old. She had checked to see if her sister, May, was awake. Yes, she was lying on her back, stock still, with her eyes wide open.

"Hey," Celia said. "Da is home."

"I know," May said. "Keep quiet."

Celia, who was about the height of a doorknob and as light and slender as a board, always slept between May and Annie on the floor opposite the door. A funnel of light from the streetlight lit up the narrow bed beneath the window, and Celia could see her mother curled up there.

The door swung open, and her father stumbled in. He shuffled to the shelves over the sink and rummaged around. "Evelyn, where'd you put the money?"

As their mother raised herself up on the bed, its springs creaked. "Quiet! The girls are sleeping."

"I will not be quiet. I know you're hiding the money."

"There isn't any. I spent it on groceries. Come to bed."

Her father teetered toward the bed. "Get up, goddamn it, or I'll deck you."

May grabbed Celia by the arm. "Come on. Bring your blanket. You, too, Annie." May pulled her sisters to standing and dragged them to the door.

Their father swung his arm at them as they passed by, clipping May's shoulder. "Get out of my way, you."

Just as May pulled Celia out the door, Annie slammed it behind them. Their father's shouts sounded down the hallway of the tenement building. "I told you to get me the money."

Celia asked May, "Where are we going?"

"To the cellar."

At the end of the hallway, they rounded the stairwell and plodded down the steps. It was dark, and Celia had to grope her way down the staircase. When they got to the bottom, Celia couldn't see anything in the pitch-dark space. It smelled damp and musty.

"I can't find the light switch," May said. Celia heard her patting the wall, and then a light bulb dangling from the ceiling flicked on.

In the room overhead, Celia heard her father crashing around and her mother and father hollering. The words were muffled, but she could tell they were fighting, maybe even throwing things at each other.

Annie said, "One of these days, Da's going to drink himself to death."

"Let him," May said. "We'd be better off without him."

Celia looked at the cement walls and metal chute high up on one wall. A big pile of coal spread out over most of the floor below the chute. Black soot was everywhere. She lifted a foot and examined her sole. It was covered with soot.

May went over to a folded-up hunk of canvas in the

corner and picked it up. "Help me with this, will you, Annie?"

Annie grabbed one side of the canvas, and she and May unfurled the canvas and walked over to the coal pile. They spread it out and draped it over the coal. Then May and Annie climbed on top of the coal pile and stomped around on top, smoothing the top out into a level area.

"Come on up, Celia," May said.

Celia hopped onto the canvas and joined her sisters on top of the mound.

"It's nice and level here," May said, patting a space in the middle. "You can even wiggle around and make it fit your body if you want."

May climbed down, turned off the light, and joined them on top of the coal pile.

Celia lay down on the canvas, and May and Annie nestled on each side of her. She spread her blanket over her, turned on her side, and dug out a hollow for her shoulder. Sure enough, the coal shifted around beneath her.

"That was a good idea, May," Annie said, "plucking this tarp out of the garbage."

"Yeah, this beats getting stumbled over in the night."

Celia asked, "Can this be our new bedroom?"

"Sure," May said, "it's nice having it to ourselves, isn't it?"

Her sisters' bodies warmed her up in no time, and even though she could still hear her parents shuffling around and arguing above them, she fell into a nice, deep slumber. In the morning, they folded up the canvas and put it on the floor in the corner—knowing they might be back.

Celia had the time of her life picking out furniture for their new home, buying big-ticket items like a maple bedroom set. Ed was a real gentleman, letting her pick out whatever she wanted—a green sofa, an easy chair, and an oval rug. When she asked Mr. Schwartz if he had any lamps with colored-glass shades, he said, "Tiffany style? Oh, yes." And they bought one of those, too. Everything came to a little over a thousand dollars.

Ed was about to put down half the whole cost, but that would have wiped out almost all their stash. Celia had seen a sign in the window that said 'Installment Plans Available,' so she asked Mr. Schwartz, "If we bought it on the installment plan, how would that work?"

Mr. Schwartz tapped his pen on the paper. "You could put down two hundred now, and I would arrange for the rest to be paid in fifty-dollar installments. Would that be acceptable?"

She looked up at Ed and raised her eyebrows in question.

"Sure," Ed said. "Go ahead and write it up."

Mr. Schwartz offered to deliver everything the next day, and Ed said, "That'd be great. Celia can let you in."

Celia was on cloud nine when they left the store. Growing up they only had secondhand furniture bought off the street. She was sure coming up in the world. And fast.

The next day, she stuffed their clothes into a big laundry bag and packed everything else up in boxes. That took about ten minutes. After work, Eddie planned to borrow the boss's Oldsmobile and pick up their belongings.

She visited their landlady and told her they were moving.

"Well, it's been a pleasure having you and Ed," she said.

"Thank you," Celia replied. "You've been nothing but nice to us. Maybe I'll stop by and see you sometime."

Celia knew she'd never see her again. What reason would she have to return to this rundown heap of rooms? But she did mean it about the landlady being nice to them. The woman they'd rented from before her had kicked them out, claiming Celia had stolen twenty dollars from her. That was a lie. She'd taken a dislike to Celia because she'd complained about her renting to lowlifes who raised a ruckus every hour of the night when decent working people were trying to sleep.

At noon, Celia walked over to the new apartment and waited for the delivery men. They were very polite and knew just how to do their job. Every time they brought in a new piece of furniture they asked her where she'd like it placed. They started with the rug, and she told them to center it on the parlor floor. Then they carried in the bedroom set, which they easily maneuvered through the parlor. Next, they arranged the sofa, easy chair, and lamp in the parlor and then brought in the dining room set. She gave them fifty cents for a tip.

After they left, Celia walked from one room to another admiring their new home. Everything was so shiny and new and sparkling she could hardly believe it was all theirs. When she was a kid, her mother was always slaving over a washtub and telling her to go play in the street. But their baby would have a nice home and a mother and father to take care of her. (Celia was sure it'd be a girl.)

Being a mother wasn't something Celia had thought about when she was growing up. She never even played with dolls. But since she'd married Ed she began to think it'd be swell to have a kid of their own. And she couldn't think of anything more adorable than her big lug of a man snuggling a tiny baby.

She wanted to celebrate having a new apartment, so she went to the nearest grocery store, which was three blocks away, and bought a porterhouse steak to surprise Ed. She didn't know why guys liked eating beef so much. Once, her sister May had taken her on an errand to see a lady who had a milking cow. She often thought about that cow and her sad eyes. But chickens are dumb. She didn't mind eating chicken.

When Ed got home Celia let him carry in their belongings. She unpacked their plates and silverware and started cooking dinner. She was glad all their things fit in the drawers and lower cupboards because she couldn't reach the high-up ones. The thing that bothered her most about being short was not being able to reach high shelves and such and having to ask for help.

"Hey," Ed hollered from the bedroom, "what's that heavenly smell?"

"Never mind, buster," she cracked. "Get washed up for dinner and come see for yourself."

She set the table, and they sat down kitty-corner from each other. She had tried to make french-fried onion rings to go with the steak, but they turned out soggy.

Ed didn't mind. He plopped down at the table and grabbed his fork and knife. "Hot diggity dog. Look what my little wife fixed up."

While they were enjoying dinner she said, "Would you be happy with a baby girl?"

"Sure I would. She'd be sweet like you. But if it's a boy I'll teach him how to catch and throw a ball."

"A baby can't play ball."

"I know that. And when he's old enough I'll take him to the ballpark."

"Eddie, don't you think we should've bought a crib, too?"

"No, doll face, there's plenty of time for that. And, besides, we fibbed to Mr. Schwartz about not being married yet."

Ed had planned that out before they got to the store. He said little lies like that would keep the cops off their tail. After all, it wasn't every day a couple walked into a furniture store and bought a houseload of goods.

"I'm awful happy with this new place, Eddie. But now we owe fifty dollars a month for the furniture and twelve dollars for my fur coat. Maybe I should go back to the laundry."

She missed her pals at Foster's Laundry, Em and Rosie. On hot summer days, when the owner made himself scarce, they'd flick water at each other for fun—and to keep cool. They shared stories about fellas who'd asked them out and laughed at all the ways they gave them the slip if they didn't like them. Plus she'd been thinking about all their bills and the rent on this new apartment all day. There were so many things she still needed to buy—sheets and towels and some more plates and silverware. They simply couldn't manage it all on Ed's thirty dollars a week.

Ed finished swallowing a chunk of beef. "For a lousy twelve dollars a week? No, I won't have you working with a baby on the way."

"But how are we going to afford this place?"

"Look here, sugar, that money got us a new start, but we got to think now."

"What do you mean?" But she knew what he was getting at, and she didn't see any other way out of the fix they were in.

"You saw how easy it was. But we didn't get enough. We got to do it again. Maybe we can score another big roll, and then we'll quit and be square."

"Okay, Eddie, but we got to be smart about it. Smart like Sherlock Holmes."

Making Headlines
Brooklyn, January 10–13, 1924

After dinner, the next night Ed said to Celia, "Okay, princess, it's time to learn how to handle that twenty-five."

"But I don't want to shoot anybody."

"Yeah, but you got to carry it real sure-like and know how to aim and shoot. You don't want to accidentally hurt anybody, and if somebody tries to pull something, you'll know what to do."

"What's that?"

"You fire a shot over their head and say, 'Listen up, next time I won't miss.'"

"Right," she said, "just to show 'em who's boss."

They walked down to the cellar and leaned a board with a circle on it against the wall. Celia stood at the other wall and practiced aiming for the bull's eye. She expected the gun to make a big bang, but the sound was more of a pop, like a balloon busting.

Ed told her to treat the pistol like an extension of her hand, and after a few practice shots, she got the hang of it. Ed explained that if there was a gun in the store it'd be behind the counter. So she should be sure she could see the clerk's hands before she pulled anything.

When they went upstairs Ed sat her down at the dining table. "I want you to promise me something."

"Sure, what's that?"

He leaned across the corner of the table and clamped his big hands around hers. "Promise me you won't never shoot anybody. I don't care how hot things get. The gun is just to make people pay attention. Will you promise?"

"Yeah, sure. You know I will."

Come Saturday night she was raring to go. Like Ed said, it was easy dough, and if they made another big haul, they'd be ahead of the game. She told Ed, "It makes me nervous sitting at home waiting for you. Let me go with you to get the car."

They strolled the few blocks to Horgan's Garage. Ed said they'd use a Ford that was in for repair this time. He took its license plates off and put the fake ones on.

"Those plates sure look real, Eddie."

"I took two different sets of plates, cut them in half, and welded them back together. So we have two sets of fake plates."

She thought up a little poem and recited it for him. "No one can say my man's not clever. Nope, not ever ever."

They hopped in the Ford and cruised around Brooklyn's Brownsville neighborhood. Ed stopped in front of an Atlantic and Pacific Grocery on Ralph Avenue and said, "This'll do."

He kept the engine running. "Okay, kid, let's make it snappy."

Celia wasn't nearly as nervous this time. They marched into the store like big-league thieves and sized up the situation. The store was clean and well lit, and the shelves were jam-packed with goods. Celia's mother used to cut up limp greens and vegetables and make a bland soup, but Celia was looking forward to lining her kitchen shelves with cans of Campbell's Soups ready to heat up.

A couple stood eyeing the glass case of baked goods and desserts, and four clerks were scattered around the aisles. Celia walked up to the man at the cash register and spoke boldly. "I'll have a dozen eggs."

He asked if she wanted anything else and then wrapped up the eggs, staring into space like he was daydreaming about a summer day. While his hands were occupied she pulled out her gun and said, "Stick 'em up, and make it quick."

He jumped like he'd been plugged and bugged his eyes out. A gun sure was a good way to get a fella's attention, she thought, even when it was only a pipsqueak like her handling it.

Ed waved two guns and hollered, "Get to the back, all of you, and turn your faces to the wall."

The lady shopper didn't budge. She turned to her husband and said, "Hey, what is it? What do they want?"

Jeez, did this dame think they were inviting her to a picnic?

But the lady's husband knew the score. He shot his hands up and said, "They're robbers, don't you understand? Put your hands up or we'll both get killed."

"Well," she said, sticking her nose up in the air, "it's plain this is no place for me. I'll never shop at this store again. Come on, John." And she actually headed for the door.

Celia looked at Ed, who stood there with his mouth hanging open. He pointed his guns at the woman and yelled at her. "For God's sake, lady, this ain't a joke. Move it."

That stopped her in her tracks. "Very well," she said, mincing beside her husband and grumbling. "I can't believe this. Where are the police when you need them?"

Celia kept her gun on this cheeky lady and the guys while Ed dipped into the cash register. After a minute Ed said, "Keep the change," and she knew he was done.

They backed out of the store, keeping their eyes on the people, hopped in the car, and tooled around two corners.

Ed eased off the gas and steered one-handed like he usually did. "Well, darlin', we didn't get much there, less than a hundred."

"Gosh," she said, "I thought they'd have as much as Roulston's, being a big chain like they are."

"Maybe they stashed some of the day's take in a safe."

"That woman got a good look at us, and she's just the type to hound the coppers until they nab us."

"We can't worry about that now. You had your collar turned up, and I kept my hat cocked low."

He was probably right. "Not even a hundred. That's not much help." *Look at me,* she thought—*pooh-poohing a hundred bucks.*

"Say, we got plenty of time, and everything's all set. What do you say we hit another store?"

"Sure," she said, "I just hope we don't run into another persnickety dame." But they had their routine down like clockwork, and the car plates couldn't be traced, so she figured they might as well.

Ed drove to the Bedford neighborhood, and they soon spotted another grocery store, H.C. Bohack Company. Ed slowed down so they could get a good look.

"It's real quiet inside," she said. "Let's go."

The dozen-eggs line was getting stale, so this time she asked for a pound of ground beef. When the clerk stepped out from behind the counter she pulled out her gun and told him, the two customers, and the two other workers to line up.

While she covered them, Ed got to work on the cash register. He was struggling to open it and cursing at it like it was a stubborn mule. Sweat beaded up on her brow. The clerks and customers started shifting from one foot to the other and giving each other the eye, like maybe they were thinking of jumping her. She wondered if she should fire off a shot, like Ed said, to scare them a little. But her palms had gone clammy, and she was afraid she wouldn't be able to keep a grip on the gun.

"Hurry up," she hollered at Ed. He was taking too much time. What if some cop on the beat wandered by?

Ed finally got the register open and stuffed his pockets. When they left the store Celia looked up and down the street. She didn't see any coppers, just a couple all bundled up and not paying them any mind. They got in the car and headed for home.

"That was the longest we ever took, Eddie. We can't be spending that much time in a store."

"I know. I couldn't figure out the darn register."

They scored about two hundred at Bohack's, so

altogether they brought in three hundred that night. After they counted it up at the dining room table, Ed wagged his head in disgust.

Celia told him, "It's all right. We just can't spend it all at once like we did our first haul."

The next morning after Mass, they bought two Sunday newspapers, and Celia hard-boiled some eggs and made coffee. They got comfortable on their new bed.

Celia wondered how many other couples in the city were relaxing on a roomy bed with breakfast and the news. This was the life for her. And she felt lucky having Ed by her side, him being a hard worker and polite and all.

The year before she met Ed she'd taken up housekeeping with Clarence Cherison. Her friend Rosie at Foster's Laundry had introduced them. Clarence was dapper and full of swagger, with jet-black hair and a pencil mustache. He fancied himself a lady's man and ogled and flattered every girl who crossed his path.

Even though Celia had never really invited him to live with her, they somehow ended up together in her one-room place on Franklin Avenue. He had gradually moved his clothes in and started spending every night there. So by the time she'd known him for two months, he'd become a permanent fixture in her life.

Not that she'd welcomed him with open arms. Sure, they made a fine-looking couple, but his boasting, blustering, and complaining got on her nerves. He worked at a service station on Atlantic Avenue and constantly bellyached about his boss ordering him around like a step-and-fetch dog and expecting him to take extra shifts whenever another guy didn't show.

The worst part was he demanded she fix him dinner every night, even after she'd put in a long day at the laundry. She rarely bothered with anything special for herself in the evening, usually just heated up a can of beans or soup. But that wasn't good enough for Clarence. No, he said, a good woman ought to spoil her man. Celia told him she'd spoil him once he started taking her out on the town and springing for some groceries, too.

Finally, after putting up with Clarence and his chiseling ways for a year, she'd had enough. After work one night Celia stopped at the grocery store to pick up a few items and asked for two large paper bags. Back in her room, she stuffed his clothes and razor and toothbrush in the bags.

When Clarence came waltzing in that evening, she said, "Hey, Clarence, it's time you found yourself a woman who'll spoil you. I'm not good enough for you."

"Now, baby, don't be that way," he said, coming up to her and putting on the squeeze.

She shoved him away. "I mean it. I ain't what you're looking for, and I don't like how you treat me. So just scram and don't make a fuss about it."

Celia had told the fella who lived in the room next to hers, Joe, that she was going to give Clarence the heave-ho and asked him to come around if he heard any trouble. Joe was a quiet guy, and she'd gone out dancing with him a time or two, but they were pals more than anything else.

But Clarence said, "All right, if that's how you feel, I'd hate to cramp your style."

She handed over his bags of stuff. "Here you go. I think I got everything."

He puffed himself up and gave her a little salute. "See you around, baby."

Whew, she thought, *that wasn't so bad.* Still, she decided she'd been a sap to take up with him in the first place and promised herself she wouldn't be fooled by a bounder like him ever again.

Then, a little over a month later, she'd met Ed. It was a Saturday night, and she was feeling lonely, so she decided to blow thirty cents on a night out. She took herself to the Fulton Theatre to see *Adam and Eva* with Marion Davies and, when she funneled out to the lobby, she spotted her friend Joe. He was talking to a tall, brawny guy with ginger-colored hair—a clean-cut fella wearing a snappy coat with a belt in the back and a striped silk shirt. The guy was a real looker.

She strolled over to them and said, "Hi, Joe, you here alone?"

Joe slapped this guy's shoulder. "No, shake hands with my friend Ed Cooney."

"Hello, Mr. Cooney. Nice to meet you," she said, offering her hand. His grip was firm, and his smile a mile wide.

"This is my friend, Celia," Joe said. "Lives in the same building as me."

Celia decided to dispense with the mister. "Where do you live, Ed?"

"A couple of blocks from here, with my mother. Just got out of the Navy a few months ago, and I'm still getting settled in."

"Say," Joe said to Celia, "we were going to grab some chow down the street. You wanna join us?"

The three of them visited over chop suey and then took to the dance floor. Celia made a point of dancing with Joe most of the evening. She had her eye on Ed but didn't want to seem overeager. He was handsome and had a neat haircut and didn't bluster like a lot of other fellas. She knew right away he was the one for her.

Afterward, Ed walked with them back to their building. When they were saying their goodbyes, Ed turned to Celia. "You haven't said when I can see you again."

Playing hard to get had sure enough done the trick. Plus, she had only let on about particulars she was proud of—like how she and the girls at the laundry razzed each other about their boyfriends, and how she had older sisters who'd taught her how to cook. And she asked Ed lots of questions because it's always smart to learn more about the guy than he learns about you. That way you make him want to solve the mystery that is you.

The more time she spent with Ed, the more sure she was. He had a soft voice and opened doors for her like a real gentleman. She could hardly believe it when he asked her to marry him. She looked him in the eye and said, "You wouldn't be joshing me, would you?" Clarence had said a few times that they ought to get hitched, but she never believed him; it was just his way of stringing her along. But Ed whipped out a ring with a red stone and said, "Here's how serious I am." So she figured he was for real, and she was about as thrilled as a kid in a candy store. What could be better than loving someone who loves you back? He was always gentle as a teddy bear and never hollered or got mad at her, even when she ruined dinner. Four months after they met they got married at St. Augustine's Church. It was the happiest day of her life, and she felt like God was smiling down on her and giving her a fresh start. She never trusted anybody in her life the way she trusted her Eddie.

When they were meeting with the priest to set the date for the wedding, Ed asked if she wanted to invite her parents or brothers or sisters. No, she said, there's not enough time. Ed said they could put it off for another week or two if she wanted. "No, Eddie," she'd said, "my parents are getting up there in years. And I lost touch with my brothers years ago. Maybe I'll ask my sisters."

Celia figured her parents were still living in Manhattan, scrimping and cheating and scheming like always. She didn't want Ed to know she hadn't seen them in years—and didn't care if she never saw them again. They were an embarrassment to cavemen. She'd last seen her sisters May and Annie about five years ago, when she was fifteen, and they were living together in Brooklyn. May had married Walter, a cobbler, and he decided to lay the law down for Celia, ordering her to come straight home from her job at the brush factory instead of hanging out with 'harlots and sailors.' Celia said she'd been taking care of herself since she was old enough to suck lollipops and didn't need anybody telling her when she could come and go. She went to live with her mother for a while and then she got a room of her own. She figured her sisters had their lives and she had hers. She wasn't interested in going back in time. She had Eddie, his family, and her pals, and that was good enough for her.

When Ed and Celia finished reading the funny pages she took their breakfast dishes back to the kitchen. She was up to her elbows in suds when Ed called out, "Holy Toledo, come here and listen to this."

Celia turned off the faucet and trotted to the bedroom. Ed sat cross-legged on the bed. He held up the front page of *The New York Telegram*, and in letters as big as her thumb it said, "Bob-Haired Bandit Robs Two More Shops." She grabbed the paper and read as fast as she could.

She looked up at Ed. "Gosh, the cops kited all over Brooklyn in their flivvers looking for us last night—while we were home in bed sleeping."

Ed scooped up another paper. "Look at *The Brooklyn Eagle*."

The big headline on that paper said, "TWO STORES HELD UP BY ARMED WOMAN AND CONFEDERATE."

She pressed a palm to her cheek. "Imagine that—us on the front page, just like Howard Carter and King Tut."

They gobbled up those stories like strawberry jello, every now and then reading lines to each other. Celia could hardly believe all the fibs that got printed, like how she drove the getaway car or darted onto the running board of the speeding car or was in charge of the whole operation, "brandishing her gun and gruffly warning the victims she'd fill them full of lead." Mr. Gibbons, the husband in the A & P Grocery, even said he wanted to grapple the gun away from her, except she wielded her pistol like she'd blow his head off if he tried.

She waved the paper like a newsboy hawking his wares. "Gee, Ed, I'm famous. Who would've thought little old me would make the headlines? I'm the bob-haired bandit."

Ed gave her a crooked smile. "Yeah. And I'm your sidekick."

It sounded like Ed was sore that she got all the ink, so she thought she'd tease him a little. "And don't forget it, you galoot. I'm the big cheese in this outfit."

"Come on, Celia, I don't think you understand what we're up against."

"What do you mean? I know we're wanted by the police."

He folded up the newspaper he'd been reading and handed it to her. "Read this here part."

She read the end of the column, about how Brooklyn detectives plus scores of plainclothes cops would be hanging out in the stores to deter robbers or catch them in the act.

She said, "So anybody in the store could be a bull and they could round us up on the spot?"

"Yeah." Ed crinkled a corner of his mouth and shook his head, like he was saying 'ain't it a shame.' Then he snapped his head up. "Hey, there's no law says a guy and his doll can't go shopping after dark. If you see somebody in the store who looks like a cop you just smile real nice and order a pound of butter. Then you skedaddle out of there, and we're in the clear."

"But what if he gets smart and tries to search me for the gun?"

"Well, then you'll have to pull it on him and back him off."

"Sure, Eddie, I can do that."

Gosh, she thought, *maybe we ought to lay off the stick-up business.* Then she looked around at their bedroom furniture and brand-new sheets and pillows. They still owed a bundle of money, and she figured Schwartz's furniture guys would come knocking if they didn't keep up on the payments. Then where would they be? The way she saw it they were in pretty deep.

Suspect in Custody
Manhattan and Brooklyn, January 14, 1924

Captain William Casey stood before Commissioner Richard Enright's paper-strewn desk, trying like the devil to swallow his exasperation. He had better things to do than get chewed out by Enright. And he felt oafish standing there with his pudgy hands clasped over his protruding belly. The commissioner always dressed natty as a movie star. But despite putting on a fresh shirt every morning, Casey's suit and shirt always looked rumpled. He didn't give a damn, either. He was a detective, not some Macy's store-window mannequin.

The radiator in the commissioner's office pinged away, cranking out steamy heat, which made him sweat all the more. But he wasn't about to shed his wool coat. He wanted to clear out of Enright's office as quickly as possible and get back to work. Didn't the commissioner realize he was wasting his time admonishing him like he was some chump who didn't have a clue about how to do his job?

Because the commissioner had been promoted from the ranks, he was forever trying to prove himself to the mayor or defend himself against charges of cronyism and corruption in the force. Now he was on a campaign to clamp down on speakeasies and counter accusations of a crime wave sweeping the city. Casey was his favorite punching bag when it came to goings-on in Brooklyn.

These damn politicians sure knew how to grandstand, but put them on the street and they wouldn't know how to catch a criminal if he walked right up and snatched their gold watch.

Enright shook his fist in the air and put on a bulldog scowl. "Look here, Casey, it's not just New York papers carrying this story. It's papers all across the country."

"I know, sir, but they're getting the story all wrong, playing it up just to sell papers. Like saying the dame's the one toting two guns. And giving different descriptions of her and her pal."

"Do you think the mayor gives a damn whether this lady bandit carries one or two guns? The press is having a holiday with this story. And they love making us look like Keystone Cops."

"The newspapers are egging each other on, sir." Christ, he hated how Enright made him squirm like a schoolboy caught fibbing. "The stories are full of inaccuracies, which complicates our work. We've got tips coming in from as far away as the Bronx, and it takes time to sift through them."

The thing was, a lot of the tips were pranks, like 'My granny came home late last night with a dozen eggs, you better bring her in for questioning.' Or 'Have you staked out the beauty parlor on Seventh Avenue? I hear they give a good bob cut.' The damn telephone made it too easy for these jokesters to needle the police.

Enright snorted. "Regardless of what the papers are

saying, you need to track down these robbers and get them off the streets before someone gets killed. And don't tell me there are more serious crimes that need investigating. The newspapers are using this one against us for all it's worth. And, frankly, this bob-haired dame's repeat robberies make us look inept."

"Yes, sir, I'll give it my highest priority."

"Fine, and keep me posted." Enright waved a hand in dismissal.

As Casey trundled along on the subway he tried to cool down. Enright's campaign to shake up the force wouldn't last forever, he told himself. He needed to keep his head down and get this job done. Once he caught the bandit couple, he'd ask for the vacation time Fiona had been badgering him about.

He walked the two blocks from the subway to Brooklyn Headquarters, leaning into the stiff January wind howling down the streets. He was looking forward to sitting down at his desk and reviewing the latest tips and reports over his sack lunch—a roast beef sandwich slathered with horseradish and a thermos of black coffee. He pushed open the door and shed his coat, hat, and gloves.

The front desk dispatcher greeted him. "Hiya, Bill. Frank needs to talk to you right away."

"Thanks, Elmer. Is he in his office?"

"Either there or the interrogation rooms."

Casey wound his way to Frank Gray's office and knocked on the door.

Gray called out, "Yeah, come in."

Casey swung the door open. Gray cupped his hand over the phone's mouthpiece and said, "We got her, Bill. There's a car going out to arrest her right now."

"The bob-haired bandit?"

"Yup, the very one. Just got a confession from the accomplice."

Gray motioned Casey in and turned his attention back to his phone. "On the double," he said. "Captain Casey just returned."

Gray hung up and updated Casey on the developments.

Casey hurried to his office and gulped down his sandwich and coffee. Fifteen minutes later, he walked into the interrogation room. In addition to his second-in-command, Frank Gray, there were three other detectives: McGowan, Fox, and Dwyer. Across the table from them sat a slight brunette with rosy cheeks, her hands demurely clasped on her lap. He had to admit she was a pretty little thing. He'd have never pegged her for a bandit, but then none of the murderers he'd put away over the years sported a devil's horns and tail, either.

Gray said, "Helen, this is Captain Casey. Captain, meet Helen Quigley."

Casey pulled out the chair beside Gray and plunked down. "Yes, is it Miss Quigley?"

"Yes, sir," she said, calm as could be. He could tell she was a cool customer.

"How old are you, miss?"

"Twenty-three."

"Where do you live and with whom?"

"I live with my father at 63 Eighth Street."

"Are you employed?"

"I'm my father's housekeeper."

She'd neither hesitated with her answers nor shown a hint of apprehension. He had to give it to her: She had poise, confidence, and ice-blue eyes—the perfect temperament and looks for someone who needed to stay calm under pressure.

He asked, "Did you and a male accomplice rob Roulston Grocery on the night of January fifth?"

"No, sir."

"Did you, on Saturday night, January 12, enter the A & P and Bohack's Grocery and bark orders at the clerks while pointing an automatic pistol at them?"

"No, I did not."

"I'm told a Mr. Vincent Kovalski has identified you as his accomplice in these three robberies."

She smirked. "You mean Apples Kovalski?"

"Yes, Apples—or whatever his name is—has told us you accompanied him on these robberies."

"Well, the dirty rat's lying."

"You do know Mr. Kovalski?"

"Yeah, I know him, but I ain't proud of it."

"How do you know him?"

"I met him at a speakeasy in Brooklyn."

"And on how many occasions did you meet him there or elsewhere?"

"Just that once."

"And why would he lie about robbing stores with you?"

"I don't know. Maybe he's sore at me. I was supposed

to go out on a date with him last Saturday night, but I gave him the slip."

Casey rubbed his forehead. He'd have to review the confession and question this Apples character to get to the bottom of their stories. But first, they'd grill this girl some more. He and the other detectives fired questions at her for the next two hours, gathering more background and asking her where she was the last two Saturday nights. She admitted it was her practice to let her hair down on Saturday nights at a neighborhood speakeasy. She liked a few drinks of whiskey and could hold her liquor as well as any fella. She was willing to admit to frequenting speakeasies but not to robbing. She was a canny one, all right.

Before questioning Helen, Gray had called in the bob-haired robber's victims and asked them to report to the precinct at four o'clock for a line-up. After getting nothing but smiles and denials from Helen Quigley, Casey informed her they'd brought in witnesses for a line-up. She grinned and asked if she could powder her nose first. So she was a smart aleck, too.

At five o'clock on Monday, Bill Casey called the commissioner's office to report that the bob-haired bandit, Helen Quigley, and Vincent 'Apples' Kovalski had been positively identified by several storekeepers. They had procured a confession from Kovalski, who had named Quigley as his accomplice.

The Brooklyn Standard Union, Pages 1, 18
January 15, 1924

EX-CHORUS GIRL ARRESTED
AS CHAIN STORE BANDIT

Helen Quigley, who, it is said, formerly graced the boards of the burlesque stage, faced the strangest audience in her career today.

Fifty men gazed intently upon her. There was no applause or catcalls. For the audience, it seemed as if the last curtain had fallen, but throughout the performance, in the detectives' room at Atlantic Street headquarters, the principal character never lost her bearing.

When the men—detectives—filed out, their places were taken by a score or more of small storekeepers, victims of the numerous holdups staged within the past few weeks. Several identified the young woman, who is only twenty-three years old, as the bob-haired bandit for whom the police have been searching.

"You got me wrong," emphatically declared the well-dressed prisoner. Then she smiled.

Keeps Father's Home

The arrest of the young woman is the outstanding development in a new series of crimes which have occurred in Brooklyn and Queens during the past twenty-four hours. A number of holdups have been reported and the amount of loot gathered by thieves will reach several thousand dollars.

Detectives McGowan, Fox, and Dwyer of Fifth Avenue station arrested Helen last night at her home, 126 Eighth Street, where she acts as a housekeeper for her widowed father, Michael.

"This is the most ridiculous predicament I've ever been in," she said immediately after the line-up.

Despite these protestations of innocence, police officials believe they have in custody the female bandit who has struck terror to those merchants she has visited in company with a young man. It is the latter, the police say, who is responsible for Helen's present plight. In the vernacular of the police department, he is said to have 'squealed.'

Claim Youth 'Squealed'

The youth in question is Vincent Kovalski, nineteen years old, of 336 Seventeenth Street. He was picked up early yesterday morning. Confronted by half a dozen sleuths, Kovalski is said to have revealed the identity of his alleged companion.

According to the police, the pair entered a store together. The young woman promptly displayed her weapon, covering the prospective victims, while her accomplice did the actual robbing.

"Why, I'm so afraid of a gun I can hardly look at one," the girl told the authorities today. "And the only occasion I ever use a knife is when I am eating."

Throughout most of the night and early morning hours today, the young woman, interrogated by detectives, stoutly denied any connection with the holdups. She is said to have admitted an acquaintance with Kovalski, known to his familiars as 'Apples,' and she said she had a date with him for last Saturday night but did not keep it. It was on Saturday night that the two groceries were robbed by a man and a woman.

Fashionably Gowned

The girl, attired in a short sealskin coat with a large beaver collar, black and white striped dress, flesh-colored stockings, and brown pumps, looked more like a society debutante than a bandit. Her face was continually wreathed in smiles, and her eyes sparkled. The small black velvet hat, trimmed with silver ornaments and worn jauntily on the back of her head, displayed her brown hair, cut in the latest mode of the flapper.

Kovalski presented a somewhat different picture. Highly nervous, his six feet two inches of height quivered with emotion, and occasionally tears came to his eyes.

But for 'Smilin' Helen,' the ordeal apparently held no terror. When Barnett Kennedy and Lester Lowden, employees of the Roulston store at Seventh Avenue and Seventh Street which was held up on Jan. 5 and robbed of $680, identified her and Kovalski as the bandits, her smile broadened.

"You're all wrong, mister," was her retort.

Identified by Victim

A minute later, John Dodenhoff, manager of the A and P Store at 367 Brooklyn Avenue, picked out the young woman as the gun toter who visited his place Saturday night with a tall young man and relieved him of $200 at the point of a gun.

Several of the victims were unable to pick out the prisoner. Richard Ohlandt, manager of an A and P Store a 451 Ralph Avenue, was one of them. He was positive Miss Quigley was not the gunwoman. Then Capt. Casey produced Thomas Gibbons and Enoch Turpin, who happened to be in the store at the time of the crime. Gibbons could not recognize the young woman, but Turpin identified both her and Kovalski.

Signs Up in Chorus

The line-up at an end, the girl was taken to an adjoining room. As she ate she talked freely with police and reporters, smiling all the time. She said she left school when she reached the seventh grade and that her mother died several years ago. For a time, she remained at home, keeping house for the rest of the family.

Then she had an ambition to become an actress and signed up with the 'Parisian Whirl,' a burlesque company, as a member of the chorus, she said. The show swung around the circuit and finally reached Brooklyn. Helen says she did not want her friends to know she had gotten no further than the chorus so she quit. She returned home, she said, as housekeeper for her father.

The Wrong Dame
Brooklyn, January 15–16, 1924

Ed was all smiles and good cheer when he got home from work Tuesday. He sloughed off his coat and said, "Hey, doll, everybody at the garage was talking about how the coppers arrested the bob-haired bandit. Look at this."

Ed handed her the *New York Herald*. The bold headline on the front page read, "Bob-Haired Girl Captured as Store Bandit."

"Well, I'll be a son of a gun," she said.

Celia had spent the day washing and polishing the floors in their new apartment and hadn't gone out at all. So she was behind on the news. She usually read a paper or two every day. Celia had never told Ed, but she hadn't gone to school until she was nine, when her Aunt Margaret, who had moved to Brooklyn, took her in. Neither of her parents knew how to read or write, and between begging and scrounging around the streets for food, there was no time for schooling. But Aunt Margaret signed her up for the parochial school at St. Matthew, and she wore a blue skirt and white blouse, like all the girls. Her classmates all knew their letters, and some of them made fun of her and called her a dunce, but Aunt Margaret made the nuns help her, and she picked up the alphabet in no time.

She'd gotten the biggest charge out of learning how to read and write. It was like knowing a secret; she could do something her parents couldn't do—read store signs and write notes. When she turned fourteen, her mother took her away from her aunt and that was the end of school. That's when she started working at laundry jobs. But she never quit using her reading and writing and enjoyed dime-store novels and magazines.

She plopped down at the dining room table and ran her finger down the column. Ed sat down and sidled up close to her, following along. He tapped out a Chesterfield and lit up.

"Ha," she said, reading out loud, "South Brooklyn merchants, terrorized the past few months by a girl robber and her male escort, may breathe easier hereafter. The Brooklyn police have arrested the gun-toter, a wisp of a girl, slim and scarcely five feet tall. Several storekeepers picked her out of a line-up, down to the fur coat and tam-o'-shanter."

Ed asked, "What do you think of her picture? Does she look like you?"

"I don't see it, except she's short and wears her hair the same. I guess those shopkeepers didn't get a good look at my face."

"Must've been too busy staring down the barrel of the pistol."

She winked at Ed. "She's pretty though, just like me."

Ed looped his arm around her shoulder. "Nothing like your kind of pretty, doll face."

She turned back to the story, reading to the end. "Holy

cow. She and this Apples fellow are being held on ten-thousand-dollar bail. The dirty rat squealed on her." She looked Ed in the eye. "Why in the world would he say he robbed the places we robbed? And bring this poor girl down with him?"

"Beats me. Either he's some kind of fool or the police badgered him into it. But it keeps the heat off us."

"Well, the papers have been saying some pretty rough things about the coppers, like claiming Brooklyn's streets are as dangerous as the Wild West and wondering how one girl could buffalo the whole police force. But it ain't right—them hauling in some poor girl with a pretty face who never did anything worse than dance in a burlesque show."

"This is good for us, sweets. Those shopkeepers couldn't even finger the right girl."

"I know, but I won't stand for it—her going to the penitentiary when she's innocent. We got to do something."

Being wrongfully accused was not something Celia took lightly. She was only six years old when a shopkeeper grabbed her arm and accused her of stealing an orange. Her sister May got in the guy's face and told him that was hogwash—that she'd asked Celia to pick out an orange, and here was the money for it. He apologized and let her go. But Celia never forgot May sticking up for her like that, and she wasn't about to let Helen Quigley take the rap for something she did.

Ed said, "It'd be pretty dicey—getting mixed up in this business."

"We could write a note to the police saying she's innocent."

Ed leaned back in his chair and crinkled a cheek, giving himself time to think. "Maybe we can take the heat off this Helen and throw them off our tail at the same time."

"Sure, how would we do that?"

"I'm going to get washed up and think some more."

"Okay, Eddie. I'll get dinner ready. Then we can figure out what to put in the note."

Still, she'd been worrying about the stick-up business the last few days. The coppers' plan to place plainclothes men in the stores and on the streets gave her the heebie-jeebies. But she and Ed had gotten away with every job so far, and they had their routine down. She figured if they spotted anybody giving them the eagle-eye they could just turn tail.

Over their pork chops and green beans, Ed grinned and said, "Let's go out tonight and pull another job. They won't expect us on a Tuesday night. And then they'll know they've got the wrong gal, since Helen is sittin' in a jail cell right now."

"And I can leave a note for the police, just in case they have any doubts."

They borrowed the Oldsmobile Six again and cruised around the Clinton Hill neighborhood. At the corner of Dekalb and Ryerson Celia spotted a Weinstein's Drugstore. They were in and out in no time. They only brought in fifty dollars from the drugstore, but it was worth it to rile up the bulls with that note.

The next morning, Celia went out and bought two newspapers. Sure enough, right there on the front page of the *Brooklyn Standard Union,* it said 'Girl Bandit Leaves Note Saying Police Made False Arrest.'

The other paper even printed Celia's note, which she had to admit she was proud of:

You dirty fish-pedling bums, you got the wrong dame! Leave this inocent girl alone and get the right ones, which is nobody but us. We are going to give Mr. Hogan, the maneger of Roulston's, another visit, as we got two checks we couldn't cash that we need to change for some dough. And tell Bohack's maneger we're sorry if we ruined his cash registir. We'll stop by real soon to see if he bought a new one. We defy you fellas to catch us because we are profesional crooks.

The Bob-Haired Bandit and Her Man

Putting on the Heat
Brooklyn, January 16, 1924

The morning after the Weinstein Drugstore robbery, Bill Casey telephoned Commissioner Enright to update him on the crime, the note left at the scene, and other robberies in Brooklyn. "I can't say for sure," Casey told him, "but if that note's from the actual bob-haired bandit, then Helen Quigley is innocent."

Enright huffed, "Here we go again, with another round of news about police ineptitude."

As Enright predicted, the newspapers took the most recent reports as more evidence of an unchecked crime spree. Enright claimed the rampage was manufactured by the press, and he said he had the statistics to back up his claim. But the newspapers weren't buying it, and Mayor Hylan didn't give a damn about statistics. During his interviews and speeches, he pontificated about 'keeping the streets safe for decent citizens' and pledged he'd go all out 'to take the fight to the criminals.'

Of course, Enright had been the one to put the screws on Casey and the other precinct detectives to throw the hoodlums in jail and get them prosecuted. And this business with the bob-haired bandit and her note claiming they had the wrong dame frankly made him and his team look like a bunch of bunglers.

He'd gone around and around with Fiona on the matter of asking for a month off. That morning, he'd begged and cajoled to get her to relent. "Listen, dear, once we catch this bob-haired bandit Enright will let up on me, and I can put in for that vacation."

She gave him the squint-eye. "You promise?"

"Yeah, I promise."

"Okay, and you better not weasel out of it, either. Because if you do, I'll be spending the summer in Boston with Jenny."

"The whole summer?"

"You heard me right."

Casey hated the idea of kicking around by himself for three months—and not seeing their daughter, who usually visited them in Brooklyn in July. He needed to track down this damn bob-haired nuisance—or he'd be subsisting on cornflakes and salami sandwiches all summer.

Casey summoned two of his lieutenants, Frank Gray and 'Mac' McGowan, to his office. Gray and McGowan shuffled in and plopped down in the seats in front of his desk.

Casey steepled his fingers and eyed the men. "Okay, this is what we've got—one confession and two identifications from the line-up. But the manager at the A & P and Mr. Gibbons claiming Helen Quigley is absolutely not the woman who robbed that store. So was the note left at Weinstein's Drugstore last night from the real bob-haired bandit, or is it some copycat trying to throw us for a loop? Do we now have two women thumbing their noses at us?"

Gray shook his head and snorted. "And if you consider the rat's nest of victims' descriptions, we could have as many as three women robbers on the loose."

"Look here, it's not just the women," said Casey, swatting the air. "It's like every thief in the city decided if we can't catch a dame, they might as well get in on the act."

Mac spoke up. He was tall and lanky as a street post and looked goofy folded up in his chair. "I don't know how to account for the disparities in the line-up identifications, other than to say it's happened before, and we still got convictions."

Gray, always quick to cut Mac down to size, swiveled toward him. "Quigley and Kovalski are out of our hands now. Let the District Attorney deal with those two."

Mac was a strictly by-the-books guy who relied on odds and numbers, whereas Frank, the more cynical of the two, went with his gut. That made them a good team, even though they frequently sniped at each other. But this was no time for quibbling, not with Enright and the newspapers putting the heat on them to solve this case. "Listen up, you two. I'm asking what you make of the note."

Gray smoothed a hand through his black hair, which was forever flopping over his forehead. "I think we've got three different duos out there. At least we ought to assume that's what we've got—and spread the net wide."

Casey poked his chin at McGowan.

"I think Quigley is guilty. And once she gets wind of this note saying she's innocent, she'll milk it for all its worth."

It was Casey's turn to be annoyed with McGowan. "That's not what I'm asking about. What's your assessment of this note?"

Mac shifted in his seat. "Chances are it's a new dame, some wiseacre playing cat and mouse with us."

Gray chimed in. "Yeah, the bob-haired bandit has favored chain stores and Saturday nights, and this pair picked on a drugstore. On a Tuesday."

McGowan drew in his bony elbows. "I hope this note doesn't influence the DA. What if he releases Helen Quigley?"

"It'd make us look like a bunch of idiots," said Gray.

Casey waved them off. "The DA will do Enright's bidding, and that includes keeping Quigley in custody. He understands we can't release her while the press is questioning whether we even got the right dame."

Mac screwed up his face. "It's possible she's innocent. That Kovalski set her up, like she says, maybe to protect somebody else."

Gray scowled at McGowan. "Playing both sides of the fence, are you?"

Damn these two and their needling. Casey jumped in. "Never mind that. I spoke with the commissioner this morning and asked if we could beef up our plainclothes presence. He's given us the go-ahead to hire twenty more men."

"Humph," Gray snorted. "Our knight in shining armor rides to the rescue."

McGowan wagged his head. "Well, let's get them on

board as soon as possible. And station them in business districts, especially around the chain groceries."

"Right," Casey said. "Mac, you get the word out and hire the men. Frank, call in everybody we can spare for plainclothes duty and start posting them tonight. Make sure the blues and them are out in force come Saturday night. Let's put the heat on these crooks."

McGowan and Gray stood and headed for the door.

Casey called after them. "And I want results, you hear?"

Good Night, Boys, Hello, Girls
Brooklyn, January 20–21, 1924

Poor Helen Quigley was still under lock and key, and Celia was absolutely disgusted. The authorities even doubled her bail to a whopping twenty thousand. It was disgraceful, her being accused of their robberies, especially after they'd left that note. Were the coppers going to lock up every bob-haired girl they could find until the robberies stopped? Celia was itching to leave another note and needle them about their big-time bungling. But Ed said they should skip Saturday night because that's when the cops would be expecting them.

But Sunday seemed like a good time to go out on the town. They waited until ten thirty, when there wouldn't be many people, including coppers, on the streets. Most businesses were closed by then, but after cruising around they spotted a drugstore on New York Avenue at Union Street with the lights blazing.

The only people in the store were the clerk and his mother, who was in the back room doing paperwork. The clerk pleaded with them not to hurt his mother and obeyed all their orders. And Celia was learning how to keep people in line with her little helper. So it was an easy robbery, all in all.

When they were leaving, Celia took out her scribbled note and slapped it down. "This here's for the coppers. Tell them I left it, with my compliments."

She and Ed hopped in the car, and Ed squealed out, rounding the first corner they came to. He slowed down after a couple of blocks. "Okay, it's less than a mile now."

They kept their eyes peeled the rest of the way home. Whenever they spotted headlights coming their way or a car approaching from behind, Celia ducked down in case it was a bull. But the streets were quiet that Sunday night. By the time they'd dropped the car at the garage and walked the block to their apartment, they'd spotted only a half dozen cars on the street, and only one was a cop car.

Back at their place, they counted up the evening's take, which amounted to a hundred-fifty-five dollars. Celia tucked it away in their new hiding spot, the slats under the bed.

"We better get some shut-eye," Ed said. He had to open the shop, as usual, at eight o'clock sharp Monday morning. They crawled into bed, and Celia went to sleep thinking about the note she'd left:

Well, I'm sure having a fun time with you donut munchers, don't you think? Give it up boys, because you'll never catch me. I will use my pistol on you if I have to, so watch your step. And let that poor Helen Quigley go free. She's inocent, you buffoons. I'm telling you we're using the money for a good reeson, and we'd hate to have to spend it on a lawyeur. So good night, boys, but don't forget—you'll be hearing from us again soon.

The Gun Girl And Her Tall Man

Celia got the idea during the drugstore robbery—when she spotted bags of rainbow-colored gumdrops. Monday morning she went to her neighborhood drugstore and asked what candies they sold. Sure enough, they had gumdrops, so she bought some. They were coated with sugar sprinkles and came in red, yellow, orange, white, green, and black.

She knew when Em and Rosie would be on their lunch break at Foster's Laundry, so she arrived there at noon sharp. Mr. Foster always went upstairs and had lunch with his wife. So she could visit with her friends then without getting them into trouble.

She opened the door to the basement, and a wall of warm moist air greeted her. The sharp smell of lye reminded her of all the things she hated about slaving over laundry. It was sure enough back-breaking work.

Em and Rosie sat at the table in the rear and spotted her right away.

"Celia," Rosie called out. "Haven't seen you in a string of Sundays."

Celia sauntered over to them and sat down next to Em. "Hello, girls. You staying out of trouble?"

Em flounced her blond hair off her shoulders. She was proud of having a wavy head of golden hair. "Not if I can help it."

"I brought you a treat." Celia put the gumdrops in the middle of the table and opened the bag.

Rosie popped a black one in her mouth. "Mmm, licorice."

Em leaned back a little and sized up Celia. "You're starting to show. How many months is it?"

"About four. Going on five."

Rosie asked, "You been to see a doctor about the baby?"

"No, why should I spend money on a doctor? It's not like the baby'll listen to what a doctor says. She'll come when she comes."

Em asked, "You think it's a girl?"

"Sure, that's what I'm hoping. Eddie said the guys at the garage wanted to start a betting pool, but I told him he can't be spending money on such foolishness."

Rosie laughed at that. "I heard Clarence took up with some theatre type. You know anything about that?"

"He's old news. I don't care if he marries the queen of England." Celia helped herself to a red gumdrop, letting the sugar dissolve before she chomped down on it.

Em said, "Rosie's found herself a new beau, a six-footer."

Rosie smirked and shook her head. She was a tall beanstalk of a girl and didn't like dating guys who were shorter than her. "Only saw the guy twice. I ain't jumping into anything."

Celia looked at Em. "How's your mother?"

"Not getting any better. My sister stays with her during the day now, and I take care of her at night."

"Well, if you want some help, just let me know." Celia figured she could spare a little time for her friend. She'd never have to take care of her mother or father.

Rosie asked, "What's your secret, Celia? To landing a man like Ed?"

"Well, maybe I learned something from taking up with that skinflint Clarence. I'd say don't be too quick to let a fella know you're interested."

"Yeah," Em said, "most guys are just looking for a girl to get in bed and aren't thinking about getting married."

"Maybe it was just dumb luck, me finding my Eddie. If I hadn't met him, I might be stuck with some guy like Clarence. A girl can't get ahead on her own, she has to get married sooner or later. And if she chooses the wrong guy, like my mother did, her life will be miserable."

Em wagged her head like she was skeptical. "Where am I supposed to meet a decent guy like Eddie? You can't trust the guys at the speakeasies, and it's not like I got a ticket to the places the upper crust hang out."

"I say keep an eye out for a guy come back from the war. Somebody who served his country and learned discipline. Eddie said the Navy woke him up to how to work hard and make something of yourself."

"Easy to say," Em said. "But lots of guys never came back from the war. And some of the ones that did are damaged goods."

"Yeah," Celia said, "three of my brothers went over to fight, and I heard not one of them came back."

"Were you close to them?"

"Never really knew 'em. By the time, I came along they were long gone." Celia smiled. "I got some news. Me and Eddie moved into a three-room apartment and bought a set of brand-new furniture. You ought to stop by and visit."

Rosie whistled. "Well, listen to you. You rob a bank or something?"

"Bought it on the installment plan. You can do that now." Of course, Celia would never tell them she and Ed were committing robberies. They'd agreed it was their secret. Then she wondered: What would Em and Rosie think if they knew? And that made her feel a mixture of shame and embarrassment—just like she'd felt when she started school and the other girls made fun of her haircut, which wasn't really a haircut, just handfuls of hair hacked off at different lengths.

Em hunched a shoulder. "I got an uncle who says you should never buy anything you can't pay for all at once— that people are getting suckered into buying stuff they can't afford."

Celia recalled a sermon by Father Mulvaney about it being easier for a camel to get through a needle's eye than a rich man to get into heaven. She asked, "Is your uncle a priest or something?"

"No, he's a communist."

Celia asked, "What's that?"

Em said, "You know, like those Russians who killed the Czar and his wife and kids."

"Well," Celia said, "that ain't anything to be proud of—killing somebody and his family."

Rosie said, "I don't know anything about that. I just want to find a fella who'll treat me right and buy me stuff, like Celia's Ed."

"Yeah," said Celia. "All I want is for my kid to sleep in a nice crib and have toys and all."

A Barrel of Fish
Brooklyn, January 22, 1924

Come the end of January Celia's baby bump started to show pretty well. Her sealskin coat was roomy enough, but she figured they couldn't do too many more jobs before it'd be obvious she was pregnant—and that'd make her an easy target for the gumshoes.

Over dinner Tuesday night, she said, "Eddie, we got to get enough money so we can pay off our bills before the baby comes. What do you say we do another job tonight?"

Ed scrunched up a cheek. "Are you sure, doll? You been awful moody, and I don't want you blubbering in the middle of a holdup."

"I know, seems like I'm either laughing or crying lately, but it'll be all right. I promise."

"Well, if you're sure you can handle it."

"Yeah, I'm sure. Just one more big job and we can lay off for good."

They walked to the garage in the freezing cold. Ed put the fake license plates on a black-as-night Ford, and around ten o'clock they rolled onto Brooklyn's streets. They found a corner grocery store just a few blocks from the drugstore they'd robbed Sunday night. Ed had a good route picked out to get them back home on less-traveled streets, and they only had a dozen blocks to cover anyway.

He parked the car, and Celia went in first. There was one man at the counter, a short fella with a toothy smile. He rubbed his hands together and said, all cheery, "Good evening, miss. How can I help you?"

"I'd like a bar of Fels Naptha, please."

While he was fetching the soap, Celia noticed a fishy smell. She turned around and spotted a big barrel of dried fish. She never liked fish, especially smelly fish, and they looked disgusting, wrinkled up and yellow, brown, and black. But all of a sudden she wanted to grab one of those fish and stuff it in her mouth.

"Hey, mister," she said, "what kind of fish is that?"

He strolled over to her. "Why, those are herring, the finest quality and very reasonably priced. Would you like any?"

Her mouth was watering something fierce, and all she could think about was chowing down on some fish. "Will you wrap a big one up for me?"

Then she heard the door open. Ed strolled in and gaped at her with his mouth open, and his brow furrowed. That woke her up.

While the clerk was bending over the barrel wrapping up a fish, she pulled out her gun and tickled his ribs with it. "This is a holdup, mister."

He stuck up his arms. "Oh, lady, please don't shoot."

"Just keep your hands up, and move it." She motioned to the back of the store and he marched down the aisle. She made him stand behind a partition in the rear so nobody could see them from the street and waited for Ed to call for her.

She heard the door open and a woman's voice say, "Oh, hello, is Mr. Fishbein in?"

She wondered what Ed was going to do. She stepped back so she could see what was happening, keeping her gun on the clerk.

The woman looked at Ed, who was busy rifling through the cash register and said, casual as could be, "I need a pound of butter."

Jeez, couldn't she see this was a holdup? Why did the women always cause trouble?

Ed shook his head like he couldn't believe this batty dame. He pulled out his gun and said, "You can get your butter later, lady. Now move it." He waved his gun at her, and the woman did like he said.

When the lady saw Celia covering the clerk, she came and stood beside him and asked, "Are you all right, Mr. Fishbein?"

"Yes," he said, "just do what they say."

"That's the right idea, folks. Nobody needs to play the big hero. We aren't going to hurt you." Celia was getting the hang of this stick-up business. And she was finally earning some respect, like she wasn't just a two-bit shrimp. At her parochial school some of the girls in her level had teased her about being a skinny runt. But once, after school, when a boy called her and some other girls tramps, she slugged him in the nose. The girls quit making fun of her after that and even started calling her Toughie.

"Okay," Ed hollered.

Celia backed away from the twosome. But she hadn't

forgotten about that barrel of fish, and as she passed it she reached in and grabbed the half-wrapped fish. She held the door open and called out, "When the cops wake up tell them this is how a good job is done. I didn't have time to scribble a love note for them. I got a date tonight."

As they drove away, Ed grabbed the steering wheel tight and high with both hands. "What the hell were you thinking—chatting up the clerk like that?"

"I just wanted to know what kind of fish it was."

"You can't let people get a good look at you like that. I mean it, Celia."

"All right, don't be making such a fuss."

"You want us to get caught or something?"

"No, that's stupid."

"We can't be taking risks like that. You hear me?"

"Yeah, sure." She couldn't wait any longer. She unwrapped the dried fish she'd grabbed on the way out and started munching on it.

Ed said, "That thing stinks to high heaven."

But Celia paid him no mind. It tasted scrumptious.

In The Commissioner's Backyard
Brooklyn, January 23–24, 1924

William Casey tossed the Wednesday morning newspapers on his desk. He knew he couldn't trust a damn word the newspapers printed, but he had to be prepared to counter the inaccuracies when reporters came around. It seemed everybody in the city was talking about the bob-haired bandit's robbery spree—and the police department's ineptitude. He was so desperate to crack this case he was dreaming about speeding after these two in a wild street race and, when they crashed into a lamp post, yanking them out by the collar.

This dame and her companion were wily, but they were bound to slip up sooner or later. And given all the press they were getting, they might start bragging around town. Or somebody who knew them might put two and two together. He'd gather all the descriptions they had so far and call a press conference. Maybe getting the right details out there would lead to the tip that'd crack the case.

The Brooklyn Standard Union and *Brooklyn Citizen* trumpeted the Fishbein grocery robbery like cops and robbers was a sporting event. He plowed through the columns, and then he saw they'd brought Commissioner Enright into the picture: "Strangely, all the bob-haired robberies have been perpetrated in the Atlantic Avenue

Precinct, within the confines of which Richard E. Enright and Capt. William J. Casey, who is in charge of the detectives of Brooklyn and Queens. In fact, Enright's home is in close proximity to the places robbed."

He scrambled to the door and called down the hall, "Frank, get in here, right now."

Frank Gray marched in and closed the door behind him.

"Have you read *The Brooklyn Standard* article about the Fishbein robbery?"

Gray sat leaning over his knees. "Yeah, I read it. And then I threw it in the trash."

"You saw they reported all the robberies are in Enright's backyard?"

"Sure. Have you heard from the commissioner yet?"

"I expect the phone'll ring any minute. You got any updates for me?"

"Nothing more than I put in my report."

Damn it. He expected his second-in-command to do some thinking for himself. "And what's your next move?"

"I was planning on knocking on some doors in the neighborhood this morning to see if anybody has a description of the car."

"While you're at it, canvas neighborhood stores, too. Find out if they've seen anybody flashing money around lately. Maybe these crooks live in the neighborhood they're robbing, and that's why they're getting off the streets so fast. They have to be spending all that dough somewhere."

"Sure thing, Bill. Is that all?"

Casey drummed his fingers on his desk. "Not unless you got any other ideas for collaring these two."

"I'll let you know if I think of anything else."

"Yeah, do that."

Gray stood and made for the door, then swung around. "You worried about your job, Bill?"

"Nah, we'll get these two soon enough."

"Yeah, sure. I'll check in with you this afternoon on what I find."

But Casey was worried. Commissioner Enright had recently made a show of housecleaning throughout the department. A few weeks ago, he'd charged twelve police inspectors with neglect of duty, grandstanding about how he wasn't afraid to fire, demote, transfer, or indict underlings guilty of wrongdoing. Since then the twelve men had kept a low profile—and their jobs—and Casey hoped Enright was just posturing for the press.

Casey figured if he didn't catch this girl bandit and her accomplice, Enright wouldn't hesitate to put him back on the streets to make an example of him. That'd mean a cut in salary. And no vacation for Fiona. And problems paying for his son's education. Damn it, he needed to snare these two before they made his life a living hell.

He finished reading the newspapers and traipsed down the hall to McGowan's office.

"Hey, Mac, what other ideas you got for catching this bob-haired pain in the ass?"

Mac stretched out his lanky legs. "I was thinking we could set up some roadblocks in the neighborhood and check cars for twosomes that match the description. We know the girl is short and always wears a fur coat. And the tall guy has a brown overcoat."

"When Frank gets back this afternoon let's talk about setting those up."

"Of course, Captain."

"And put the word out to the newspapers that I'll be holding a press conference tomorrow afternoon at three. Since they insist on giving this bandit front-page coverage we might as well tell our side of the story."

Casey returned to his desk and phoned the commissioner's office. He decided beating Enright to the punch was the best way to handle his aggravation about this case.

When Enright's assistant put him through, Casey said, "Hello, sir. I wanted to give you a quick update. We'll be setting up some roadblocks over the next few days to try to apprehend the bob-haired bandit and her companion."

"Sure. Say, I asked my assistant to map all the robberies those two committed, and there's a definite pattern."

Honestly, did the commissioner think he was an imbecile? "Yes, we have them mapped, too. It's like the papers say: All the robbed stores are in proximity to the Atlantic Avenue Precinct."

"And my home, too. You think this couple is thumbing their nose at me?"

"My theory is they live in the vicinity, sir."

"Well, it seems odd that they're operating right under your nose and you can't catch them. Could they be part of some gang that's buying protection?"

"It's always possible, but I think it's unlikely."

"Then how in the world do you explain the officers in your precinct not apprehending them when the store owners call right after the robberies?"

"My hunch is they're getting off the streets quickly because they reside in the neighborhood."

"If I find out they're paying off some officers in your precinct, there'll be hell to pay, Casey. You better at least check that angle."

"Yes, sir. I'll do that."

Casey knew there were some rotten apples here and there on the Brooklyn force, but they mostly took payouts from speakeasies and rum runners, not two-bit thieves. Still, he'd check the time sheets and see if there was any pattern to officers on duty the nights of the bob-haired robberies—in case they were looking the other way for some reason.

The next afternoon, Casey held his press conference. He made a point of articulating clear descriptions that all the victims of the bob-haired bandit agreed on. He also put out the theory that these two lived in the vicinity of the Atlantic Avenue Precinct and urged anyone who lived in the neighborhood to come forward with any pertinent clues—information about spending sprees or boasts of newfound riches. He imagined his appeal would bring in a flood of irrelevant tips. Still, he held out hope that one precious nugget might emerge.

All in the Family
Brooklyn, January 25–26, 1924

After the Fishbein job Celia and Ed decided it would be best to lay low for a while. Besides, Celia wasn't herself these days, what with worrying about their bills and the coppers. They'd paid the rent for February, but their money was running low, and she'd been pinching pennies all week. Good thing Ed got paid on Friday.

"Eddie, I need some new clothes. My dresses are too tight. Can we go shopping tomorrow?"

"I suppose, kitten."

"And we need to buy some more plates." They'd invited Ed's mother and brothers over for dinner on Saturday night. Celia had spent the whole week scrubbing the walls and polishing the furniture so everything'd be perfect for company.

On Saturday morning, they borrowed Mr. Horgan's Oldsmobile and drove to the Frederick Loeser Department Store. When she held up two maternity dresses—one dusty-blue and the other jade—he said she looked beautiful, that the colors showed off her complexion and chestnut hair. Celia loved shopping with Ed. He always flattered her when she dressed up.

The only other person who had made her feel that way was her Aunt Margaret. Celia remembered when her aunt gave her a brand-new dress and told her, "Don't you look darling."

Celia had almost burst with happiness. She fingered the three shiny white buttons on the sleeves of the blue cotton dress and smiled. It had a frilly white collar and fit her perfectly. She was seven, and this was the first time she'd had a dress that wasn't a hand-me-down.

Earlier that morning her mother had ordered her and her two older sisters out to the streets. Celia had told May and Annie, "I don't feel like begging today. I'm going to visit Aunt Margaret."

May, who was twice the age of Celia but just as spindly, said, "Don't be silly. You can't go all that way by yourself."

Twelve-year-old Annie, who always did what May said, piped up. "Yeah, Ma'll be furious if you go wandering off."

So Celia pretended to tag along for a few blocks, but when they were gabbing to each other, she turned tail, ran to an alley, and hid behind a garbage can. When she was sure they weren't coming after her, she headed out for her aunt's apartment.

Aunt Margaret was her father's sister, and Celia had last seen her when she and her mother and sisters went to Sunday Mass at St. Peter's Church. Celia had sat next to Aunt Margaret. She felt special sitting on the smooth wooden pew in church and doing just what her aunt did— standing, kneeling, or sitting. Some of the church windows were tilted open, and she liked the smell in the air, like fresh trees from outside and sweet burning wood inside.

Her aunt had told her when she turned eight she could be confirmed and start taking communion, and Celia was looking forward to marching up the aisle with the other kids and grown-ups. The priest said God was everywhere and loved everybody, and when Celia heard the choir singing and the sun lighting up the colored windows, she could feel God all around.

After Mass, her aunt told her and her mother she'd made a dress for Celia and that her mother should bring her by for the fitting. But that could be forever because her mother hardly ever took her to see Aunt Margaret, and she didn't want to wait. So that morning Celia walked the twelve blocks to her aunt's apartment and, sure enough, her aunt was home.

When Aunt Margaret answered the door, she said. "Well, goodness gracious, did you come all this way by yourself?"

Celia nodded. "It's not that far."

Aunt Margaret invited her in and said, "How about a warm mug of milk and some cookies? And then I'll walk you home."

Her aunt lived alone. She was practically a widow because the man she was going to marry worked construction jobs and died when some scaffolding gave way. She had a sewing machine in her bedroom and used it to make dresses for ladies.

Her aunt's apartment was the nicest place Celia had ever seen. It was always neat and clean, and the couch and stuffed chair in the parlor were the same color, a pretty green, and there was a lamp with a shade made of yellow, orange, and brown glass. When the lamp was turned on the glass shade gleamed like the stained-glass windows in church.

Aunt Margaret sat them down at the kitchen table and stirred some sugar into Celia's mug of warm milk. "Celia, if your father ever pushes you down the stairs again or hits you, you let me know."

Celia had smarted off to her father, and he got mad and shoved her down the stairs. She had a big bruise on her arm, but it had turned yellow. "How did you hear about that?"

"Your sister told me. If something like that happens again, will you come right over here?"

"Okay." But Celia wasn't sure she should tattle on her father because then both her mother and father would be mad at her.

When Celia finished her milk and cookies, Aunt Margaret cleaned her face with a washcloth and helped her into her new dress.

"Can I keep it?" Celia asked.

"Of course you can. It's too small for your sisters. It's all yours."

Her aunt said, "Celia, you can't be coming all this way by yourself without telling your mother. She'll worry about you. Will you promise you won't do that again?"

"Okay," Celia said. "Do you think I could come live with you?"

"No, I'm sorry. You belong with your family."

There was a knock on the door, and her aunt answered it.

Celia's mother barged in and said, "Celia, what in the world are you doing? You can't run off like that."

Aunt Margaret smiled at her and said, "No harm done. I was going to walk her home. We've had a lovely time."

"Celia, come here," her mother said.

Celia looked at her aunt. She wanted to stay and eat more cookies. Her aunt's apartment was clean and smelled like perfume. And she loved nestling into the corner of the soft, cozy couch.

Her aunt said, "Go ahead, Celia. I'll see you at church."

Her mother scowled at her aunt. "Where's the dress she was wearing?"

Aunt Margaret plucked her old dress off the chair and handed it to her mother.

Her mother took her by the hand and said to her aunt, "Next time, ask before you steal one of my kids."

All the way home, her mother mumbled things like, "How dare she," and, "you can't go running off like that, Celia," and, "you ought to be ashamed of yourself, leaving your sisters to do all the work."

When they got home, her mother said, "Take that dress off this minute."

"Do I have to?"

"Yes. Come here."

Celia walked over to her mother. She twirled her around and undid the buttons on the back of her dress and pulled it up over her head.

"Here," she said, handing over her old dress.

Celia stepped into her dirty brown dress and wriggled

it up over her shoulders. It was baggy and hung on her like a sack. She hated it.

"Aunt Margaret said I could keep my new dress."

"It's too nice for grubbing around in. Now go find your sisters."

Her mother gave her a little shove, and Celia marched out the door. She wended her way along Lafayette and veered off onto Second Street.

She spotted May and Annie sitting on the steps of the library. They waved to her, and she trudged up to them and plunked down, spreading her dress over her crossed legs to make a place to catch coins.

May rumpled her hair. "Gave us the slip, did you?"

"I visited Aunt Margaret," Celia said. "And had warm milk and cookies."

"Did you bring us any?" Annie asked.

"No, Ma came and dragged me away."

May said, "You know she hates Aunt Margaret. Says she's a meddler."

"She gave me a new dress. It was blue and had frills on the sleeves and collar."

"Oh, yeah," May said. "Where's it now?"

"Ma made me take it off."

May humphed. "Well, you can kiss that dress goodbye. She'll sell it."

Celia knew her sister was right. Her mother never let her keep anything.

After purchasing two maternity dresses, Celia and Ed visited Woolworths and Celia picked out a set of six dinner plates—they were pearly white plates with scalloped red edges.

She held one up to the light. "Look how shiny they are. Won't they look swell on the dining room table?"

Their last stop was the neighborhood grocery store, where they picked up a pot roast, some vegetables, and a Hom-Pak of Vernors ginger ale. Celia asked the butcher how to cook the roast so she'd be sure to fix it just right.

By the time Mrs. Cooney, Owen, and Willy showed up at five o'clock, the oven had warmed up the kitchen and parlor. Celia was so happy to be hosting an honest-to-goodness family gathering. Mrs. Cooney sometimes had her and Ed over after Mass or for Sunday dinner, and Celia was pleased she could invite her to their new home.

Celia hadn't seen her parents in years. She'd gotten out from under them and their miserable ways long ago. Sure she was proud of Ed, and sometimes she thought of showing him off to her parents, but she figured they wouldn't care so why should she bother. There wasn't any kind of family feeling there. She was the youngest of eight and the runt of the family, and nobody had paid her much mind. She did miss May and Annie, but May's husband had ruined the chances for any kind of good times with them by ordering her around like a drudge. She'd learned to manage on her own, and maybe that was a good thing. She'd done all right by herself and wasn't a bit like her Ma or Da. She was no shirker or chicken-heart. And she always said if you can't find something to smile about you'll miss the sun when it shines.

"Welcome to our new home," Celia said. Ed took all their coats and piled them over his arm.

"Hello, dear," said Mrs. Cooney, giving her a kiss on the cheek. She was always sweet to Celia. And Owen and Willy hugged her. Owen was older than Ed and Willy younger. They were both as tall and handsome as Ed, except Willy had a birthmark on his forehead, an oval splotch that he partly covered with his curly blond locks. Owen was a real smart aleck, always joshing and teasing.

"Sure smells heavenly in here," Owen said. "Like Ed's not doing the cooking."

"Celia's been getting ready all day," Ed said.

Celia and Ed toured them around their apartment, stopping in each room so they could take it all in. First, they showed off the dining room set, next, the bedroom furniture, and finally, the couch and easy chair in the parlor. Celia was so proud she couldn't stop beaming.

Owen whistled and plunked down on the sofa. "You ought to have Mr. Schwartz come over and take pictures for his advertisements."

Ed grinned. "Nothing but the best for my honeybunch."

Celia asked Mrs. Cooney, "Will you help me check on the roast?"

Celia and Mrs. Cooney left Ed and his brothers to talk about cars and baseball and such. The three of them were big fans of the Brooklyn Robins. Celia liked baseball all right, and she'd even gone to a game once in the summer with Ed, but she usually stayed home and read when Ed went to the ballpark.

Celia opened the oven door, and she and Mrs. Cooney bent over and looked at the big pot, which she'd borrowed from Mrs. Cooney. Hot steam came rushing out of the oven and warmed and moistened her cheeks. The potatoes, carrots, and onions nestled around the roast. It all looked delicious.

Celia closed the oven door, and Mrs. Cooney stood up and asked, "How many pounds is the roast?"

She was a bit taller than Celia and plumpish. Celia looked into her smiling blue eyes. "Four pounds. I've been cooking it since two o'clock."

"Another half hour or so, and it'll be just right. Let's just you and me visit and leave the boys to themselves."

They sat down at the dining room table, and Mrs. Cooney asked her, "How are you feeling these days, dear?"

"Well, I'm hungry for the oddest things, like yesterday I got this craving for sweet corn, so I had to go to the grocery store and buy a can to gobble up."

"Yes, that's perfectly natural. I remember craving sauerkraut, and I don't usually like it." Mrs. Cooney scrunched a corner of her mouth the way Ed did when he was pensive. "Tell me, have you been to a doctor yet?"

"No, everything is going along fine." She didn't much care for doctors and hospitals, and they didn't have money to spare anyway.

"Well, it'd be good to visit an obstetrician. You ought to have one lined up for the birth so you know which hospital to go to."

"Oh, I'm sure we'll go to Kings County. And Ed can always borrow a car from the shop to get me there."

While they visited, Celia could hear Ed and his

brothers jawing and every now and then laughing. She felt warm all over—happy Ed had his brothers, and she had Mrs. Cooney, and they were all having a special dinner together. The guys all got along swell, even if they did cuss at each other sometimes.

Celia and Mrs. Cooney set the table and took the pot roast out of the oven. Celia plopped it in the middle of the dining room table and called the guys in.

She had put glasses on the table and an open bottle of ginger ale beside each glass. When the guys came in Owen pulled a flask out of his pocket. "Who wants a splash of gin?"

"Oh, Owen, must you?" said Mrs. Cooney.

"Come on, Ma, how often do we get to celebrate with Ed and Celia?" He poured some gin in his and his brothers' glasses and held the flask over her glass. "How about it, Celia?"

"No, I better not." She'd never tasted booze, and if Mrs. Cooney wasn't going to have any, she didn't want any either. But she didn't mind if the brothers celebrated, so she said, "You fellas can go ahead and have a drink."

They had such a nice dinner together. Of course, Owen teased Ed every chance he got. Ed, who was the quietest of the brothers, just smiled, and Willy, who also took his share of Owen's ribbing, laughed and changed the topic. Willy was a real softie and always stuck up for Ed when Owen teased him. Ed usually looked at his feet when Owen started in on him. He wasn't the arguing type.

When they were finishing dinner, Owen said, "Hey, Ed, what about all this new furniture? You trying to make the fellas at the garage jealous?"

Ed hunched a shoulder.

"I tell you what, wise guy," Celia said to Owen, "while you're at our dinner table, you show your brother some respect, or I'll box your ears."

Everybody laughed, including Owen, who held up his hands like he was crying uncle.

Celia and Mrs. Cooney gathered the dishes and brought them to the kitchen counter. The guys went back out to the parlor and lit up cigarettes.

Mrs. Cooney said, "You just sit and visit while I do the dishes, dear."

Celia relaxed at the table. Mrs. Cooney told her what she'd need to have on hand when the baby came—talcum powder, plenty of diapers, and wash cloths. "And you're bound to get tired because you'll have to get up in the middle of the night to feed the baby. So you'll need to take naps during the day, and I can watch the baby sometimes, too."

Mrs. Cooney was about as sweet as could be, and Celia knew she'd help her out if she had any questions about how to take care of the baby.

"Well," Ed said after they left, "that was real nice, doll. Everybody loved your pot roast."

"There are leftovers for you to take to work."

"You want to play some cribbage?"

"No, I'm tired. I'll just tidy up the kitchen and go to bed."

"I'll keep you company." Ed pulled out a chair and plopped down. "You and Ma get along real well, don't you?"

"I really like her. She's just how a mother should be." Celia thought Ed was lucky to have a mother like Mrs. Cooney. She had the sweetest face, round and with eyes that crinkled when she smiled. She'd make a swell grandmother for their baby. She once asked Ed about his father, and he said he wasn't around much and had died in an institution years ago, so there wasn't much to say about him.

"I got to tell you something, honey."

Mrs. Cooney had arranged the plates and glasses on a towel to dry. All Celia had to do was put them back on the shelves. "What's that?"

"I told Owen and Willy."

She whipped around and looked at Ed. "You didn't."

"Yeah, well, I didn't plan to, but Owen figured something was up. Can't keep much from him."

"But we decided we wouldn't tell anybody."

"I know. But you don't need to worry. They won't breathe a word."

"What if your mother finds out? What would she think of us?"

"They won't tell her. I promise. It'd break her heart."

"Oh, Eddie. I wish you hadn't. I was real careful when I visited the girls at the laundry not to give anything away."

"Look, they told me they'd protect me if things heat up, like give me an alibi. They're family, Celia."

She'd worked all week to make their dinner party perfect, and then Ed went and ruined it. She crumpled into a chair and cried.

Life Goes On
Brooklyn, February 2–3, 1924

It had been twelve days since their last robbery, and the Brooklyn newspapers hadn't carried a story about them for a full week. Celia imagined it was a good thing. Maybe curiosity about them had petered out. She hoped the coppers would forget about them, too. At first, she was thrilled by all the ink, but the bulls clearly hated the press portraying them as bunglers.

Even though she fretted about the coppers wanting to catch them, she was worried about their money running out. The first payment on the furniture was due in a week, and Celia wanted to buy some towels and a coffee percolator. It was funny; just when she thought they were all set in their new apartment she saw something in the newspaper ads that she wanted. It was like buying things was an itch she couldn't stop scratching.

They were reading the Saturday paper over breakfast, and she told Ed, "We're running out of money again. But with me showing and all, I don't know if it's a good idea to be going out on the town."

Ed plunked down his coffee cup. "In your sealskin coat you just look a little roly-poly. Who'd ever think a pregnant lady would be holding up joints?"

She fiddled with her wedding ring, twisting it around. "Do you think you could ask for a raise at work?"

"I got one before we were married. And even if I asked again, it wouldn't be more than a buck or two a week."

"How are we going to make that furniture payment?"

"We need to score another big haul. Like that first job. If we could get anywhere near that much we could knock off for a while. Or maybe for good."

"I'd be terrible ashamed if Mr. Schwartz and those nice delivery men came around and took our stuff."

"Yeah, I know. How about we go out on the town tonight? Maybe hit another one of the chain grocery stores. Do you think you can handle that?"

"I guess I'll have to. And maybe with people all worried about President Wilson the reporters won't pay us any attention."

All week long, the newspapers had reported that President Woodrow Wilson was losing his battle with death. With the president's story grabbing the headlines, Celia hoped the press would move on from the bob-haired bandit.

They waited until late, a bit before ten, before they walked to the garage. Ed dug the fake license plates out of his scrap bin and put them on a yellow Cadillac.

"Gosh, Eddie, don't you think this jalopy's a little flashy for robbing in?"

"Nah, we'll just use it this once. I been itching to take this baby out on the road."

They spotted a Bohack Grocery store on Hancock Street and Ed pulled up in front. "Go on in, sugar," he said. "I'll give you a minute to get things under control."

"Sure thing." For Ed's sake, Celia always pretended she was sure of herself. But she didn't feel that way. She'd been scouring the newspapers trying to find out what happened to people caught robbing. The only articles she could find were about forgery, extortion, or murder, which usually meant spending years in Sing Sing, except most of the murderers got the electric chair. She figured that's why Ed had made her promise to never shoot anybody. So she didn't really know what'd happen to them if they got caught robbing, but she figured it'd mean doing some time. She didn't breathe a word about this to Ed. What good would it do? They needed the money and couldn't quit until they got themselves set up for the baby. And turning all fraidy cat wasn't going to help.

Celia marched into that store like she owned it and looked around. There were three customers in the aisles, but she only saw two clerks, one at the cash register and another behind the meat counter. Just when she was getting ready to ask the butcher for a chicken, Ed burst in.

He grimaced and waved at her, and she stopped in her tracks. He came up to her and whispered, "A cop just cruised by so I killed the engine. Let's get out of here."

The clerk at the cash register was eyeing them. Maybe he was wondering if they were the bob-haired bandit and tall companion. Celia figured she and Ed weren't the only ones paying attention to all the newspaper stories about their robbing spree.

They headed for the door, and as they passed by the clerk, she grinned. "Can you believe my husband forgot his wallet? And it isn't even the first time."

She rolled her eyes to see if she could get a smile out of him.

"I've seen it before," he said with a chuckle. "Good evening to you, folks."

They hopped in the car and Ed eased out onto the street. He wagged his head. "Of all the rotten luck. We better find a different store."

"If the cops pull us over they'll find our guns."

"Yeah, we just got to do the job and get off the streets."

After driving around a few minutes, they spotted another Bohack store on Lafayette Avenue. In she went. There were five clerks and three customers in the store, but everybody did as she instructed, and they were in and out in a few minutes. They were home by ten-thirty.

Celia had turned superstitious about asking how much money they'd scored while they were driving or walking back to the apartment. She thought they should act innocent as angels while they were on the streets, and she'd asked Ed to do that, too. But as soon as they walked in the door, she asked him about the haul.

"Not enough," he said. "Nothing near what we need." He emptied his pockets onto the kitchen table and took off his coat. They sat down and smoothed out the bills and counted them.

"A lousy hundred-forty-eight dollars," she said. "What are we going to do?"

"We'll make that furniture payment. And then we're going to be real smart about our next move. Don't worry, kitten. Everything'll be all right."

On Sunday morning after Mass, they picked up *The Standard Union* and *The Brooklyn Citizen*. Celia thought maybe they wouldn't be in the news because of President Wilson. But no, they were on the front page of both papers. *The Brooklyn Citizen* said, "GIRL BANDIT AND HER AIDE BACK AT WORK," but their headline was much smaller than the big news, "WILSON SINKS INTO STATE OF COMA."

BOB-HAIRED BANDIT MAY BE
A BOY; CUSSES LIKE SAILOR
BUT HAS FEMININE FEET

The enigma of the hour in the Police Department is: Who is the bob-haired bandit who pens such defiant and sarcastic notes to the police after a holdup, who wields a gun with the easy nonchalance which another woman displays in using knitting needles?

The latest suggestion, one that the police have devoted more than a little attention to, is that the pert bandit with the black, half-portion hair is not a girl at all, but a young man masquerading in girl's clothing.

In support of this theory, it is recalled that in a recent instance in the West, a bandit persistently reported as a girl turned out on apprehension to be a man. It would be comparatively easy for a slimly built youth to successfully counterfeit a girl, and a sealskin coat might readily be stowed away in the tonneau of the bandit car to be slipped over the shoulders as occasion required.

The police admit that the bob-haired bandit, who has them fairly stumped, may turn out to be a young man, although they are inclined to think that the weight of evidence favors the suggestion that the bold person is a girl.

Her Feet Are Feminine

They have thrashed over at length the possibility that the evasive letter writer may be a cleverly disguised man, but it sticks in their memory that certain women witnesses who have seen her describe the bandit's feet and shoes as typically feminine and her walk as characteristic of a member of the weaker sex.

But weak the bandit certainly is not. In the more than half a dozen holdups in which she has figured she has carried out the harsh, dominating role of a thoroughly hard-boiled stick-up man to perfection. Her ready gun has not wavered ever so slightly in her hand, and the language she uses in ordering a hapless victim into a back room would awaken boundless envy in the heart of a deep-sea sailor. It is unprintable and torrid.

Her notes reveal no distinguishing marks which would aid the police in finding her. They are all printed by hand on paper of a common type, which yields no clues either in the handwriting or the make of the paper.

The police are in hope that she may betray herself in the end for she has written to the newspapers as well as the police and evidently glories in the notoriety she has attained. Someday this petite person with the winning manner and old salt way of speaking may let a hint drop in the letter which will help to unravel the tangled skein of circumstance that now makes her a puzzle to the entire Police Department.

Casey couldn't figure it out. He doubted there was any kind of protection scheme at work. He'd checked the time sheets, and there was no pattern to officer shifts the nights of the bob-haired robberies. Still, in the most recent robbery, the manager at the Bohack store on Lafayette had phoned the precinct minutes afterward, reporting the bandits made off in a yellow Cadillac. Three police machines quickly converged on the scene and combed the surrounding streets, but the getaway car had vanished.

Casey had hurried to the store that night to interview the clerks, and the descriptions matched up with those given by other victims. He knew without a doubt the kind of coats this duo wore and that the guy was six feet and the dame a foot shorter. He was sure now that the crooks lived in the neighborhood where the robberies were committed.

But the young twosome had never before been spotted in a yellow Cadillac. Maybe they were part of a gang that traded off cars. He'd have Frank run a check on getaway cars and see if any repeats showed up in recent robberies. But he'd probably have remembered a yellow Cadillac. Something wasn't adding up. How many cars did these two have access to, and where were they stashing all of them?

Plus, the handwriting and tone of the notes mailed to the precinct and to newspapers didn't match the two the bob-haired bandit had left at the scene of her earlier holdups. Casey was inclined to think the other notes were penned by jokesters for kicks. And in the last week, there'd been reports of robberies by a woman with two men as well as another female-male team. The descriptions of these five didn't fit those for the bob-haired bandit and her pal. It looked like the gun girl and her tall man were inspiring a bunch of copycats. Damn these two.

On Monday, he'd line up all the notes side by side and check the handwriting and type of paper used. And also comb through the descriptions of all groups of robbers that included a dame. But first, he'd have a relaxing weekend. These bandits rarely struck two nights in a row, so maybe he could actually stay home and laze around for a change. It'd happened before: While spending a day resting and letting the wheels of his mind mull over a crime, the pieces of the puzzle sometimes fell into place.

Sunday morning, he and Fiona went to nine o'clock Mass at St. Augustine's and afterward Fiona cooked a batch of fluffy pancakes. They settled at the dining room table over *The Brooklyn Citizen* and *Brooklyn Daily Times*.

"President Wilson isn't long for this world," said Fiona. "And now all anybody wants to talk about is how he helped those European countries after the war."

Casey was only half-listening to his wife. "Yes, dear, that'll be a big part of his legacy."

He was focused on the article about Enright's demotion of numerous detectives. He'd told Fiona about it on Friday, and he wasn't surprised that both the Sunday papers carried the story. One of the headlines read, "DEMOTION OF FOURTEEN SLEUTHS OF OLD SCHOOL AND PROMOTION OF NEW MEN STARTLES POLICE," and the other, "FOURTEEN DETECTIVES OUSTED HERE IN SHAKE-UP."

"I tell you," he said, "if Enright intended to undermine every detective in Brooklyn and set them to skulking the streets like a pack of hungry dogs, he couldn't have found a better way to do it."

"Do you think he'll demote any more detectives?"

"God, I hope not. If he expects these greenhorns fresh out of training to crack all the outstanding cases, he'll be in for a surprise. Nothing beats experience when it comes to chasing down clues."

Fiona reached out and patted his hand. "I know you'll catch that bob-haired bandit, dear. You'll show those new recruits how it's done."

"It's just a matter of time now."

"And then we can take our vacation. Do you think you'll catch them by April? That's when I'd like to make our plans definite."

"Yeah, they can't get away with such bold robberies much longer. They'll get sloppy sooner or later."

He sure as hell hoped he'd snare these two in the next few weeks. He knew the kinds of stores they robbed. His team had continued to map out the neighborhood they operated in. He had clear descriptions. In the coming week, he'd post plainclothes men around stores and schedule some raids and more roadblocks in the neighborhood.

The inevitable came to pass later that day. Casey was listening to a radio broadcast of the New York Yankees and Philadelphia Phillies ball game when the announcer broke in: Woodrow Wilson has died; the nation is going into mourning. But Casey wouldn't let that deter his quest to capture the bandits who'd become a thorn in his side. It was time to tighten the noose.

The raids he ordered on Monday morning netted two women suspects, a Mary Cody and Rose Moore, and Casey phoned Enright with the good news. But after he called in the store clerks for a line-up, Casey was forced to release Rose Moore. And given the uncertainty among the clerks about Mary Cody, he wasn't convinced she was their gal either. Helen Quigley was still in custody, but she was probably innocent, too.

Casey called Frank Gray and Mac McGowan to his office. He was too flustered to sit still. He parked a buttock on the corner of his desk and nervously swung a leg.

"We need to catch this duo. I want results out of you two."

Gray flicked his black locks off his forehead. "I say we keep stopping cars with bob-haired girls, especially after dark. Maybe we'll get lucky and apprehend her on the way to a job. If we catch her and her chum with their guns, all the better."

The spindly Mac swiveled around and looked down his nose at Frank. "Sure, and meantime the papers can mock us for bringing in every flapper in Brooklyn."

Casey glared at Frank. "We can't let press reports

deter us. The newspapers harp about us not catching these two and then turn around and criticize our tactics for trying to catch them."

Mac said, "It's a numbers game at this point. We've got plainclothes men keeping an eye on the stores. Sooner or later, one of them is going to catch this girl red-handed."

"Let's hope so," Casey said. "Frank, I want you to visit boarding houses and ask the proprietors about any girls who stay in during the day and go out at night. Or engage in any kind of suspicious activity."

"Sure, I'll start knocking on doors today."

Casey rubbed the back of his neck. "I'm starting to think we've got a female Jekyll and Hyde here—someone who puts on a show of respectability during the day but turns into a cunning robber at night."

Mac nodded and pushed out his lower lip. "That's a possibility. And if you're right, then we really need to catch her in the act. I'll look at the map again and see if I can spot any pattern. Maybe that'll give us some ideas about where to concentrate the plainclothes guys."

"Okay, men, get on it. I've got a press conference."

"Better you than me," said Frank. "I'd end up mouthing off at the buzzards."

Eleven reporters from Brooklyn and Manhattan newspapers waited for Casey in the bullpen. He tried to keep his head while they fired questions at him, knowing full well they'd mangle his answers whenever it suited their whim to add color to their stories.

"Detective Casey," one of the younger ones hollered, "what do you say about people calling this woman a female Robin Hood? Is that interfering with police efforts to apprehend her?"

"I don't see why it would. All the shopkeepers have promptly phoned in the robberies. The force is committed to catching this woman and, for that matter, all thieves who jeopardize public safety. I appeal to anyone who sees this duo at the scene of a crime to get their license plate number."

A bald fellow seated in the front waved a hand and, when Casey nodded at him, asked, "Given the hires of all these detectives fresh out of training, is the force using any newfangled tactics?"

Casey knew Enright might very well read whatever he said, but he was tired of catering to the commissioner's fancies and political posturing. "Detective work is methodical. It requires good analytic skills and the ability to comb through copious clues. Experience counts in this business."

The same fellow followed up. "Then how do you explain not catching such a singular pair of bandits?"

Casey paused to swallow his aggravation. "Think about it, gentlemen. The population of Brooklyn is well over two million. And there are thousands of stores. There simply aren't enough men in blue to canvass every store every hour of the day."

Another reporter called out, "What kind of profile has emerged of this thief? Is she a professional?"

"Without a doubt, this is a seasoned criminal we're dealing with. Perhaps a female Dr. Jekyll and Mr. Hyde. She quickly and efficiently rounds up the clerks and is in and out before victims can recover from their surprise and get a good look at her."

A reporter sporting a *Brooklyn Citizen* card on his hat rim asked, "What do you mean by a Jekyll and Hyde type?"

"The notes she leaves are misspelled in a studied way, as if a respectable and well-educated person is trying to appear unrefined. She may put on a different front during the day. A woman of two faces, so to speak." Casey scanned the expectant faces of the reporters. "But I promise you, we are closing in on her. I expect a break in the case over the next week or two."

Casey took a few more questions and then begged off.

On Wednesday morning, he summoned Gray and McGowan for a check-in meeting. Frank reported that his interviews at boarding houses hadn't yielded any suspects. "But," he said, "the proprietors are at least on the lookout for anything fishy."

"And what about your review of getaway cars?"

"I can't find any commonalities between the cars used by the bob-haired bandit and other thieves. Getting a license number would sure help."

Casey turned to Mac, "I hope you have some good news for me because these two are giving me a headache."

McGowan brushed a hand over his pointed chin. "We've got the plainclothes men concentrated in the radius of previous robberies. None of the shopkeepers reported any unusual purchases. A few of them got smart with me and said it wasn't their job to keep track of ordinary citizens buying big-ticket gowns or couches."

Casey shook his head. "Yeah, well, they squeal plenty when they're robbed, though, don't they?"

Late that afternoon, Enright phoned and told Casey to report to his office first thing Thursday morning—and to bring his file on the bob-haired bandit with him.

Over dinner he told Fiona, "Sounds like Enright wants to look over my shoulder on this case. I should be spending my time tracking these two down, not pandering to his misgivings about the case. If he's got some bright idea about capturing them, I'm all ears."

The Brooklyn Citizen, Page 1
February 8, 1924

ENRIGHT TAKES CHARGE
OF GIRL BANDIT HUNT

Police Commissioner Enright has taken personal charge of the pursuit of Brooklyn's most prominent and elusive criminal, the bob-haired girl bandit. It has been learned that the Commissioner, dissatisfied with the manner in which the case is being handled by Brooklyn police, has taken over the matter himself and will give it his personal attention until the girl and her male companion or companions are brought to justice.

It is authentically reported that Mr. Enright has notified Captain William J. Casey, commanding detective in Brooklyn and Queens, that in the future, he will personally supervise all work on this particular case.

It is believed that the case has annoyed the Commissioner as much because the girl has been operating almost exclusively in and near his home precinct as because the police do not seem able to put the cuffs on the daring, good-looking gun girl and her tall companion.

Police of Brooklyn today extended the sphere of their activities to territory outside of New York in their search for the elusive girl bandit, who has been robbing chain stores with monotonous regularity and success. Where the latest clue has led them officials declined to state. They were hopeful, however, that the young woman they want will be in custody within twenty-four hours.

Though two of the three bob-haired young women taken into custody on suspicion still are being held, police are of the opinion that the real girl bandit has not yet been arrested. One of those held is Miss Helen Quigley, twenty-three; the other is Mrs. Mary Cody, twenty-five, arrested in a raid by detectives on an apartment at 333 Thirty-ninth Street. The third suspect, Miss Rose Moore, nineteen, was released soon after her arrest, police admitting they had nothing on which to hold her.

Captain William Casey's theory that the girl bandit may be a feminine edition of Dr. Jekyll and Mr. Hyde—a respectable, normal girl worker in the daytime and the consort of bandits at night—has started police working along new lines. With this theory in view, they have appealed to owners of boarding houses to report the names of boarders who do not leave their rooms during the day or who act suspiciously.

They have also made a request to the public that police headquarters be tipped immediately if anyone answering the description of the girl bandit and her tall companion are seen near an automobile. It is thought the bandits are using a Cadillac sedan and a Ford touring car. Police believe if someone would note the license number of automobiles carrying bob-haired girls and tall companions the bandit would sooner or later be arrested, merely as a matter of elimination.

Authorities resent the allegation that they are not

putting forth their best efforts to apprehend the girl bandit. Everything possible has been done to capture her, they said, yet she has eluded police traps and police bait with consummate ease. The fact is being borne in upon them that they are opposing a super-criminal, according to one official.

One thing which is handicapping the police is the lack of enough patrolmen and detectives to make the activities of the stick-up gentry more hazardous. There are but one hundred forty detectives in the whole of Brooklyn, and there are several thousand stores to be guarded against the descent of the girl bandit and her tall accomplice. Moreover, police say the open-mouthed astonishment or admiration with which victims of the girl bandit submit to her demands is not aiding them any in the task cut out for them. If one of the victims would only hurl something through his window as soon as the bandits leave, thereby attracting attention, the robbers would be in custody in a comparatively short time, they declared.

The theory that the bob-haired girl is in reality a man in disguise has been all but discarded by police. All her victims, they point out, are certain that the voice of the bandit, though gruff and commanding, is that of a girl, and her general appearance is almost certainly that of a girl.

Getting Smart
Brooklyn, February 11–16, 1924

Celia wanted to pay off their furniture and buy a set of shiny new pots and pans, but she knew they needed to be careful about their next move. She was getting bigger and bigger around the middle, and her back ached if she stayed on her feet too long. She figured the baby would be born in early May. If they could make one more big haul in the next few weeks they could retire from the stick-up business. They'd be in the clear, and Celia could stay home, see her man off to work, and get their apartment ready for the baby.

After Ed went to work, she bought three different newspapers and a box of crayons. She'd saved all the earlier stories about their robberies, and she spread them and the new dailies out on the roomy dining table and got to work. All week long she scoured the newspapers, using her crayons to mark anything about the bob-haired bandit and police tactics to catch them. At the end of each day, she stacked the newspapers on one side of the table and got ready for the next day's batch. She arranged the papers at angles so she could keep track of the different days.

She got a charge out of what the reporters were saying about her, like claiming she cussed like a sailor. But she was also plenty worried about how desperate the cops were to catch them. She even cried over one of the stories. But she dried her eyes before Ed got home because she knew they were in the stick-up business now and had to finish what they'd started.

Ed was curious about what she was doing. "Hey, baby doll, what are you learning from all those newspapers?"

"I'm making a study of us and the police. I'll show you everything on Saturday when I have it ready."

She outlined all the stories that mentioned them with a purple crayon. Anything about how the police were trying to catch them she outlined in red. She planned on organizing them so she and Ed could figure out their next move. And she couldn't ignore all the advertisements, so when she spotted something she wanted to buy she circled it in green—like a shiny percolator for a dollar-eighty-nine and a cute baby crib with a mattress for five-ninety-nine.

When the weekend rolled around, Ed said, "Hey, sugar, you finally going to show me what's in these papers?"

"Hold your horses, buster," she said. "First I have to get some breakfast in me." She brewed a pot of coffee, fixed their food, and set the table.

Ed tucked into his meal like he was a growing boy. Celia was always hungry herself these days. She'd fried six eggs for them and buttered a big stack of toast. It sure was nice being able to afford to fill her belly with home-cooked food.

Ed leaned back and smacked his lips. "Now can we go through those papers?"

"Right after I clean up the dishes."

She had put the newspaper articles in an order to tell a kind of story about them and how the cops were trying to catch them. She figured she'd save the worst news for last so it wouldn't ruin the comical parts. After she cleaned off the dining table and washed the breakfast dishes, she sat down beside Ed and pulled the stack in front of them.

First, she showed him the *Brooklyn Standard Union* article about a Saturday night robbery. "Looks like we're not the only team with a bob-haired bandit. Here's a dame with three male accomplices. They even robbed a Roulston's, just like us."

"Well, what do you know?" said Ed. "Maybe if they track down these other robbers they'll lay off on us."

"I don't like these fakers nosing in on our act and making off with loot. Once we pull off one last big job and retire, we can be the famous bob-haired bandit and tall companion that stumped the whole police force."

Ed chuckled. "We ought to save these articles so we can look back and have some laughs."

Next, she showed Ed the column headlined 'BOB-HAIRED GIRL BANDIT KEEPS THE TOWN GUESSING.'

"This one takes the cake," she said. "Listen to this."

She trailed her finger across the lines and read. "What type of individual is the elusive bob-haired girl bandit? Is she a young woman of refinement who was reared in a good environment who is committing depredations for the thrill and excitement? Is she found in cheap dance halls? Or is she in love with her tall companion and under his mysterious hypnotic power? The cleverest sleuths are baffled, and none of the experts can agree."

Ed looped his arm around her shoulder. "We got all them educated experts scratching their heads, don't we, pet?"

"Yeah, it's funny. They're getting all tangled up in these fancy notions. And all the time it's just little old Ed and Celia Cooney setting up a nice home for their baby."

"I say let's keep 'em guessing."

She turned back to the story. "It says here lots of experts think I'm addicted to narcotics because no other kind of woman would so brazenly rob one place after another with such calm and courage. And one detective who wouldn't even give the reporter his name said he has no doubt that if one of my victims gave me a hard time I'd kill him in cold blood."

"Humph," Ed said, tossing his head back. "They got us all wrong, doll. And I don't mind one bit. Means we can go about our business, and they'll never suspect it's us."

She didn't want to show Ed the rest of that article because of what it said about him—that he kept at a safe distance until she'd subdued their victims and, when there was no danger, entered the store and took the money. It called him weak-kneed and yellow, a cake-eater type. Celia pretended that part of the story was nothing special and skipped ahead to the next paragraph in purple. "This here reporter is calling me 'Little Miss Jesse James' and says the only difference between us is Jesse James used a horse."

"Jesse, my little Miss Jesse. You just got a new name,

darlin'."

She gave Ed the stink-eye. She was still sore about him telling his brothers about them. "Don't you be calling me that in front of your mother. Or anybody else either."

"Hey, don't get so hot. I'm only having fun with you." He gave her a peck on the cheek. "Okay?"

"Okay." She and Ed needed to stick together, and she always felt like a louse when she bickered with him. She said, "You want to hear my favorite line in this whole article?"

"Sure."

"'This veritable will-o'-wisp goes on successfully outwitting several thousand policemen.'"

"They got that right. You're one smart cookie."

"And they say I keep changing my personality. How about that? This Detective Casey says I'm a Dr. Jekyll and Mr. Hyde.

Ed asked, "What does that mean—Jekyll and Hyde?"

"I don't know. Maybe the bulls are calling me dirty names because they can't catch us."

"Yeah, next thing you know they'll be saying we're devils from the deep."

She read the next bit. "This flatfoot Casey says I can speak in a soft, smooth voice and suddenly change to a coarse tone and that I even patted a woman customer on the back once and said 'Don't worry, dear.'"

"Did you do that? Say that to a lady and pat her on the back?"

"Sure I did. I don't like scaring people. Unless I have to."

She was coming to the hard parts, about how the coppers and detectives were trying to nab them. "But it looks like they've got a good description of me, and they're splashing it all over the newspapers. Like it says here I'm between twenty and twenty-eight, five feet one or two, with dark brown or black hair and big black eyes."

She looked up at Ed. "At least they don't say anything about me being pregnant. One clerk even said I'm a peach, and when I first came into his store, he wanted to put the make on me."

Ed crinkled up his nose as if he was trying to look mean. "Let him try."

She patted the stack of newspapers. She didn't want to frighten Ed, but she didn't want him thinking this was a joy ride either. "The thing is, Eddie, we're big news. And now every cop and gumshoe is gunning for us."

"Yeah, we just got to get ourselves set up so we can quit."

"This Commissioner Enright is getting antsy. Says here he's not happy we've been operating unmolested for a whole month. He's ordering some new detectives, a hundred and fifty recruits fresh out of training school, to track us down."

Ed flattened his palms on the table and spoke slowly. "Well, at least we know, sugar. We'll be careful. Real careful."

She pointed at the next paragraph. "Says here that most of the detectives on the hunt are assigned to the Atlantic Avenue Precinct since that's where the girl bandit has most frequently appeared. It also says those new recruits will be covering all the groceries and drugstores in the neighborhood."

Ed scratched his cheek like he was puzzling this out. "You done good, doll, finding all this out for us."

She was down to the last article, the one in the *Brooklyn Standard Union*. She gulped and pulled it in front of them. "This is the one that worries me."

She took in a deep breath and started reading. "Commissioner Enright has ordered the police to shoot to kill on sight—all two hundred fifty detectives and the cops on the street, too."

That wasn't even all of it. One detective said that the cop who tried to arrest her would have to either get a good drop on her or wound or kill her. She decided not to show Ed that part. She was already spooked enough for both of them.

Ed pushed out his lower lip and nodded. "Damn cops and politicians. Always flapping their mouths. Making us out to be cold-blooded murderers or something."

She looked Ed in the eye. "They wouldn't kill us, would they? Can they really shoot us just for robbing?"

"One thing I learned in the Navy is orders are given to be obeyed."

"What're we going to do, Eddie?"

"We stick to our plan. And we take it real slow and careful."

"We don't have to go out on the town tonight, do we?"

"No, sugar, it's too hot on the streets right now. We'll stay home tonight and play some cribbage, okay?"

Enright Calls the Shots
Manhattan, February 16, 1924

Casey was still smarting over Enright's most recent dressing down: The commissioner would call the shots until the bob-haired bandit duo was apprehended. Although Casey was still in charge of daily operations, he was expected to give Enright regular updates on all estimable tips and tactics.

Now Enright had scheduled a special headquarters conclave—of every single detective in the force. What the hell was that supposed to accomplish?

Casey emerged from the subway that chilly February morning and threaded his way toward Manhattan headquarters. As he approached the imposing columned stone building at Centre and Broome Streets, he joined a stream of morose suited men trudging through its wide doors. Who wanted to spend their Saturday morning being chastised by Enright like a bunch of wayward children?

Commissioner Enright's memorandum had ordered all hundred and fifty first-grade detectives to report to police headquarters at ten sharp. The missive was labeled 'Strictly Confidential' and indicated the meeting would be held in the auditorium on the main level. Given the secrecy, Casey wasn't surprised there were no signs outside the meeting room. He made his way along the tiled floor, listening to the men's heels clicking and echoing down the wide hallway.

He decided on a seat about halfway back, off to the side, not so far away from the stage that he couldn't hear well, but hopefully not close enough to be spotted or singled out. Of course, all the other detectives from his precinct would be in the crowd, but he preferred to sit alone. Since he'd been as good as demoted, McGowan and Gray had turned cool toward him, as if the smudge of shame might rub off on them. It seemed that he was Enright's primary target when it came to complaints about Brooklyn crime in general and this bob-haired bandit in particular.

Fiona had thrown a fit when he explained that asking for any vacation time was out of the question now that Enright had sidelined him. "Well," she'd inveighed, "don't be surprised when I up and go to Boston for the whole summer." Like he needed another kick when he was already down.

Casey shifted in his seat and looked to his side. He vaguely recognized the fellow on his left. "Say, aren't you Roger Wilson from Queens?"

Wilson offered his hand. "Yeah. I remember you from that double-murder case we worked on a few years back."

"Sure. Great way to spend a Saturday morning, isn't it?"

Wilson gave a little snort of disgust. "Any idea how long this meeting'll run?"

"Depends on how wound up Enright is. I heard he's

summoned all seven hundred second-grade detectives to be here at twelve-thirty, so I figure he'll dismiss us before then."

By the time Enright strode to the podium on the stage, it was ten-fifteen and Casey was as jumpy as a jackrabbit. Damn Enright—telling them to be there at ten sharp and then keeping them waiting while he preened.

"Welcome, men," he sounded out, "to the first special conclave of the department. I call you together at a time when the force is at a crucial crossroads. The recent surge in criminal activity has everyday citizens concerned for their safety. After consulting with Mayor Hylan, I have decided to call all of you together to renew our commitment to combating this crime wave."

Good God, Casey thought, did Enright imagine his corps of detectives didn't read the newspapers? Every one of them knew that ruffians had been emboldened of late, robbing stores and people on the streets with abandon, possibly because they figured if a woman could get away with robbery, so could they. Sure, there were some corrupt cops who looked the other way and took payouts from mobsters and rum runners, but a public scolding from Enright wasn't going to deter them—or spur the honest ones to work harder. He and all the other on-the-level men on the force were already spending long hours combing through tips and hustling to crime scenes when calls came in.

"I am charging every man on the force to work assiduously with the Special Service Squad to eliminate violation of the Volstead law. In view of the brazen infractions observed this past New Year's Eve and, for that matter, every day since then, the squad has been asked to double their efforts. We've got speakeasies operating with impunity throughout the city, and it's not just illegal sale of alcohol they encourage but other forms of vice as well. I am announcing this day that the squad will exercise all means at its disposal to shut down these dens of iniquity. And I will not look kindly on anyone in the force who obstructs apprehension of booze runners or in any way benefits from the operation of runners or speakeasies."

Casey had heard all this before, and, frankly, he didn't put much stock in the Volstead Act. Not that he looked the other way, he just had higher priorities—like catching thugs and murderers. The Volstead law had been folly from the beginning. He could have predicted the campaign to stamp out booze would fail. Sure, some guys overdid it and drank up their paycheck while their wives scraped to get by. But to deny every single man a glass of beer or shot of whiskey after a hard day of work was downright fool-headed.

"Now," Enright droned on, "there is another pressing matter about which I speak to you. The crime statistics for the month of January have now been tallied: There was more criminal activity in January than any other month in the duration of my six years as commissioner."

Enright squared his thick shoulders and thumped the podium. "Robbers are running roughshod across the boroughs. Businesses have suffered the loss of thousands of dollars. Shopkeepers live in fear that they will be the next burglary victim. Three churches in Brooklyn were robbed. Think about that—these criminals are so depraved they stoop to taking goods from our places of worship, churches which ought to be able to keep their doors open to those who wish to light a candle or kneel in prayer."

It was just like Enright to play the sanctimonious protector of the citizenry. He sounded more like a politician than a cop. No doubt he and the mayor had cooked up these choice lines because they were worried about the security of their positions and paychecks. And he and all these other detectives had given up a Saturday morning to listen to this tripe.

Enright grumbled and groused about the number of murders across the city, and Casey tuned him out. The fact was the force did a decent job of tracking down the worst of the criminals, and he personally believed his time was best spent bringing in murderers and hardened criminals who were desperate enough to commit murder. He counted the bob-haired bandit among the latter group. She and her companion wielded three guns between them, and sooner or later someone was going to get killed—either them or one or more of their victims. They'd lain low for a little over a week now, but he knew they were bound to strike again before long. They'd brought in a whopping six hundred eighty dollars on their first job, but only a smattering of that on subsequent robberies. He figured they were getting pretty hungry about now. He'd put as many plainclothes men as he could spare on Brooklyn streets between the hours of eight and midnight, which was the prime time for these two. And, under orders from Enright, he'd station a fleet of high-powered automobiles at precinct stations and in areas with high concentrations of businesses.

When he heard Enright mention the bob-haired bandit, he snapped to attention.

"I'm particularly distraught about this bob-haired bandit and her tall companion. How in the world can two such obvious thieves—who we have the most detailed descriptions of—operate with complete license in a circumscribed part of Brooklyn? It defies understanding.

"Not only does this bob-haired girl take delight in thumbing her nose at the department, but the newspapers are undermining public confidence in the force."

Enright's gaze circled the hall. "That means each and every one of you. This depraved twosome and their crime spree is an insult to every Brooklyn man in brass and blue. I have personally taken over the case, and I will not rest until we catch these two. Your first order of business is to bring this couple to justice.

"I'm telling you now if you do not clean up the streets and drive out the riffraff, I will shake up the whole force. Unless I see some immediate results in Brooklyn, every single post in every single precinct will be subject to review. That's a guarantee."

<h1 style="text-align:center">The Dragnet
Brooklyn, February 18, 1924</h1>

Enright ordered a dragnet of Brooklyn crime haunts and told Casey he expected not just arrests but plenty of confessions and convictions as well.

In the early hours of Monday, starting at two in the morning, police fanned out to all of Brooklyn's known dives and underworld rendezvous joints and rounded up every suspicious character on the premises. In anticipation of the frenzy of booking and questioning, Casey rose early and reported to the station at five.

Casey greeted the night-duty dispatcher. "Hiya, Al. No sleeping on the job for you last night I bet."

"No, Bill, it's been Grand Central Station for hours. The place is crawling with desperadoes."

"Any dames?"

"Yeah, three bob hairs."

"How many men?"

"Frank told me they'd booked eighteen hoodlums."

Casey hoofed it to his office and grabbed his notepad and booking sheets. He'd asked Gray and McGowan to report early, too, so he struck out in search of them. They weren't in their offices. He made his way to the interrogation rooms. Yup, there they were, across the table from two fellas who looked none too happy to be in their company. Casey would let them finish. In the meantime, he'd set up interviews with the women, who he'd planned to handle personally.

The first one shuffled into his interrogation room ten minutes later. Julia Sciretta was petite and clothed in a shabby, wrinkled dress. She walked hunched over and appeared meek, even scared. He'd bet the farm she wasn't the bold and elusive bob-haired bandit.

"Hello, Miss Sciretta," he said, rising. "Please have a seat."

The file said she was fifteen, but she barely looked that. "I see you told the booking officer you're fifteen. Is that right?'

She folded her hands on her lap and looked at him with bowed head. "I just turned fifteen."

Casey glanced at the booking sheet. She'd been brought in from a billiard hall along with two young men and another female. "That's pretty young to be out into the wee hours of the morning at a billiard hall."

She barely looked up. "Yes, sir. But I work there, and I can't go home until everyone leaves."

"And where is home for you?" The booking sheet explained she had recently run away from her parents' home in Bayonne and was living in a rented room on Cumberland Street.

"My parents live in New Jersey, but they don't really want me there. I moved here and found this job."

Casey knew he was wasting his time on this youngster. She'd stand for the lineup with all the others. But he doubted she'd be identified, so afterward he'd release her.

The second bob hair was also only fifteen, a Mildred Kostloski, apprehended at the same billiard hall. It turned out she was hanging out there with her friend Julia Sciretta, the employee there. And she was on the tall side, so Casey figured she wasn't a good candidate for the bob-haired bandit either.

But the third woman looked like she might fit the bill. She was slender, no taller than five foot two, and held herself erect and proud. The booking sheet had her down as Mrs. Jean Scharfman, age twenty-one, of 91 South Ninth Street.

She strode into the room like it was her personal parlor.

"Good morning, Mrs. Scharfman. I'm Captain Casey. Won't you have a seat?"

She huffed. "Well, Captain, I don't see why I'm here."

"If I understand correctly, you're employed at a shirt-waist factory."

"Yes, I have a respectable job. And a husband. How long are you going to keep me here?"

"Well, you're being held on suspicion of robbery. Along with your husband. You'll be here until we learn you're above suspicion." Her husband, John Scharfman, had a criminal record and was known as Detroit Red on account of his flaming hair. He was suspected of having committed a robbery of a Brooklyn restaurant with two other men. A woman supposedly drove the getaway car. Although no one had reported that the bob-haired bandit's accomplice was a redhead, it was possible this woman was one half of that duo, perhaps operating with one of her husband's cronies.

"Tell me, Mrs. Scharfman, did you and your husband rob William Yarrington, owner of the Atlantic Cafe, on the evening of February 9?"

"No, I work all day, and at night, I cook dinner for my husband. I don't go around robbing joints. And neither does my husband."

"Do you and your husband own a car?"

"No."

"Do you know how to drive a car?"

"Never drove one in my life. Never even set foot in a taxi. They cost too much."

"Have you ever engaged in a robbery of a chain grocery store or drugstore?"

"No."

"You do understand you'll be standing for a lineup later today. And that we'll be bringing in shopkeepers who've been robbed over the last several weeks?"

"I don't care if you bring in Jesus Christ himself. I'm no thief."

This dame was sassy enough to be the bob-haired bandit, but she obviously wasn't going to confess. Casey figured he'd stick her in the lineup and leave it to the shopkeepers to finger her. If nothing else, he could keep her locked up for a while and see if that took the bob-haired bandit out of commission. Still, he had to admit that keeping Helen Quigley behind bars hadn't done any good. He almost felt sorry for her. Clearly, she wasn't the bob-haired bandit, but Enright insisted on keeping her locked up, just because this half-wit Apples Kovalski had confessed she was his accomplice.

Casey trudged back to his office to look over the tip sheets from the weekend. He'd asked Gray to report to his office after he finished his interrogations, which took him most of the morning. Finally, around noon, Gray knocked on his office door.

"Come in," Casey called.

Gray sauntered in and, with a snap of his head, threw back his wavy locks as he sat down in front of Casey's desk.

"So, what's the yield, Frank?"

"Eleven confessions. And seven accomplices to round up."

"Any of them own up to associating with the bob-haired bandit?"

"Not a single one."

"Damn. What are the prospects for convictions on the confessions?"

"If we get positive identifications in the line-ups, I'd say very good. But some of them are roughed up from the interrogations. A few guys clammed up until I applied a little pressure."

"Okay, we'll charge them after the line-up. Have you had a chance to look at the weekend's tip sheet?"

"Yeah, I came in last night for an hour or two."

Casey ran his finger down the sheet and stopped at the bottom of the first page. "Not sure there's anything solid here. A Stanley Howell says he saw his two neighbors, Mr. and Mrs. Devon, loitering in front of Weinstein's drugstore Friday night.”

“Yeah,” Gray said. “But there was no robbery of that drugstore over the weekend, so I don’t think there’s any reason to check on those two. If the place gets robbed again, we can round them up.”

Casey nodded and flipped to the second page. “Here’s an anonymous tip from a guy who says he saw a man name of Ed Cooney flashing money around. What do you think?”

Gray flicked his hand. “We arrested him last November on a minor burglary charge. He and Lyle Rickert robbed a filling station. Rickert was the ringleader and drew prison time, but the magistrate let Cooney off.”

“I remember him. Cooney’s not smart enough to pull off a string of robberies.”

“And Mr. Anonymous could have a beef with the guy.”

“Yeah, I don’t put much stock in these anonymous callers.”

Gray asked, “What about the dames? You get anything out of them?”

“Two are ruled out. But one of them is the type to cuss and order shopkeepers around. We’ll see how she fares in the line-up.”

Later that afternoon, twenty-five men and three women stood for one of the biggest line-ups ever held at the precinct. Some of the victims identified their assailants, and Casey hoped they’d easily win convictions on these. But none of the victims of the bob-haired bandit singled out her or her accomplice. Casey phoned Enright with the news.

"Well, sir, the round-up was successful, I'd say. We'll be taking a half dozen holdup gangs off the street. My guess is these guys were responsible for a good ninety percent of Brooklyn's robberies over the last few months. And I expect speedy convictions."

"Was the bob-haired gal and her partner among them?"

"No, we had most of the shopkeepers from their robberies present, so I can say with confidence she was not among the lot."

"Look here, Casey," Enright said, "I'm getting mighty impatient that you can't apprehend those two."

"No one knows that better than I do, sir. Between all the new recruits and the machines on the streets, we're well-positioned to snag them next time they attempt a robbery."

"Any good tips come in over the weekend?"

"None worth following up on. I figure these two are lying low for now. But they'll be back. And next time they strike, we'll be ready for them."

Mrs. Dougherty Comes Calling
Brooklyn, February 22, 1924

Mid-afternoon Friday there was a knock on the door. Celia froze. She hadn't expected anybody to call. Could it be the cops? Think, she told herself. The guns—yeah, they're hidden in a shoebox in the closet. And the money from the last job is tucked in the slats under the bed.

She couldn't escape. There was no other way out of the apartment. And if it was the cops, they could just break down the door. She took a deep breath and marched to the kitchen.

Plastering an innocent smile on her face, she swung the door open. "Oh, Mrs. Dougherty, hello."

"Hello, Mrs. Cooney. Do you have a minute?"

"Of course, come in." Whenever Celia visited Ed's mother, she was offered a cup of coffee so Celia thought maybe that's what you did when a neighbor came calling. She stepped back to let the spindly woman pass. "Would you like some coffee, Mrs. Dougherty?"

"Oh, no, dear, don't bother. I won't be long."

"Okay, we can settle in the parlor."

Celia was glad she'd swept and mopped the kitchen floor that morning. The linoleum was sparkling clean, and she could still smell the Lysol. She led the way to the parlor and sat in the easy chair, leaving the sofa to Mrs. Dougherty, who sat down and glanced around the room. It was the first time their widow landlady had been in the apartment since they'd moved in.

"Such lovely furnishings, Mrs. Cooney. You've fixed the place up quite nicely."

"Thank you. We really like it here. After we buy a crib, we'll be all ready for the baby."

Mrs. Dougherty pushed her spectacles up on her nose. "When do you expect your little one to arrive?"

"In about two and a half months."

"Well, if I can help in any way let me know. Both my daughters have little ones now, and I must say I love rocking them to sleep."

"Thank you, Mrs. Dougherty. That's very nice of you." Celia wasn't sure exactly what kind of help she'd be needing. But Ed's mother, who lived a block away, had said she mustn't hesitate to call on her to lend a hand.

Mrs. Dougherty folded her hands on her knee tops. "Dear, I wanted to make a request of you and your husband."

"Sure, Mrs. Dougherty, we'll help if we can."

"My sister just lost her husband. She lives in Philadelphia, and I'd like to assist her with the funeral arrangements and, well, be there to comfort her. I know your rent isn't due for another week, but if by any chance you could pay early that'd help me out a great deal."

With Ed's pay they'd have just enough to make next month's rent, but then they wouldn't have anything left over. And she didn't want to admit to Mrs. Dougherty that they were limping along. "Ed will be home from work in a few hours, and I can talk to him about it."

"If it's a hardship, I will certainly understand."

"Oh, we'll be wanting to help if we can."

"That's very nice of you, dear. Now, I won't keep you any longer."

Ed was almost always in a good mood when he got home from work on Friday, and before she could tell him about Mrs. Dougherty he asked if she wanted to go out for chop suey.

"That sounds awful good, but I was planning on cooking a nice clam chowder. And we got to talk, besides."

"Okay, cookie," Ed said. "Let me get out of these grubby clothes."

She followed Ed to the bedroom. He plunked down on the bed and unlaced his leather boots. They were all broken down and splattered with grease. He always put them in the closet so she wouldn't have to handle them.

She sat down next to him. "Mrs. Dougherty came visiting today."

"Oh, yeah. Did you show her around the place?"

"Just the kitchen and parlor."

Ed stood up, slipped the shoulder straps off his overalls, and stepped out of them. He tossed the overalls into the laundry tub. He pulled his shirt over his head and threw it in the tub, too. She always soaked his work clothes overnight Friday so they'd have plenty of time to dry before Monday morning. Monday was wash day for all their other clothes.

Ed headed for the bathroom. "So what'd she want?"

Celia followed him to the bathroom and sat on the edge of the tub. "She told me her sister's husband died."

Ed stood in front of the sink, turned on the hot water, and sudsed up his hands. "That's lousy."

"She wants us to pay our rent early so she can visit her sister in Philadelphia."

"Oh, criminy. When?"

"As soon as possible."

Ed leaned over the sink and splashed water on his face and neck. He grabbed his towel and dried his hands and face. "How much do we have stowed away?"

She'd gone grocery shopping on Thursday, and it cost eight dollars to get stocked up for a while. "Only about twelve dollars. But you got thirty dollars today, so that makes forty-two."

"Oh, hell. I owed Teddy six dollars, so I only got twenty-four dollars left."

She hated it when Ed surprised her like this. He was supposed to bring thirty dollars home every Friday. "What'd you owe him money for?"

"Aw, don't get sore with me. Some of us guys were playing a friendly game of craps after work the other day. I was ahead of the game most of the time."

"Jeez, Eddie, you can't be losing your paycheck like that. We got rent and bills to pay."

Ed stomped out of the bathroom, and she got up and followed. "Now what're we supposed to do? Tell Mrs. Dougherty you gambled away our rent money?"

He pulled open his dresser drawer, took out a shirt, and gave it a snap before slipping it on. "Quit jumping all over me, will you?”

“No, I won’t quit. You lost a whole six dollars. We ain’t got money to spare with the baby coming. I want you to promise me you’ll quit playing craps.”

Ed turned around and looked at her. His head was bowed and his shoulders hunched. He took her hand and sat them down on the bed. “I know you’re right, doll. I was feeling lucky. I thought I could stretch some of our money.”

“You better promise me you won’t do that again.”

Ed wagged his head and looked down at his feet. “Okay, I promise.”

“Now we’re going to have to go out on the town to pay the rent.” It was all too much for her. She started crying.

Ed pulled her onto his lap and wrapped his arms around her. “It’s going to be fine, kitten. I been thinking about our next job. We’ll pick a new store, one the coppers won’t be expecting us to rob. And we’ll park the car around the corner so we can make a clean getaway.”

She let Ed hold her, and she nestled against his chest. But she couldn’t stop the tears. “Not tonight. I’m too upset to go out tonight.”

“Okay, kid, how about you beat me at cribbage again?”

TWO-GUN, BOB-HAIRED BANDIT
HOLDS UP SIX IN BORO STORE

Perhaps the most interesting, at all events most spectacular, crook of modern times is the girl bandit who appears here, there, and everywhere. Last night, after a three-week respite, during which many wondered if she had hung up her guns for good, the elusive and thoroughly businesslike bob-haired bandit returned to the job. She played the leading part in a chain store holdup at Dean St. and 3rd Ave. It was swiftly carried out and before the manager of the store, two startled clerks, and four customers had recovered from their amazement she and a male pal had robbed the till of $80 and melted away into the night.

Every detail of the holdup was carried out with precision, and the little group who faced two automatics, firmly held, are the authority for the statement that the twentieth century bandit is sure enough a girl and not a man masquerading in wig or woman's clothing, like several others recently apprehended. It seems there are more than a few fellows out there aspiring to emulate this pretty little holdup artist.

The store is one of the Butler chains. The holdup was

carried out shortly before eleven o'clock. Cornelius Roger is the manager of the store, and the clerks were waiting on the customers when the door was swung wide and in strode a fine-looking young woman in a three-quarter length sealskin coat and a black fur cap perched jauntily upon her bobbed locks. She might have been a customer, but this illusion faded as soon as she was well within the store.

In her coat were slits and very suddenly through those slits, two uncompromising automatics peeped out and a crisp command came in a rather coarse voice for everybody to put their hands up. Her manner was reminiscent of the gunmen of the old Western frontier who shot through their pockets.

She backed all the store occupants toward the rear, keeping them covered, when her companion entered—a man in a brown suit and cap, who also displayed a gun.

The bob-haired one told the little group that they would not come to any harm if they preserved silence. They did, for obviously she was not one to fool with. Then, while she held them the man robbed the till. No attempt was made to rob the customers.

The girl told those in the store they were not to move for five minutes. The alarm was quickly transmitted to the police of the Bergen St. Station, who hurried to the scene on the jump in fast cars, but the girl and her pal had fled on foot and disappeared into the dark.

Casey Versus the Press
Brooklyn, February 27–March 3, 1924

As Casey was wrangling his tie into place Fiona joined him in the bedroom. What wise guy, he wondered, cooked up the custom of a fellow tying a fancy rope around his neck? He hated putting on a monkey suit five days a week. Since adding extra weight, all his shirts and suits felt tight around the middle. And he knew he was no flower to look at in the first place.

"Bill, you need some new shirts."

"I don't have time to go shopping."

Fiona walked up to him and straightened his tie. "We could go Saturday."

"If I can take the day off. Enright's got every single detective in Brooklyn jumping when he says boo."

Fiona sighed. "Seems like you shouldn't let him rile you like this."

"You think I like being at his beck and call?"

"I suppose not."

"Okay, honey, I have to get going. Have an interview with a lady reporter this morning."

"I know you don't like reporters, so I hope you'll be a gentleman."

"Yeah, I will."

Casey had enough headaches without Enright

breathing down his neck and the press hounding him. The reporters who badgered him for a story didn't give a fig about all the hours he spent chasing down clues, rounding up witnesses, and interrogating suspects. They wanted the goods on this bob-haired bandit so they could sell their hopped-up stories. He could only think of a few clear-cut occasions when a newspaper story had helped him catch a criminal. Sure, tips usually poured in after a story, but most of them were useless, and oftentimes the sheer number made it difficult to separate the wheat from the chaff.

The latest in a string of reporters was this Elizabeth Smith. She perched on the chair in front of his desk like a schoolmarm ready to launch into the day's lesson.

"Tell me, Captain Casey, how you arrived at the theory that our bob-haired bandit is a respectable young lady."

Don't this take the cake, he thought, *calling this slippery eel our bob-haired bandit.* "Well, Miss Smith, I have encountered all manner of hoodlums in my years on the force. I wouldn't be surprised if *our* bandit holds down a day job as a salesgirl. She's comfortable ordering clerks around and is well-spoken when she wishes to be. But her notes look like they're written by a barely literate person, so I think she's trying to throw us off the trail."

Casey didn't know if his conjectures held water, but he figured if this bandit was a shop girl maybe broadcasting this theory would smoke her out.

"Exactly how many notes has she written? I have read reports that in addition to leaving notes at the scene, she has mailed letters to police precincts and newspapers."

"I'm sorry. I can't go into those details." Casey had compared the handwriting and paper of a few dozen notes, and he was convinced that only two matched the first note left at the scene of the crime.

"May I ask why not?"

"Look, a store owner already let the newspapers print one of those notes, and if I give you details about every single one of them, how are we supposed to keep track of those written by the actual bandit versus those penned by imitators? We have to guard certain aspects of the investigation."

"Might the notes spark someone to provide the tip that could help you apprehend her?"

Casey shook his head. He didn't have time to school this reporter on how investigations worked. "I doubt it."

"Well, then tell me what tips have proven unhelpful."

Here was a question worth answering, not that she'd print his reply. "Lots of people send us tips that are overly vague or far-fetched, like they spotted these robbers in Timbuktu or buying a ring in a jewelry store. If people would stop and think for a minute, we'd be saved from wading through the most ridiculous notions."

"How do you explain the boldness with which the robbers have operated these last two months?"

"Without a doubt, we're dealing with professionals who have thought through their every move. They're in and out of the stores in short order and off the streets before our cars reach the scene. They have access to several getaway cars. This has made it difficult to nab them. But I guarantee they'll slip up at some point."

"I understand that a special bob-haired bandit squad has been formed. What can you tell me about that?"

Oh, hell, he thought, *I wish that hadn't leaked.* It was true: Enright had assigned him and seven other detectives to a squad that was supposed to focus exclusively on this case. In the meantime, the fat cats were getting away with rum-running and big-money protection schemes.

He gave Miss Smith a tight-lipped smile and said, "I'll tell you what it means, Miss Smith. Criminals who brazenly terrify the city's businesses ought to sit up and take notice. While the newspapers may think it's great sport to report on their crimes, the commissioner and the police force won't rest until these two and their ilk are taken off the streets."

"Has this squad made any significant progress in identifying suspects?"

"That I can't speak to." The fact was, they hadn't, but he wasn't about to admit that.

"I must ask you, Captain, why are you so reluctant to go into details on this case?"

Casey let out a sigh. "Let me explain. I don't want any girl getting bandit ideas from an interview with me that ends up in the papers. Just last week, we arrested a thief who said he'd been reading about how easy it was to stick up people. I'm in the business of staving off crime, not emboldening criminals."

"Isn't there anything you'd like to say about these particular robbers, Captain? Something that might alert the public to the danger they pose?"

"Yes, I'd like to urge the public to record the license

plate number of any car speeding away from a crime scene. That's the kind of help we need."

"All right, but can't you say anything else about these two?"

"No, I'm sorry, Miss Smith. There's nothing more I can share at this time."

Casey should have known that whatever story this lady reporter put together wouldn't show the department in a favorable light—or help the cause of tracking down this duo. And sure enough, when the paper came out the next day, her story claimed the bob-haired bandit had the Brooklyn boys in blue running in circles and, furthermore, the police force was unwilling to admit their failings.

As to the bandit, this reporter wrote: *She might be some brave and daring soul with an outsized sense of adventure or perhaps someone purely and cussedly bent on devilry.* Elizabeth Smith even called her 'some girl,' as if she was a heroine among flappers and female criminals. As far as Casey was concerned, it was bad enough that women were drinking, driving, and smoking. Did they have to butt in on the crime racket, too?

Casey decided not to grant any more newspaper interviews. It looked like the bob-haired bandit enjoyed taunting the police and wallowing in the publicity. Maybe denying her the newspaper coverage she craved would push her to take even more risks and put her on a collision course with the force.

He expected Enright, who famously avoided the press, would agree with him on this assessment. So Casey was surprised when the *New York Evening Post* reported the commissioner had shown reporters around his map room. And he gave reasons galore for why the force faced obstacles containing crime: New York City was the 'hardest nut in the world to crack' and had more than four thousand automobiles and over six million residents. He claimed he'd need over a thousand more cops to effectively combat the pestilence of crime and snarled-up traffic.

It looked to Casey like Enright was starting to worry about his own neck, especially with the mayor returning from a six-month convalescence in a few days. *Good,* he thought, *let Enright get a taste of his own medicine.*

A Thrill A Minute
Brooklyn, March 5, 1924

When Ed came home from work Celia said, "Hey, Eddie, the cops won't be expecting us on a Wednesday night. What do you say we hit the streets?"

Ed scooped her into his arms. "You've got guts, kid. There's not a dame in this city who can hold a candle to you."

She gave him a playful shove. "You smell like a grease monkey. Go clean up for dinner."

Between handing over the rent early, stocking up on groceries, and paying off Celia's sealskin coat, the eighty dollars from their last job hadn't lasted long. Now that March had rolled around they owed fifty dollars on the next furniture payment. That last job had been a cakewalk, but it didn't leave them flush. Celia kept hoping for a big haul like their very first one. She wondered if this was what it felt like to be a gambler—always staking your dreams and hopes on hitting a big kitty.

Part of her knew it was wrong. She had quit going to confession because she was too ashamed to tell Father Mulvaney she was stealing. Sure, she'd need to confess sooner or later, but first she wanted everything to be perfect for the baby. Wouldn't God and the priest understand they just wanted to give their baby a proper start in life?

Still, another part of her got the biggest charge out of robbing—being famous and having people snap to when she gave orders. She wasn't proud of it, but heck, the money was easy. And they weren't putting anybody out of business—only taking a day's worth of sales. The stores could open the next day and make up their loss.

After they paid off the furniture and bought a crib, she figured they could retire from the business. With a little one cradled in her arms, who would suspect she was the daring gun girl? They'd raise their baby in a nice apartment with furniture in every room. And their little kiddo would have a grandmother and uncles to spoil her rotten.

Celia had cooked a meatloaf and planned on making meatloaf sandwiches for Ed's lunches Thursday and Friday. He liked them smothered in ketchup on Wonder Bread.

Over dinner she told Ed that lots of thieves had disguises. "I went out to the five and ten today and bought a blond wig. Everybody says I have dark hair so that ought to give the cops conniptions."

"That's smart, doll, real smart."

"And I'm going to talk like that girl from Georgia I knew at my old rooming house." She put on a southern drawl. "Won't that be a dandy trick?"

Ed laughed and slapped a hand on the table.

"And I bought a nail file and fixed up my nails." She held her fingers up for Ed to see.

He took her hand and gave it a kiss.

She laughed. "You're just like one of those Frenchies in the movies."

After dinner, they suited up, her in her roomy jade maternity dress and wig and Ed in a clean shirt and tie. She tucked the thirty-eight special and twenty-five in her coat pockets, and they picked up the Ford from the garage.

Ed pulled onto the street and said, "Okay, doll, let's go find a pile of dough."

"And watch out for the plainclothes coppers." She knew Brooklyn was crawling with guys just waiting to pounce, jawing with the clerks and maybe hiding in corners or lurking in aisles.

They cruised down Sumner Avenue until they spotted a drugstore on the corner of Sumner and Jefferson. The lights shone brightly inside, and gleaming green and yellow glass balls lined shelves in the window display. She looked across the street and noticed a large brick building with wide windows and all its lights on.

She gave Ed a nudge. "Will you look at that?"

There were scores of cops inside and even more streaming into the building.

"Uh oh. Looks like a convention of coppers." Ed sped up and swung the car around the corner. "I guess that drugstore is safe from the bob-haired bandit tonight."

They'd gone about three blocks when an idea struck Celia. "Hey, Eddie, I bet there aren't any plainclothes cops in that drugstore. We ought to hit it. Wouldn't that be a sweet joke?"

Ed scrunched up a side of his face. "You sure, doll?"

"Yeah, who'd expect us to pull a job on a street

crawling with coppers?"

Ed swung around the corner and headed back to the drugstore. They usually picked quiet streets, but here there were taxis coming and going and lots of people on the sidewalks. Celia figured that with all the commotion they could blend into the scenery.

Ed parked the Ford around the corner from the drugstore, out of sight. "Okay, kitten. Show time."

"Be sure to raid the safe, too. We need a big haul." She hopped out of the car and headed into the store.

The man at the counter looked up and smiled at her. "Hello, miss."

She walked up to him and asked for a tin of tooth powder. He retrieved it, and when she saw his hands were occupied she said, "Hands up, mister, this is a stick-up."

There were two phone booths on the side of the store and Celia heard voices coming from them, so she showed the clerk her guns and marched him to the booths. Sure enough, both of the phone booths were busy with girls yakking away.

Ed marched in and headed for the cash register.

She told him, "I got everybody covered here."

Celia tapped her pistol on the glass of the first phone booth. A curly-haired girl looked up at her, and her eyes widened.

"Come on out, you," she told her.

The girl hung up the phone and opened the door. Looking at Celia's guns and then at Ed, she said, "Oh, robbers. Are you the bob-haired bandit?"

"Don't be getting smart with me." She waved her gun.

"This ain't a Vaudeville act. If you don't want to get hurt get over there and keep your mouth shut."

About now the girl in the other phone booth caught on to the situation and cowered into the corner.

"Get out here, you," Celia said, giving the door a kick in the middle to open it.

This girl started crying and said, "Don't shoot. Please don't shoot."

"Just do like I say and you'll be fine," Celia said.

Then the front door jangled and in walked two men. Darn it, Celia thought, *I hope they aren't bulls with guns under their coats.* She aimed her twenty-five at these two and said, "Hello, fellas, I got you covered so get back here and behave yourselves."

The guys joined her party, and she lined up the five of them against the wall and trained her guns on them. "Now isn't this a thrill a minute? Everybody, just stay nice and quiet. There's nothing to be afraid of."

Ed came over to her and said to the clerk, who was wearing a white jacket. "Show me the safe."

The clerk said, "It's back here, but there's no money in it."

Ed poked his chin at the guy. "Just do like I say."

The clerk headed for the back of the store, and Ed told him, "Open it, and take it slow and easy."

Celia heard the clip-clop of footsteps behind her. She whirled around and noticed stairs on the other side of the store and a woman walking down them. *Just what I need,* she thought, *another dame.*

When the woman got to the bottom of the stairs, she

looked over the scene and said, "What's going on here?"

"Nothing, lady. We're just robbing the place."

The woman's eyes darted from Celia to the clerk, who was kneeling down in front of his safe. "What in the world? You can't get away with this."

Ed swung around and looked at Celia, his mouth gaping like he didn't know how to answer this lady.

Celia decided she better step up and handle the situation. "I'll take care of her. You just hurry up and finish."

Celia waved her pistol at the woman. "Okay, sis, shut your trap and join the party here."

That did the trick. The woman marched to the line-up and fell in beside the others. Celia glanced at Ed, who was fumbling around in the safe. Finally, he pulled something out.

Ed gave her a nod and headed for the door.

"Listen to me, all of you," she said. "Stay right here and be nice and quiet. I don't want to get rough with you, you understand?"

She backed away, and when she reached the door she gave them a hard look to show she meant business. She didn't want them waving down any bulls, not with a whole convention of them across the street. "Remember now, no funny business."

Ed got to the car first and, as soon as she hopped in, he steered out onto the street. She heard people yelling, "Thieves, stop them."

She swiveled around and saw all six of the people from the drugstore standing on the sidewalk hollering and waving their arms.

"Hurry up, Eddie," she said. "Or we're going to have coppers on our tail."

Ed stepped on the gas, and the tires squealed. They sped down Jefferson Street. He hunched over the steering wheel and held it with both hands as if he was telling the car to giddy up. "Maybe we ought to ditch the car."

"No," she said. "If they find it, they'll figure out where it's from. We got to get it back to the garage."

Ed concentrated on driving, and she kept quiet so he could do his job. She heard sirens blaring from cop cars, and her heart started beating a mile a minute.

They came up behind a slow-poke sedan, and Ed thumped the steering wheel. "Damn it, mister. Move your ass."

"It's not far, now," she said. She'd never seen Ed so flustered. "You're doing swell."

Those last four blocks seemed to take forever, but Ed finally pulled up in front of the garage. He hopped out, looked up and down the street, and swung open the wide garage doors. Rushing back to the car, he nosed it into the garage, braking and killing the engine.

He got out and slammed the garage doors closed. Celia jumped out of the car, too. Ed leaned against the garage doors like he was holding back a horde of invaders. The only light in the shop came from a streetlight outside the windows. They stood in the dark looking at each other with big eyes and breathing in the stink of gas fumes and grease.

Celia felt as jumpy as a grasshopper. It was only a

block to their apartment, but with cop cars on the prowl, she was nervous about them showing their faces. "Let's stay here until the streets quiet down."

"Okay," Ed said. "I need a cigarette."

She knew he was rattled because he didn't call her doll or anything. "Come on," she said. "We can get comfortable in the car and count the loot."

They got back in the Ford, and Ed lit up a smoke and clamped it in the corner of his mouth. He emptied his pockets onto his lap, and she could see his hands were shaking. There was some cash and two envelopes. He opened the first one and looked inside. "Nothing here but some war medals."

He reached into the second one, pulled out a ring, and handed it to her.

She held it up to catch what little light there was. "Looks like a diamond. But it won't pay the bills."

Ed shuffled through the cash. "Damn it, all we got was a lousy thirty-five dollars. This business is giving me ulcers."

She felt like a balloon that'd lost its air. "I know. These two-bit robberies are a lot of bother for hardly any loot. We got to figure a way to score big."

Ed's hands were still shaking, and he kept flicking his cigarette out the window even though it had hardly burned down between flicks. Celia scooted over next to him and put her hand on his thigh. "Imagine all those coppers out there scampering around like a bunch of confused cockroaches. Ain't that a kick? And here sits the gun girl and tall guy, calm as can be."

GANG OF BOB-HAIRED BANDITS HERE; TWO-GUN BLOND CULTURED, BRUNETTE NERVY

Has Brooklyn a gang of bob-haired bandits? It is becoming evident daily that more than one young woman is operating in the borough, with five hundred cops on their mettle and the public awaiting the outcome with mingled indignation and amusement.

For the descriptions of the victims do not agree. A number of girls, rather than a solitary bandit, are responsible for the holdups that have baffled the police since January. Brooklyn, in fact, is experiencing a feminine crime wave greater than any it has undergone before. The holdups take place within the period of ten to fifteen minutes, the getaway is a Ford car, usually a sedan, and is affected so quickly that the police seem powerless to catch the girls who may or may not be working in cahoots.

Descriptions of
Bob-Haired One Differ

The victims do not agree on the girl's description—which seems to prove that more than one girl bandit is at work. There is only one item on which all agree: the girl is short, a few inches over five feet. On every other point, they are at issue.

"There must be more than one girl bandit operating in Brooklyn, but I claim the original one robbed this store," said Louis Hecht today. Hecht is the clerk in the drugstore of Leo Weinstein at 259 Ryerson St.

"I looked at the girl for five minutes at least. She was dark, short, and chunky. Her feet were fat. Her nose was round and fat. She was five feet three inches tall, her skin was olive, her eyes were dark, and her hair was black. Her weight was easily 135 or 140 pounds. She wore no hat, and she was cool as you please. There is no doubt in my mind whatever as to her looks."

Different Girls Here

Two blocks away, at the corner of Lafayette and Grand Aves., Peter Kossman, manager of the Bohack store, was equally positive in his description of the bob-haired bandit—and a woman customer who was in the store at the time of the holdup corroborated Kossman's description this morning.

"I don't know about the other girl bandits, but there's one thing certain about the girl who held us up on Feb. 2. She was thin and hungry looking, a little dark thing with thin features. She didn't weigh a hundred pounds. Her voice was high-pitched, and she seemed excited. She was very slim, and she had a black hat and a dark coat."

"There was a red rose on the right side of her hat," added the customer. "She wasn't chunky; she was skinny."

The girl bandit who held up the drugstore of Samuel Weiss at Jefferson and Sumner Aves., when one hundred fifty police reserves were drilling in the 13th Regiment Armory, was of an entirely different type from the two just described by her victims. The girl who held up the Weiss store was a cultured girl, with well-groomed hands and a slightly Southern manner of speech. She was genial and plump—not underfed.

"She has bleached blond hair and is about five feet three inches tall," says Miss Adeline Weinstein, one of the customers in the store.

"She has a charming voice, and her hands showed grooming," said Mrs. Mary Freitag, another customer. "She had blond hair, very coarse. It was not natural looking and was either bleached or a wig. Her English was good. She called me honey and suggested I take a seat while waiting under her revolvers as her male companion robbed the cash register."

According to Sam Weiss, the robbers netted $35 from the cash register, his Spanish-American war medals, and a $425 diamond ring belonging to his wife.

The Damnedest Thing
Manhattan, March 5–6, 1924

On the night of the Weiss Drugstore robbery, Casey and Gray rushed to the scene and interviewed all six people at the store—the owner, the owner's wife, and four customers. Their descriptions convinced him that the job was the work of the bob-haired bandit. Sure, they all said the girl was blond, but the women agreed she was probably wearing a wig. He figured she had donned a disguise to complicate matters. *Humph,* he thought, *she'll have to do better than that to outfox me.*

When the wife of the owner, Mrs. Weiss, told him she'd memorized the license plate number on the getaway car, he nearly jumped out of his skin. Finally, someone had the presence of mind to hand over the detail that could break the case. Casey carefully recorded the plate number and asked Mrs. Weiss not to give that detail out to reporters. Publicizing the plate number would give the thieves time to cover their tracks.

Casey could hardly wait to get to the vehicle bureau the next morning and identify the registration for the plate. A phone call wouldn't do; he wanted to be there in person to lay eyes on the registration form and then run down the bandits.

He'd hold off on telling Enright until he'd pounced on the criminals. After insisting on daily briefings for the last three weeks, Enright had recently loosened the reins. Quit bothering me with all this unnecessary minutia, he'd harped, like he'd forgotten he'd been the one asking for that. Just call me when you get somewhere, he said. And, for Chrissakes, don't take forever.

First thing Thursday morning, Casey took the subway to the Bureau of Motor Vehicles in Manhattan.

"Good morning, Al," he said. "I got a plate I need to check the registration on. From a crime scene last night."

"Sure thing, Captain. You want a cup of coffee while I look it up?"

"If it's all the same to you, I'd like to see the registrations with you."

"Sure," Al said, and Casey followed him to the records room.

"Okay," the clerk said. "What's the number?"

Casey pulled the notebook out of his inside pocket. "327 639."

"327," Al said, scanning the file boxes. He pulled out the box labelled '325–340 Prefixes.'

Al shuffled his fingers to the 327 section. "Give me the last three digits again."

"639," Casey said, looking over Al's shoulder.

Al fingered his way through the stiff registration cards. "Did you say 639?"

"Yeah."

Al shook his head. "Nothing here. That plate number is not currently in use."

"Are you sure?" Casey showed him the number written in his notebook.

Al glanced at it and looked back at the drawer. "I have a 327 637 and a 327 640 but nothing in between."

"Could it be misfiled?"

"I doubt it. The clerk in charge of maintaining these files is as fastidious as a dog on a bone."

"When a number goes out of use, what does that mean?"

"Sometimes the car was in a wreck and damaged beyond repair. Or sold."

"Can you check on who it was previously registered to?"

"Yeah, I have to go down to the archives for that. You might as well have that cup of coffee."

"Can I use your telephone to make a call?"

"Sure thing."

The clerk left Casey in his office, and Casey rang up Sam Weiss's drugstore.

"Is Mrs. Weiss available?"

When the owner's wife came to the phone, Casey said, "Hello, Mrs. Weiss, this is Captain Casey. I'd like to check with you on that license number."

"Yes, Captain, have you found the robbers?"

"Not yet. Say, are you sure that was a New York license plate?"

"Oh, yes. I'm positive."

"And what about the number? Is it possible you got it wrong? A couple of digits mixed up or something?"

"Well, I kept saying it to myself until I could write it down. I think I got it right."

"But are you positive?"

"I was, but now you've got me wondering. Is there some problem?"

"No, just thought I'd check to be sure. Once again, I have to ask you to not mention this to any reporters. Okay, ma'am?"

"Certainly, Captain."

Casey fidgeted in Al's office, looking through his notes while he waited for Al to return. Maybe the thieves were driving around with expired plates, which wasn't exactly a genius move.

Finally, Al returned.

Casey sprung up from his seat. "What'd you find?"

"That plate was first issued in 1918 to the owner of a Ford truck in Cortland. It failed to renew as of 1922. So it's been out of commission a few years."

Casey scratched the back of his neck. "Jeez, Cortland's halfway across the state. But that number was spotted on a Ford sedan last night. How do you explain that?"

"Maybe the truck was stolen at some point, and the plates removed. Or maybe it was damaged beyond repair, and somebody hung onto the plates or found them in a junk yard."

"So there's no way to know who's using that plate now?"

"That's right, Captain."

Well, this was the damnedest thing. Just when Casey thought he was about to break the case wide open, he was back to square one.

Lying Low
Brooklyn, March 6–23, 1924

The close call at Weiss Drugstore scared the wits out of Celia and Ed. Over the next few weeks, hardly a day went by without some newspaper story about the bob-haired bandit or police dragnets to catch her and all the other 'depraved criminals running roughshod over the city.' Brooklyn was crawling with bulls. And plainclothes men, too.

The way the papers told it, every cop in Brooklyn was itching to lower the boom on them. Any bob-haired girl who looked at a store clerk cross-eyed or drove a car fast was dragged in for questioning. Plus, the papers said the courts were processing lots of convictions and sending busloads of guys to Sing Sing. Or maybe the bigwigs were making the newspapers print those stories to scare them— and any other thieves planning stick-ups.

But it wasn't just the cops gunning for them. On Friday afternoon, about two weeks after the Weiss job, Celia went to their neighborhood butcher to buy a steak for Ed. Right there on the counter was a steel-blue forty-five big enough to blow the head off a horse. The papers said some stores were closing early to avoid late-night robberies. Celia never imagined they'd get to be such big news or make all of Brooklyn skittish over a string of robberies that didn't even make them rich. Heck, they were more in the hole now than when they started.

Ed had turned gloomy after the drugstore robbery, and Celia tried to cheer him up by showing him some of the funny bits the papers were running. She especially liked how one person said she was thin and hungry-looking and others claimed she was chunky or plump. Nobody had figured out that she was pregnant.

When Ed was chewing down his steak dinner that night, she said, "Listen to this," and read to him from *The Brooklyn Eagle*. "What could be more unjust than the complete attention paid by the police to the operations of the bob-haired bandit? She is getting all the publicity, and sincere and hard-working yeggs, holdup men and gunmen who take pride in their work, are passed over unnoticed. None would blame the police for suspecting she is at the bottom of everything, since she appears to be everywhere at once. Nevertheless, impartial justice demands they pay more attention to masculine criminals."

Ed chuckled. "Well, maybe I'm safe for now. But you've got a price on your head."

"Oh, honey, are you feeling left out?" Celia pretended to chide him.

"Nah, the less they say about me the better. But you better not show your face." He grabbed her around the waist and gave her a smack on the cheek.

They both laughed, but Celia couldn't shake her uneasy feeling, and she suspected it was the same for Ed. All this attention meant the coppers were dead set on tracking them down.

For over a week, they had barely left the house, and Celia was beginning to feel like she was already in jail. Ed moped around like his Brooklyn Robins had bit the dust. She beat him game after game of cribbage. He just wasn't himself.

On Saturday morning, when the sun came out, she asked Ed if he wanted to waddle to Prospect Park with her. (She was starting to walk like a duck because of her big belly.) The expansive park about seven blocks from their house had a little pond and benches to relax on.

"I don't want to go out in public. And I don't want you out there either."

"But I have to go shopping every few days."

He shot her a mean look. "You're just going to our neighborhood stores, aren't you?"

"Sure, just like you said. But can't we go to the park?"

"No, it's too hot on the streets. Go read a magazine or something."

She and Ed usually went on some kind of outing on Saturdays, like window shopping or visiting a five-and-ten-cent store where she could look at magazines and books. She did all her cleaning during the week so they'd have the weekends free. And with the weather finally warming up, she was itching to get some fresh air.

"What are we going to do all day?" she asked Ed. "I don't want to just sit home."

"I don't feel like doing anything."

"Oh, Eddie, don't be like that."

"I'm trying to think. Leave me alone, will you."

It made her miserable having Ed sore at her, but she knew it was because he was scared. She was, too. The bulls were probably mad as hell about looking like brass monkeys. She figured she hadn't helped matters by writing those notes, calling them fish-peddling bums and donut munchers. But she'd only written the notes to help that poor Helen Quigley, who the coppers had finally released. And she'd only left three notes. But she must have started something, because the papers said the police were flooded with letters jabbing at them. And they were probably about as fed up as could be with all that taunting and jeering. Celia figured that arresting them wouldn't be good enough; they wanted to fill them with lead, just like in the Wild West.

After lunch, she said, "Hey, Eddie, I need a haircut. Will you trim my hair?" Usually, she and Rosie traded haircuts because they both wore their hair in bobs, but she knew Eddie wouldn't like her going out. So she told him how to cut her hair, and he took it real slow. That kept them busy about a half hour.

The rest of that day, Ed traipsed around the apartment, sometimes sitting in the parlor and reading the newspapers, sometimes lying on the bed and staring at the ceiling. Celia tried to read her Sherlock Holmes book, but her eyes kept wandering over the words, so pretty soon she gave up. She decided to clean out the kitchen cupboards to have something to do. Ed came and kept her company, smoking a few cigarettes but not talking much.

Ed still allowed them to go to Mass, which made sense because not showing up to Mass would be more suspicious than skipping it. They had gone to nine o'clock Mass at St. Augustine's every Sunday for almost two years, ever since before they were married.

After Sunday Mass, they visited Ed's mother and brothers. Mrs. Cooney made a pot of coffee and served soda bread with raisins. Ed's brother Owen was poking fun at him, as usual, asking him how many Fords and Dodges he'd welded together lately and whether his cheapskate boss was ever going to give him a raise. Ed didn't say much, but Willy stuck up for him and told Owen he was jealous because Ed had a nice steady job.

Celia could see Ed was trying to let Owen's ribbing roll off his back. But after a while he got up and took his cup of coffee over to the window and just stood there, looking out at the street.

She went over to him. "You okay? You want to go home?"

"Yeah, in a minute."

She stood beside him looking at the big brick building across the street, the National Biscuit Company, which took up a whole block. He kept staring at the building, and she could tell his wheels were turning. He always went quiet when he was trying to puzzle something out.

When they got home, Ed told her they needed to talk. They took off their coats and went to the parlor and sat down beside each other on their stuffed sofa.

"Look, baby," Ed said, "we're in the Dutch. It's all over for us here. We can't stay in Brooklyn no more. The coppers will find us. They got the heat turned up real high."

Celia's heart sank. She knew Ed was right. What had started as a lark had turned into a dangerous touch-and-go contest. "What should we do?"

"We got to get out of town, go some other place and start over."

"Like where?"

"I was thinking Florida. I was in Jacksonville during the Navy, and it was a real friendly place. You can go to the hospital and have the baby, and maybe I can buy into a shop. We can go straight."

"What about all our furniture? And your family?"

"There's nothing we can do about that. We got to get out of town."

"Gosh, Eddie, I never lived anywhere but New York. And your mother was going to help me with the baby."

"I know, I know. I don't like leaving behind family, either. But we can't stay. The coppers will find us if we stick around." Ed heaved out a sigh and ran his fingers through his hair. "Only it'll cost us to move down there and get a start."

Celia scratched her cheek. "I figured we'd have to do another job sooner or later. We'll need a big haul if we're going to move all that way."

"We been playing a piker's game. I'm thinking we could do a payroll job. I read in the papers that three men held up a plumbing shop in Brooklyn and got away with over four thousand. We could go after the payroll at the National Biscuit Company."

"But it's all closed down at night. And probably locked up real tight."

"We make it a day job."

"Gosh, that sounds pretty risky." The National Biscuit Company was right in their neighborhood. Maybe some of the people who worked there even knew Ed.

"Yeah, that's why we got to be real smart and real careful. I got it all figured out. Down to the brass tacks."

She and Ed spent all day Sunday going over every single detail of the plan. She tried to think of things that might go wrong so they could figure their way around them. She was proud of how careful they were being, but she was still mighty nervous.

"You know, Eddie, the coppers will be all over us if we make one wrong move."

"I know, doll. You got a better idea?"

She nibbled her lower lip and thought for a minute. "No, we need the dough to start over. Let's do this job."

Prowling Around
Brooklyn and Manhattan,
March 23–March 31, 1924

Celia wrote down each step of the National Biscuit Company holdup, and she and Ed memorized the plan. Then she tore the paper into tiny bits and threw it away. Ed recorded a few details they didn't want to trust to memory in a notebook, which she would keep in her pocket in case they needed it.

Ed would go to work that week as usual while they smoothed out all the details of the job and their great escape. Their loot was running low, and they needed Ed to collect his thirty dollars on Friday so they'd have some spending money before the job.

On Monday, Celia bought a suitcase—nothing fancy, but big enough to hold some clothes, the guns, and their take. They decided what outfits to wear, and Celia waited until Wednesday to do laundry so they could put on fresh clothes. On Wednesday evening they went shopping. Ed bought a new hat and tan coat, and Celia found a hair net and thick veil for her face.

Celia couldn't bear to think of leaving Brooklyn without seeing her Aunt Margaret one last time. On Thursday, she bought a Cadbury chocolate bar—because the clerk said it was the very best chocolate—and boarded a bus for her aunt's apartment near St. Matthew's Church. While she was bumping along on the bus, she looked around at the other passengers, most of them dressed in well-worn duds, a few spiffed up in fairly new coats. They were either looking out the window or staring at their laps, probably reading or daydreaming. She figured most of them had regular jobs they went to day in and day out. Were they bored or happy? She wished she was bored right about now—instead of worrying about pulling off a big job and blowing Brooklyn.

Her aunt answered the door and whisked her in. "Well, as I live and breathe, if it isn't Celia."

Celia gave her a hug and handed over the candy bar. "I brought you a little something."

"Well, thank you. Look at you, all grown up." Margaret stepped back to take her in. "Are you pregnant, dear?"

"Yeah. A lot has happened since I last saw you."

Her aunt made them a pot of coffee, and they settled in the parlor. Celia told her about meeting and marrying Ed. "He's a swell guy—clean-cut and never drinks. Works a steady job. He made me quit the laundry as soon as we found out I was pregnant."

"I'm so pleased to hear that, Celia. You deserve every bit of happiness."

"We have a nice three-room apartment. We even bought a lamp like the one you have." Celia pointed at the Tiffany lamp in her aunt's parlor. Her aunt had always kept a nice home. *Maybe,* Celia thought, *if I'd been more patient, Eddie and I could have worked our way up to a home like this, instead of wanting everything at once.* "I always admired that lamp."

"Oh, goodness. It was a gift from my Gerry. I've had it forever."

Celia studied her aunt. Her hair was turning gray, and her jowls were saggy. "Are you happy, Aunt Margaret?"

"Sure I am. I have friends at Church, and my sewing to keep me busy."

Celia shuffled her feet over the thick maroon rug. "Do you ever see my parents?"

"It's been years. They'd never come all the way to Brooklyn just to see me, and I find their room in Manhattan terribly depressing."

"My father must be in his sixties now. Ma, too."

"Yes, your father is sixty-six, and your mother just a few years younger. You were a change-of-life baby."

Celia gave her a puzzled look. "What's that?"

"Your mother was about forty when you came along. She probably thought she was done having babies. That's why there are so many years between you and Annie."

"You think they'll ever change?"

"No, I don't believe they will. Your father loves the bottle too much, and your mother doesn't think well enough of herself to leave him."

"Yeah, that's what I think, too." Celia put her coffee cup on the occasion table and clasped her hands together. "I got to thank you for sending me to school and letting me stay with you while I went to St. Matthew's."

Her aunt hunched a shoulder. "Oh, you don't need to

thank me for that."

"Do you know what May and Annie are up to these days?"

"I haven't seen them in years. Last I knew May and Walter had another boy. And I believe Annie was still living with them. Aren't you in touch with them?"

"No, I don't care for Walter and his bossy ways."

They visited a little longer, and then Celia thought she should be getting along. "It sure is nice to see you."

"Perhaps you can bring your Eddie around sometime so I can meet him."

"Yeah, that'd be swell." A lump lodged in Celia's throat. Chances are she'd never see her aunt again. "We're thinking of moving someplace where Eddie can start a welding business, someplace where it wouldn't cost as much to get a new start."

They said their goodbyes, and as soon as Celia hit the sidewalk the tears came. Her aunt was the one person who'd done right by her, and she had probably seen her for the last time ever. If it hadn't been for her aunt she might never have learned to read and write. Or know what a decent home looked like. She hoped her aunt would never learn about her and Ed's robberies; she'd be awful ashamed. By the time she got home, she had regained her composure. Ed was her family now, and they had to build a new future somewhere else.

Friday right after work Ed went to visit his mother to ask her to call Schwartz's furniture store and have them collect their furniture and put it in storage. Celia just paced around the apartment, straightening things that hardly needed it and looking out the window while she waited for him. She had planned a simple meal that night, boiled sausage and a jar of sauerkraut, because she knew she'd be too fidgety to cook anything special.

When Ed got back from his mother's they sat down to dinner and Celia asked him what she said.

"She wanted to know why we're leaving."

"What'd you tell her?"

"I said the bulls were looking for me but that it was a mix-up, and I didn't want to be locked up while you were having the baby."

"Did she believe you?"

"I think so. I said we'd be back in a few months to clear ourselves."

"But we won't, will we?"

Ed winced and planted his forearms on the table. "No, we won't be able to come back. We got to make a clean break."

"I'll miss your mother. She's been sweet as could be."

Ed sighed and wagged his head. "Nothing to be done for it. We got to think about us and the baby now."

On Saturday morning they finished off their bread and eggs for breakfast. Afterward, they walked upstairs and knocked on their landlady's door. Mrs. Dougherty seemed surprised to see them, probably because they didn't owe the rent for another week.

"Well, hello," she said. "Would you like to come in?"

"No, thanks, ma'am," Ed said. "We wanted to let you know we'll be away for a week. I have an out-of-town job, and Celia is coming with me."

"That's just fine. Thank you for letting me know."

"You're welcome, Mrs. Dougherty." Celia tried to sound chipper, even though she felt sad. She hated to stiff their landlady for the next month's rent, but once Schwartz's furniture hauled away all their stuff, she'd probably figure out that they'd flown the coop.

She and Ed shuffled down the stairs and sat on their sofa. Celia looked around at their brand-new furniture, the ruffled white curtains on the windows, and their oval rug. "Just think, Mrs. Dougherty will rent this swell place to some other couple, and they'll fix it up like we've never even been here."

"We just got to do this one more job. Then the three of us can be a nice family moved to Florida to raise our baby."

Celia took a bath and put on her jade maternity dress. She packed her pearl-gray dress and some underclothes for herself and Ed.

While Ed got ready, she sat on the bed and looked at their maple bedroom set. Being in this fix made her feel philosophical, and she was thinking about how they'd started in the stick-up business and then had to chase after money to keep up with their bills. They'd dug themselves into a deep hole, and she wondered if it was all worth it now that they had to go on the lam.

She never wanted it to come to this, but, like Ed said, Brooklyn was too hot. She hated to think of how she and Ed wouldn't have any family to visit in Florida, and she'd never see Mrs. Cooney again. If it came out that they were the bob-haired bandit and tall man, it'd sure enough break her heart.

Finally, Ed was ready, all dressed up in his suit. He grabbed their suitcase and, as they stood in the doorway, Celia took one last look at the sparkling clean counter and beautiful dining set. She almost started crying. They'd hardly had much time to enjoy it all.

They walked to the subway and took it to Fulton Street and then up to Grand Central Station. She stuck to Ed like glue because the subway cars were crowded and her big belly made her feel tippy.

She'd never been to Grand Central Station before, and she was impressed with how enormous it was and how the throng of shoes click-clacking on the marble floor echoed off the high ceilings and walls.

"Gosh, Eddie, it'd sure be easy for someone to disappear in this crowd."

"I suppose, but you'd be surprised at how good the coppers are at finding people when they're set on it."

They wandered out front, and Ed waved down a cab. He helped her into the back seat while the cabbie swung their suitcase into the trunk.

The driver hopped in and said, "Where to?"

Ed said, "The Claman, at Forty-Third Street and Eighth Avenue."

"Times Square, huh? Going to do some sightseeing?"

"Yeah," Ed said.

While Ed held her hand she rubbernecked at the sights. Although Celia had grown up in lower Manhattan, she hadn't seen much of this part of the city. She was gawking at the tall buildings, crammed sidewalks, and crowded streets. It was mayhem, but all those people scurried along as if they knew exactly where they were going.

The taxi dropped them off in front of Claman Hotel. It must have been built recently because the brownish brick looked clean and glossy. The building was tall, about a dozen stories high and just as wide.

Ed checked them in and signed the register Mr. and Mrs. Parker from Boston. A bellhop grabbed their suitcase and led them to the elevator. He walked them up to their room on the eighth floor. It was ritzy, with a roomy bed, two glossy bedside tables, a dresser, and two easy chairs.

The bellhop flung open the maroon velvet curtains and asked, "May I offer you any other assistance?"

"No, thanks," Ed said and slipped him some change.

Celia was glad Ed knew what to do because she wouldn't have. She asked him, "How did you know to give him a tip?"

"Everybody in Manhattan has their hand out, and if you don't tip, they'll remember you. We got to blend in."

Ed went out to a deli and bought them corned beef sandwiches. Celia just picked at hers and let Ed finish what she couldn't eat. They walked to the Hudson River and bought two tickets on a Clyde Line steamship for Jacksonville. The boat was scheduled to depart on Tuesday afternoon at two-thirty.

Their hotel room was cozy and snug, and the bed was probably the nicest she'd ever slept in, fluffy and covered with crisp white sheets, a soft blanket, and a thick coverlet. Celia's mind whirred for a while after they crawled into bed, but eventually, she got to sleep and felt better in the morning.

They each took a steamy shower and got dressed.

"Okay," Ed said. "Let's take care of today's business."

They looked through the phone book in their room and found a Willmarth Chauffeur Service. Ed telephoned and asked to have a closed car sent over on Monday morning. They spent much of Sunday walking around like sightseers, but Celia got tired traipsing the long blocks and her feet swelled up, so they stopped and had coffee and grilled sandwiches at a diner. The rest of the day they lolled around their room but didn't talk much. Celia imagined Ed was getting in the right frame of mind to pull off their big heist, just like she was.

On Monday morning at nine, they went to the lobby to wait for their driver. They'd been told to watch for a black Packard with a driver named Arthur West. Ed left her sitting in the lobby and went outside. After five minutes, he came and fetched her.

"It's a Packard limousine," Ed said. "Real nice." He took her by the arm and helped her out the hotel's revolving doors and into the back seat.

"Hello, Mrs. Parker," the driver said.

Celia felt kind of shy—imagine, her sitting in a fancy limousine—but she was wearing her veil, so the driver probably couldn't see how surprised she looked. "Hello," she said, "this sure is a snappy automobile."

Ed went around to the other side of the car and slid in beside her. "We'd like to see the Brooklyn Bridge. And then have a look at a house on Dean Street in Brooklyn."

"Yes, sir," said the driver.

Celia thought that was a slick idea, pretending they were tourists who'd never seen the Brooklyn Bridge. They were sticking to all the details of their plan—making sure nobody would get suspicious.

The driver was a big guy, hefty enough to be a prize fighter, except he was too fat. He was a lot bigger than Ed, and Ed was no runt. Celia started worrying about their plan to get this guy under control. She figured she and Ed would have to jigger that part.

Ed had told the driver they were moving from Boston to Brooklyn, but they didn't want to get too friendly with him. Every now and then he'd say a few words like he was trying to make conversation, but they pretended they were busy gawking at the sights, and eventually he buttoned up.

When they got over to Brooklyn, Ed told Arthur to drive into Prospect Park. The plan was to scout a nice quiet spot there for the next day. Then Ed asked him to go to Dean Street, which was close to the National Biscuit Company, so he could get out and have a look at the neighborhood. Ed would prowl around the building and find out the best route to the payroll office. If anybody asked what he was doing, he was going to say he was looking for a job as a truck driver.

He came back after twenty minutes and told the driver he could take them back to their hotel. It was Monday and the streets were much busier than they'd been on Saturday or Sunday. Celia supposed people were hurrying to work and plotting big money deals all over Manhattan.

When the driver dropped them off, Ed said, "See you same time tomorrow."

They strolled through the lobby and to the elevator, keeping Mum the whole time.

Once they were in their room, Celia asked Ed how it went at the Biscuit Company.

"The payroll office is where I thought, on the second floor. There were lots of people in the office—loads of clerks and Janes pounding on typewriters. But I figure our plan will work."

"What about the driver? He's an awful big guy."

"Yeah, we better practice that part." He opened their suitcase and took out the rope they'd brought.

"Here you go," he said. "Tie my hands behind my back."

She strung the rope around his wrists and tied it as tight as she could. "How's that?"

Ed wriggled around, and in no time he sloughed off that rope. "It's no good. The rope won't work."

"But we don't have anything else."

Ed rubbed his fingertips over his brow. "Can I leave you here while I go find a hardware store? If I have a look around, I'll come up with something."

"Sure," she said.

Ed grabbed his coat and the room key. "Just wait here, okay?"

While Ed was gone Celia swiveled a chair around to the window to watch the people on the street. All the men and women in this part of Manhattan were dressed up in sleek fur or wool coats, dapper hats, and snazzy shoes. She'd never fit in here. Now she couldn't live in Brooklyn anymore either. She hoped the people in Jacksonville would be more regular folks, like them, and that they'd have nice neighbors and maybe even meet some other families with new babies.

When Ed came back, he had a brown paper bag. "I found just the thing, doll."

He reached into the bag and pulled out a coil of wire. "It's picture wire. This ought to work."

Ed took off his coat and sat down on the bed. He unspooled a length of wire and twisted and turned it until it broke off from the rest of the spool.

"Okay, try this." He handed her the wire and stood with his hands behind his back.

She wound the wire around his wrists and cinched it up. "Done. How do you like that, buster?"

Ed tugged and strained, but he couldn't get out of the wrapped wire. His wrists turned red.

"You did good," he said. "Let me loose before I cut my hands off."

After she undid the wire, Ed rubbed his sore wrists. "Okay, sugar, we're all set."

The Big Heist
Manhattan and Brooklyn, April 1, 1924

Celia felt like a machine as she got dressed on Tuesday morning, doing things without thinking. She and Ed had gone over their plan so many times, they knew it by heart, but she still couldn't stop playing all the details out in her head. It's all she could think about. They skipped breakfast because they didn't want to be out in public with all those eyes on the streets. They didn't even have a cup of coffee.

They fished the pistols out of their suitcase and put them in their coat pockets. Celia had a few other things in her pockets, like some powder and lipstick and their notebook. She'd stowed her purse in the suitcase because she needed to keep her hands free.

They checked out of their room and paid their bill. The driver was waiting for them outside, and they stepped into the limousine. Celia's stomach was all knotted up, and she reached out for Ed's hand. He took it and gave her a tight-lipped smile, like he was trying to buck her up. She smiled weakly and leaned back in her seat, taking in the sights. The driver had to weave his way over to the Brooklyn Bridge because the streets were jam-packed, but finally they were whizzing over the bridge and on the way to their biggest job ever.

Celia could hardly believe they were about to pull off a hard-core robbery and grand escape. If she'd known this business was going to end up with them on the run she'd have never started. They'd turned into big-time thieves without meaning to. It was like running down a hill and going so fast you couldn't stop.

They made it to Brooklyn in good time, and as they drove into Prospect Park, Ed told the driver to head for the Botanical Garden. The park was quiet and still that morning, with hardly a breeze ruffling the tree branches, and they didn't see a single person.

Ed leaned forward and said to the driver, "Will you pull over up ahead? I want to look around a minute."

When the driver parked, Ed got out of the car. He reached into his pocket and pulled out one of his guns. He opened the driver's door and held the gun to the driver's head. "Get out and do like I say."

The driver eased out and stood stock still with his hands up. "I don't want any trouble."

"Just do like we say and you'll be fine," Ed said. "Get in the back."

Arthur bent over and got into the car beside her. Ed kept the gun on him.

Celia pulled the wire out of her pocket and said, "Put your hands behind your back."

He was so big around he couldn't get his hands together behind him. Celia could tell he was trying, but it wasn't working. "It's okay," she said. "Turn around and I'll tie your hands in front."

He slowly swiveled around and held his hands out for

her as if he was praying.

She wrapped the wire around his wrists and twisted the ends together.

Ed said, "Now get down on the floor."

Arthur shifted around and eased onto the floor as best he could. He looked ridiculous trying to wedge himself into the cramped space. Ed pulled the rope out of his pocket and tied the driver's feet together. They looked him over and decided he wasn't going anywhere.

Ed slid into the driver's seat and drove the few blocks to the National Biscuit Company. Celia kept her gun on the driver in the back seat. He latched his eyes on her and raised his eyebrows like he was begging her to spare him.

Ed pulled the car over in front of the building and popped out. Celia got out, too. She kept the door open, and Ed said, "Watch him, and if he opens his mouth you know what to do."

"Sure." She slammed the door and followed Ed. They were just bluffing the driver so he'd think Celia was guarding him and would keep his mouth shut while they pulled off the job.

They headed inside and Ed stopped to tie a handkerchief over his face. Celia had her thick veil on and also a pink tam-o'-shanter pulled low over her brow. She started up the stairs, with Ed close behind.

On the second floor, they came to the payroll office. Celia could see a lot of people milling around in there, maybe fifteen workers, and she worried that it'd be hard to herd all of them out of the way. But she knew there was no turning back, and so far everything was going like clockwork. She walked in and when a clerk came up to her, she said, "I'd like to see the cashier."

The clerk called out, "Nathan, somebody to see you."

Nathan emerged from behind a wire cage. He was a broad-nosed guy, about five-feet-six, and he walked toward her in a cocky, loping kind of way. She took the envelope she'd prepared out of her pocket and handed it to him. He took it and pulled the paper out, which was a plain blank sheet. When he looked up at her she pulled the twenty-five out of her pocket.

"Everybody, move it," she said, motioning toward a room off to the side.

Ed pulled out both his guns and made sure everybody did as she'd commanded. People started herding toward the room, cramming together like a flock of frightened sheep. One guy broke away and started edging toward the safe, which was wide open. Celia called to him, "Oh no you don't, mister. Get over there with the rest of them."

Nathan was the last person they needed to get in the room, and as he walked by Celia he jumped at her and grabbed her arm. Everything happened fast after that.

Nathan lunged for her gun, and Celia lurched backward. There was a chair beside her, and she stumbled and fell flat on her back. Ed stood a few feet behind her so they couldn't see each other. Nathan careened toward the room and, as the door slammed close, Ed let two shots rip. A loud scream came from behind the door, and then it was quiet, an eerie quiet.

Ed ran over to her and helped her up. His handkerchief had slipped down, and his face was white as a sheet. "Oh,

God, I think I killed him," Ed said. "Let's get out of here."

They scrambled out of the room and hot-footed it to the stairwell. Celia heard footsteps coming up. Ed pulled out one of his guns.

"No," she said, "we got to bluff our way out. Like we planned."

Ed nodded and put away his gun. He untied the handkerchief around his neck and stuffed it in his pocket. They headed down the stairs. When these two men came barreling up the stairs, Ed pulled his cigarettes out of his pocket and said, "Got a light, buddy?"

The first guy gave Ed a startled look and shook his head no. Then he and his buddy ran past them.

Ed and Celia hoofed it to the car. Ed got behind the wheel, and Celia scooted into the back seat. The driver was still trussed up on the floor and didn't say a word, just looked at her with startled eyes and clamped lips. When they were about a block away, she heard hollering and turned around and saw three guys running after them.

She tapped Ed on the shoulder. "Hurry up."

He made a bee-line for Atlantic Avenue and turned into the traffic on the street, losing the men who'd been chasing them. The Nostrand Avenue Railroad Station was a few blocks away. When they got there, Ed snugged the car up to the curb and cut the engine. They got out, and Ed grabbed their suitcase. Yellow taxis lined up in front of the train station, and they bounded into the lead one.

Ed told the cabbie, "We're going to lower Manhattan. Take the Williamsburg Bridge."

After they'd crossed the bridge and landed deep in

lower Manhattan, Ed asked the driver to pull over.

They got out at the corner of Broome and Bowery, and Ed took her hand and pulled her along beside him, toting the suitcase in his other hand.

They walked along Broome Street for half a block.

"You okay?" he asked her.

"Yeah," she said, but she wasn't. She was flustered, but she knew they needed to play it cool.

Ed said, "Okay, we lost that taxi."

He signaled another cab and asked the driver to take them to Pier 36. They didn't say a word to each other the whole ride. Celia concentrated on staying calm and breathing evenly, even though her insides jittered like jello. When they got out, Ed took her hand, and they marched to the Clyde Line Boat that had a sign reading 'Chippewa two thirty p.m. Departure.'

Ed flashed their tickets, and they walked up the plank. At the top of the plank, another man checked their tickets. He stood in front of a board with keys dangling from rows of hooks. Reaching around, he grabbed a key and handed it to Ed. "Your room is down that set of stairs to your left and about halfway along the corridor."

"Okay, thanks," Ed said, heading for the stairs. Ed descended the narrow stairs first, holding the suitcase in one hand and the rail with the other.

Celia's legs wobbled like rubber. To steady herself, she clasped the rail as she stepped down.

"Here it is," said Ed, fumbling the key into the keyhole. As he swung the metal door open it creaked like it needed grease. Ed helped her step over the threshold and then followed her in. He flicked on the light and closed the door. The metal-walled compartment was cramped, with some built-in shelves on the wall opposite the bed and on the side wall a fold-down table and benches. The room didn't have any windows, just a light on the ceiling in a metal cage.

She looked Ed in the eye. Her heart thumped so hard she could hear it in her ears. "The coppers will be looking all over for us."

He plunked the suitcase down and slapped a hand to his forehead. "I know, and now we'll have a murder rap. It's all over for us."

"You think they'll find us on the ship?"

"Once the coppers talk to the chauffeur and the people in the payroll office, they'll be combing the city for us, maybe even ships."

Celia emptied her pockets onto the shelf and took off her coat. She looked at her pile of stuff—her gun, lipstick, and powder. Then it hit her. "I don't have the notebook."

"You sure?" Ed plunged his hands into his pockets and pulled out his guns and a handful of change, slapping everything on the shelf.

"Yeah, I don't have it."

Celia heard a man's voice outside their door. "I think it's over here."

"Oh, God," she whispered. "Could they have found us this fast?"

They froze and eyed the door. If it was the coppers they'd probably have their guns pulled. Their pieces were on the shelf, and Celia wondered if they should grab them.

But if the coppers saw them holding guns they'd probably riddle them with bullets. She stood stuck to the spot, breathing fast and shallow.

"No, it's down here," the voice said. It must have been another passenger looking for his room. She heaved out a sigh and sat down on the bed.

"Maybe the notebook slipped out of my pocket in the cab," she said. "Or maybe it came out when I fell down. Somebody's going to find it for sure."

It had the address of the hotel in it, and some other things Ed had scribbled. Although the notebook contained no names, it did connect them to the hotel. And sooner or later someone would find the limousine driver in the car at the train station, and he'd tell the cops they'd been staying at the Claman.

Ed sat beside her on the bed. "We'll be lucky to get out of this port."

Celia knew he was right. The ship wouldn't leave for another three hours. That'd give the coppers plenty of time to scour the city and maybe even put their descriptions out. If the last cabbie put two and two together, he'd know they were at Pier 36. And then it'd be easy for the bulls to check the passenger lists.

"Ed," she said, as it dawned on her. "We used the Parker name for our tickets, and the chauffeur has that name. All the cops have to do is check who bought steamship tickets for today and they'll find us."

"Oh, Christ," Ed said, pulling his cigarettes out and lighting one.

He knew she didn't like him swearing like that, but

she couldn't blame him. His hand was shaking so bad the cigarette smoke was doing a crazy dance.

The cops were sure to connect the dots between the Packard driver, the National Biscuit Company job, and the hotel. And now they'd have a murder rap. They'd be frying in the chair. Celia's stomach flipped and flopped like a fish out of water. She ran into the bathroom and vomited.

Under His Nose
Brooklyn, April 1, 1924

The call came in Tuesday morning, a little after ten thirty, from the dispatcher on duty. "Say, Bill, we just received a report of a robbery and shooting at the National Biscuit Company. The payroll office. A guy and a woman. Could be the bob-haired bandit."

"Any officers on the scene?" Casey asked. He glanced at the tattered map of Brooklyn and Queens on his wall. The Biscuit Company was smack dab in the middle of all the pins for the bob-hair robberies.

"A couple of employees ran out to flag some down. And I sent Lester over."

"And a shooting you say? Anybody hurt?"

"One guy. The ambulance is probably on the way or at the scene."

"Thanks, I'll get right over there with Mac."

Casey poked his head into Gray's office. "Hey, Frank, I'm going over to the National Biscuit Company with Mac to look over the scene. Might be the work of the bob-hair. Will you keep an eye out for any sightings?"

"A daytime job? That's a new twist for them."

"Yeah, it might not be them. But the papers will probably assume it is."

Casey swung by Mac's office. "Hey, Mac, let's get over to the crime scene at the Biscuit Company."

Casey headed for the back door to get his car.

McGowan said, "The place's only a few blocks from here. Let's walk it."

Casey would've preferred to drive, but Fiona had been hounding him about getting some exercise and shedding a few pounds.

The lanky McGowan set a brisk pace, and Casey struggled to keep up. "Hey, pal, I'm no racehorse. Give a guy a break."

As they walked up to the big building, an ambulance pulled out. Its siren sounded, and it sped away. Casey figured the driver had more important things to do than talk to the cops. He'd check on the condition of the victim later.

The payroll office buzzed with rattled employees. Three officers stood talking with a small group of them. Casey recognized all the cops; they were from his precinct.

"Hiya, fellas," he said. "What you got for me?"

Lester stepped aside with his notepad. "Lots of detailed descriptions of the robbers. They didn't take a cent, just scrammed after the shooting."

"How's the victim?"

"Shot twice, seemed to be losing a lot of blood." Lester pointed to the door. "He was shot through the door, probably with a high-caliber pistol. As they were taking him away, he said he'd made a play for the dame's gun."

Casey could see two bullet holes in the bottom of the door and a pool of blood on the floor.

"How many shots fired?"

"Just two pills. Looks like both of them hit him."

"Who fired the shots?"

"Conflicting reports on that. Some say the dame, others the guy. The door was closing as the shots were fired so nobody had a good view."

"All right, give me the descriptions."

Lester flipped back a page and checked his notes. "They all agree the woman was short, not much over five feet, wearing a sealskin coat and a pretty pink hat. Had a dark veil over her face. And pregnant. According to several of the women, very pregnant."

Casey nodded. Sounded like it could be the bob-haired girl, but pregnant? That was a surprise. "And her hair. Was it black and bobbed?"

"Dark, yes, but tucked up in a hairnet or something."

Mac asked, "Eye color?"

"Nobody could say for sure. On account of the face covering."

"And the guy?"

"Tall, blond, and good-looking. Dressed in a suit and snappy camel-colored wool coat. One lady said he was as handsome as a movie star. He was wearing a blue handkerchief over his face, but it slipped and a few people got a good look at him." Lester looked up at Casey. "And listen to this: One of the guys said the two are from the neighborhood. He'd seen them around once or twice. And some other guy said he thinks the man works at Horgan's Garage. You know where that is?"

"Yeah, I know the place. A couple blocks from here."

Casey looked around the office. There was no sign of any bullet marks on the walls. "You say they didn't take anything?"

"No, the manager said the safe was wide open, but he checked, and there's not a dime missing."

"Sounds like they got spooked," Mac said.

"Yeah." Lester nodded. "Oh, I almost forgot. They left this behind."

Lester lifted a black notebook off the desk and handed it to Casey.

Casey flicked it open. It looked like an address book. He'd study it later. But first, he'd hightail it over to Horgan's Garage and see what the score was with their employees. And then check on the victim.

He asked Lester, "What hospital did the ambulance go to?"

"Said they'd take the guy to Jewish Hospital."

"Good work, Lester. Get the names of all the witnesses. I'll see you back at the precinct."

Casey and McGowan headed out to Horgan's Garage.

Casey said to Mac, "I'm not getting my hopes up. Just because somebody thinks the guy works at Horgan's doesn't mean he really does."

"Yeah," said Mac. "Could be a case of mistaken identity."

They let themselves into the office at Horgan's. A plump, middle-aged woman sat at the desk in front of a pile of papers. Casey pulled out his identification badge, and Mac followed suit. "Hi, I'm Captain Casey. This is Lieutenant Gray. Is the owner around?"

"That'd be my husband. He's not here right now. Can I help you?"

"Did you have any employees not show up for work today?"

The woman looked at him like he was a puzzle she had to solve. "Yes, but he told us he'd be away this week. He had some family business."

"And who is that?"

"Ed Cooney. Why, is he in some trouble?"

"Not necessarily. Is he married?"

"Yeah."

"Is his wife expecting a baby?"

"Yes, she's due in a month or so." Casey gave Mac a quick look. Mac was grinning like he'd scored a big poker pot.

"What's her name?"

"Celia."

"How's that spelled?"

"C-e-l-i-a."

"Okay, thanks. That's all we need for now."

Holy Toledo. The bob-haired bandit and tall companion were under his nose this whole time. Ed and Celia Cooney. They were either hiding out somewhere nearby or making a run for it. He'd strike while the trail was hot.

They rushed back to the precinct, and he headed straight for Gray's office. McGowan peeled off to check in with the dispatcher.

Casey heard voices coming from Gray's office. He rapped on the door.

Gray said, "Come on in."

Gray was leaning over his desk, and in the chair in front of it sat a walrus of a guy.

"Captain," Gray said, "this is Arthur West, chauffeur driver. He was left tied up in his Packard at the Nostrand Train Station. He's got quite a story."

Casey grabbed the other chair in front of Gray's desk and pulled it back so he could take in both Gray and this big fella.

Casey plopped into the seat and eyed Mr. West. "Okay, what's your story?"

The guy rested his chubby hands on his hulking abdomen. "I drove those two who robbed the National Biscuit Company. They hired me to bring them over here yesterday from the Claman Hotel in Times Square. The guy walked around the neighborhood, and I took them back to their hotel. Then I brought them back here today. The guy made me drive into Prospect Park and then pointed a gun at my head. They tied me up and forced me to get down on the floor in the back. Then they drove the car a few blocks. I heard them say something about the Biscuit Company. Anyway, they parked the car and told me to keep quiet or they'd kill me. After a few minutes, I heard two shots, and they came running back to the car. They seemed pretty frazzled. The guy sped to the train station, and the little lady kept her gun on me in the back seat, resting her feet on me like I was a piece of furniture. They got out at the station and told me to take a nap. When I was sure they'd gone I kicked out the window."

Casey figured the guy was on the level. His wrists

were all red, probably from being tied up with something that cut into his skin. And he was talking a mile a minute like the adrenalin was still pumping. "What were their names?"

"Mr. and Mrs. Parker. Said they were from Boston and were moving to Brooklyn."

"Okay, Frank, get Mr. West's full statement down. I'm going over to the train station."

"Yeah, good idea," Frank said.

Casey fetched McGowan and together they drove to the station. Some officers had gathered a group of cabbies together.

Casey and McGowan slipped into the circle. One of the cabbies was jabbering about how he saw a chauffeur driver punch out the window of his car with his feet. Casey interrupted him. "Yeah, we know about that. Tell me, gentlemen, did any of you see the two that got out of that Packard?"

A gap-toothed guy said, "I saw the two of them carrying a suitcase and hopping in a cab."

Officer Jeffries spoke up. "A couple of people in the lounge said they saw the pair climbing the stairs to the elevated train."

Casey and McGowan got what information they could from the cabbies and the officers who'd questioned people in the waiting room.

Casey looked up at McGowan. "I should get back to the station."

McGowan grimaced and wagged his head. "The robbers could be on their way to Long Island or they could be God knows where. I tell you, Bill, these two are one royal pain in the ass."

"Yeah, I know. But we've got good descriptions and names of the suspects now. Why don't you stick around and see if you can track down the cabbie that supposedly picked them up here. I'll put out an alert to all the stations on the Long Island line."

"Okay, Bill. I'll check in after that."

Casey rushed back to the precinct and got the word out to the train stations along the Long Island route. It took almost two hours, but McGowan finally showed up at headquarters with the cab driver who had driven a pair matching the Cooneys' descriptions from the train station to the Lower East Side. After interviewing the cabbie, Casey was inclined to believe he'd carted the actual bob-haired bandit and her tall husband across town. They still had the suitcase they'd taken from the chauffeur's car. Why were they lugging a suitcase around? Did they change clothes after their jobs to evade identification? Or were they making a break for it?

Casey asked the cabbie, "Exactly where'd you drop them?"

"At the corner of Broome and Bowery."

"And did you happen to notice where they headed from there?"

"No, I picked up another fare right away and didn't pay them any mind."

Damn, Casey thought, *what the hell were they doing in Lower Manhattan?*

He dismissed McGowan and the cabbie and called

Jewish Hospital. "This is Detective William Casey. I'm calling about the condition of Nathan Mazo. Just brought in with gunshot wounds."

The woman who answered said, "Just a minute and I'll check."

Casey hunched a shoulder, clamping the receiver to his ear. He retrieved the notebook left at the Biscuit Company from his pocket and flipped it open. The first page listed a number of hotels in Manhattan, including the Claman, the one the chauffeur said the couple was staying at. The next page listed the names of different kinds of stores, groceries and five-and-ten-cent stores and a few others, and their addresses in Brooklyn and Manhattan. All the handwriting was the same. Was this a list of intended robbery targets? He'd put out the word for cops to be on the alert at those stores, though the two would probably lay off once they realized they'd lost their precious manual.

The woman on the hospital call came back on the line. "Captain?"

"Yes?"

"He's unconscious. The doctors are evaluating him for surgery."

"What are his chances?"

"It doesn't look good. Might be some organs involved. But please don't release that information. We've only just notified his family he's here."

Oh, hell, this might turn into a murder case. He'd known it wouldn't end well for the bob-haired bandit and her pal, not with three guns between them and the big risks they'd been taking.

Pieces of the Puzzle
Brooklyn and Manhattan, April 1–2, 1924

William Casey felt it in his bones. The pieces of the puzzle were finally falling into place.

The evening of the National Biscuit Company robbery he and Frank Gray took the subway into Manhattan. They looked over the register at the Claman Hotel. Sure enough, the signature for a Mr. and Mrs. Parker of Boston matched the handwriting in the notebook left at the crime scene. The twosome had checked in on Saturday, March 29, and checked out the morning of the robbery, Tuesday, April 1. The desk clerk rarely saw them coming or going. Casey figured they were playing it smart and keeping a low profile.

The day after the robbery Casey and Gray visited Horgan's Garage again. This time the owner, Steve Horgan, greeted them.

The three of them settled in Horgan's cramped office. It smelled like grease and gasoline, and the rat-a-tat of metal on metal drifted through a window between the garage and the office. Casey was admiring the collection of old New York license plates on the wall—all the various colors issued over the years, from brown to red to beige.

Casey asked Horgan, "How'd you come by all these plates?"

The grubby-fingered Horgan flipped off his cap, brushed his hair back, and planted his lid back on his head. "Here and there. Junkyards mostly."

"Well, we won't keep you long. We understand Ed Cooney is one of your employees?"

"Yeah, the wife said you were asking about him. He in some kind of trouble?"

"That's what we're trying to find out. How long has he worked for you?"

"About two years now. Started here shortly after his discharge from the Navy. Nice friendly guy. Good driver. Has a chauffeur license. Does most of the welding in the shop."

"I understand his wife's name is Celia. Do you know how long they've been married?"

Horgan scrunched up a cheek. "A year or so."

"Do you know their address?"

"They moved into a new apartment on Pacific Street not long ago. Don't know the address. About two blocks from here. Their landlady lives on the premises. A Mrs. Dougherty."

Well, I'll be a son of a gun, Casey thought, *their apartment is right around the corner from police headquarters.* "And I understand he has a couple of brothers. Do you know where they live?"

"Two of them live with the mother. I think there's another one, older, but I don't know much about him."

While Casey was scratching down notes, Gray asked, "Do you happen to know the mother's address?"

"It's on Dean Street, about halfway down the block

east of Franklin. A two-story green house with white trim."

Casey asked, "Your wife said Cooney was away on family business. Do you know anything about that?"

Horgan shook his head. "That's all he said."

"Does he have any family in Manhattan?"

"That I wouldn't know."

"What about the wife? She have any people there?"

"Don't know that either."

Casey and Gray wrapped up the interview and hustled back to the station. They went straight to McGowan's office.

"Okay," Casey said. "We've got this pair checking into Hotel Claman last Saturday and checking out the morning of the robbery. And Ed Cooney missing from work starting Monday."

Frank said, "Remember that tip we got in February about Ed Cooney flashing money around?"

"Yeah," Casey said. "It looks like him and his wife are our culprits all right. Let's try to find some pictures of them for the bulletins."

Gray clapped a hand over his fist. "What do you say we look in on the landlady next?" He turned to McGowan. "And don't start ragging about a search warrant. We don't have time for that."

McGowan smirked at Gray. "I'm surprised you're even bringing up a warrant."

Casey wasn't interested in Mac and Frank's running debate on the finer points of the Constitution and police procedure. "You two are like a couple of hens going at each other. Come on, Frank, let's go knock on some doors."

Casey stood and said to McGowan. "Meantime, see what you can find out about Ed Cooney. His employer says he was in the Navy and registered as a chauffeur. Maybe get over to the recruitment office and see if they have a picture. And the drivers' license bureau, too."

Casey and Gray tracked down Mrs. Dougherty at 1099 Pacific Street. They showed her their badges and introduced themselves. She invited them in, and they sat down at a square oak table in her kitchen. She leaned back against the chair, holding herself prim and erect. "How can I help you?"

"We understand Ed and Celia Cooney rent from you?"

"Yes, since January. They're a quiet couple. Fixed the place up nice and keep it spick and span, too."

"We heard they're not home now. Did they tell you where they were going?"

"Mr. Cooney said he had an out-of-town job for a week and that his wife was going with him."

"Did he say where this job was?"

"No, and I didn't ask. It really wasn't my business."

"Do they keep up with the rent?"

"Oh, yes, they always pay on time. Except this week. It's due on Friday, but I don't know if they'll be back then."

"Have you seen any suspicious activity on their part? Any unusual spending or people calling late at night? Any rowdy behavior?"

Mrs. Dougherty cupped her hands on the table. "No, they seem like a nice young couple. I hardly ever hear a peep out of them.”

Frank tapped his pencil on his notepad. “Can we have a look at their apartment?”

The landlady pushed up her spectacles. “Well, I don’t know. I hate to go in without them knowing. Is it important?”

“Yes,” Casey said, “it is. You could accompany us. We’d leave everything as we find it. We just want to see what we can learn. We’re getting discrepant reports on their whereabouts, and it might help if we had a look around.”

“Well, I suppose so.” Mrs. Dougherty fetched her key and walked them down the stairs.

The place was clean and neat all right. And well furnished. It smelled like stale cigarette smoke, but the ashtray on the kitchen counter was empty.

Casey and Gray went back to the bedroom, and Casey opened the drawers of the dresser. He didn’t touch anything. He noticed there were neatly folded clothes there, some cotton shirts, undergarments, and socks. A few pressed shirts and dresses hung in the closet. A beat-up pair of men’s leather boots and two nice pairs of lady’s shoes lined up on the floor. If Casey didn’t know better, he’d expect the couple to walk in any minute and resume their life.

They went to the kitchen and opened the cupboards. A few dishes and glasses, but nothing fancy. Casey checked the drawers. The first one held some cheap silverware and two wooden spoons. The second had a cribbage board, deck of cards, and some papers. He lifted the papers out. On top was a receipt for a furniture installment payment of fifty dollars from Schwartz's Furniture. The others were scribbled recipes. He put them back and stooped down to open the lower cupboard. The top shelf held two beat-up pots. On the bottom, there was a cardboard box, about double the size of a shoebox. He pulled it out, set it on the counter, and opened the flaps.

It was filled with newspaper clippings. The top one bore the headline: GANG OF BOB-HAIRED BANDITS HERE; TWO-GUN BLOND CULTURED, BRUNETTE NERVY.

Casey tried to keep his voice even. He didn't want to alarm—or alert—Mrs. Dougherty. "Hey, Frank, this is kind of interesting."

Gray leaned over to get a look. Casey flipped through the articles. Every single one was about the bob-haired bandit.

At Sea
The Atlantic Ocean, April 1–4, 1924

Celia and Ed locked their door and flopped down on the bed, staring at the ceiling and every now and then sharing a few dismayed words. They were so gloomy and glum you'd think they'd already been sentenced to the chair. Celia tensed up every time she heard footsteps or voices outside their door, thinking it was the coppers coming to lower the boom.

She asked Ed, "You think the ship will leave on time? Or could the bulls delay it so they can search for us?"

"Guess it depends on whether that last cabbie gets suspicious and talks. Or if the bulls start checking ship manifests."

"I'm scared, Eddie."

"I know, honey. I am, too. And I'm real sorry I ever got us started on the robbery business. It's all my fault, and now I just want to get it over with."

"It's not your fault. Don't you go saying that. And no matter what happens we'll stick together. I'll never let you down."

"But I already let you down. What kind of husband does what I did?"

"Don't you be blaming yourself. You didn't make me do anything I didn't want to do."

Ed didn't say anything to that. Celia turned to look at him and saw a tear trickling out of the corner of his eye. She asked, "What do you mean, you want to get it over with?"

"I don't know. I'm talking nonsense. Don't listen to me."

They lay there, stretched out, hardly budging for hours. They were sitting ducks, and they had no place to run. Either this ship would take them away for good or the cops would come knocking and drag them off like a couple of low-down hoodlums. Which they were. They shot a man, probably killed him, and they deserved whatever punishment got dished out.

What kind of life was their baby going to have now? While Celia wasted away in prison or fried in the chair her baby would be raised by some other mother. The nice family life she wanted for her Eddie and their new baby was ruined. All the dreams she ever had for them were drying up and crumbling like dead flowers.

Ed couldn't protect her from whatever was coming down the pike. They were supposed to be a nice young couple starting fresh in life, but they'd turned into good-for-nothing crooks. Her big strong Ed just wanted to get it over with, and she understood what he was saying. Stewing on this ship was like being tortured in purgatory. They didn't know where they were going to end up.

After what seemed like forever, the ship's whistle blasted, and she felt the hulking ship budge.

She sat up. "We're moving,"

"Yeah," Ed said, like he could hardly believe it.

"Maybe we'll get to Florida after all."

"Only they could be waiting for us there, couldn't they? If they find out we bought tickets for Jacksonville."

"Seems like it'd be pretty hard to grub through every single list of trains and buses and ships leaving New York. Maybe we got away clean."

The ship soon picked up speed, and Ed said they were out to sea and on their way to Florida.

Celia felt queasy from the way the ship was rocking and heaving—in a helter-skelter way, so she couldn't get used to it. She could hear the wind whipping around like it didn't know which way to blow. Through the metal walls it sounded spooky and far off.

Her stomach started growling. She hadn't had anything to eat since the bagel for breakfast, and then she'd thrown that up. She knew Ed was probably hungry, too, since he was usually ready to eat any time of day.

"Are you hungry, Eddie?" she asked him.

"Yeah, I am. But I can stand it. What about you?"

"Yeah, I can wait." Celia was afraid if they left the room that someone would recognize them. And then the captain would lock them up and turn them over to the police in Florida. She figured Ed was thinking that, too.

Celia didn't realize it was possible to be as miserable as she felt while that ship plowed through the ocean. It seemed like they didn't have a single thing to look forward to. Or even a plan for how to start a new life. All she'd packed was one or two pieces of clothes and a change of underwear. Their guns wouldn't do them any good. They were through with the stick-up business. Celia was never going to rob another joint, no matter how down and out they were.

And she prayed that the guy at the Biscuit Company would live. From the beginning, they said they'd never shoot anybody, just use the guns to scare people, and then the first time a robbery went haywire, they shot. She couldn't think of anything worse than killing a guy. It made her feel a sinking and sickly kind of sad. The guy probably had a wife, mother, and father. And maybe some kids and brothers and sisters.

She'd been so happy when she and Ed first got married. She thought it'd be nothing but sunny days as long as they had each other. And now they'd gone and mucked that up.

She wished she could turn back the clock and be in their one-room place again. Sure, they wouldn't have a nice apartment with all that high-class furniture, but maybe they could've stayed with Ed's mother once the baby came and saved enough money for a place of their own.

All day long she listened to the voices outside their cabin—of people walking the deck and chattering and laughing. It seemed like she and Ed had soaked up all the sorrows of everyone on that ship, for those people sounded nothing but cheery while she and Ed were weighed down with every kind of worry and fear known to mankind.

They counted their money. All they had was forty-seven dollars. How were they supposed to start over in a strange place with hardly any money? All she'd ever wanted was to give their new baby a good life in a nice home, and now they were worse off than ever. They could hardly take care of themselves. How were they supposed to take care of a baby, too?

Celia tried to sleep. What else was there to do? But whenever she dozed she had terrible dreams, dreams about voices outside their door and cops busting in and dragging them off to the clink.

Come Friday night, after two days and nights at sea, she felt the boat slow down and maneuver this way and that. It came to a halt, and an announcement blared, "Jacksonville, Florida. All travelers must disembark."

Celia didn't know what to expect when they stepped off the ship. They threw their belongings in the suitcase and stumbled off the boat into a chilly, dusky evening. She was about as limp as a rag doll from not eating and hardly sleeping. The air smelled like rotting fish, and a swirling breeze whipped her hair against her face. Waves beat at the big posts along the pier, and the water looked dark and scary—like all kinds of creepy creatures lurked in the deep.

She kept looking for a welcome party of cops with their guns pulled, but there weren't any, just a jumble of people, some of them meeting others and saying happy hellos, and others grabbing taxis and zipping off to their homes or hotels or wherever.

She asked Ed, "Now what do we do?"

"I guess we better find a place where we can stay and figure out our next move. We'll see if a cabbie can help."

"Okay," she said, trying to pick up her feet as they trudged to the taxis lined up along the wharf.

Ed helped her into a cab and asked the driver, "Do you

know an inexpensive rooming house somewhere nearby?"

The cabbie thought a minute and said, "Yeah, there's a place on Ocean Avenue. Want to go there?"

"Sure," Ed said. "How far is it?"

"About a mile and a half."

"Okay."

The driver pulled out and Celia slumped against the seat. Her feelings were all jumbled up, like she didn't know whether to feel relieved or afraid about being in Florida. Nothing was working out like they'd planned. And she was starving. Her stomach felt like a fist that'd been balled up for a week. She figured it couldn't be good for the baby to let herself get so hungry, but they didn't want anybody to see them on that boat. Maybe they shouldn't have been worried, maybe they could've had a meal or two instead of cowering like hunted animals in that room. They probably scared seven years off their lives those two days.

The cab drove through a neighborhood of run-down houses with sagging porches and here and there a junk-heap car in the yard. They pulled up in front of a two-story house that was more gray wood than white paint. Ed paid the driver and they went inside and knocked on a door that said 'Manager.'

Ed told the guy they were Mr. and Mrs. Sheehan. Celia hardly had the energy to stand so she sat down on their suitcase.

When the manager said he had a couple of rooms, Ed asked if they could take the cheapest one, the one for five dollars a week.

"Sure," the manager said. "You folks aren't from around here, are you?"

Celia figured Ed's way of talking gave them away, just like this guy's way of dragging out his words showed he wasn't from anywhere near New York.

"No," Ed said. "We're from New Jersey."

Celia was relieved to hear Ed say they were from New Jersey. Maybe he was getting back to his old self—trying to think of ways to keep the cops off their tail. Ed got the room key, and they walked up the stairs to Room Number 7. There was a lamp without a shade on a little dresser, and she turned it on.

It was the dreariest, dirtiest room she'd ever seen, worse than the one she had when she was working at the laundry. It had a dingy metal bed with a bare mattress, two chairs, and a shelf that stuck out from the wall for a table. The walls were green wallpaper, but you could hardly make out the pattern because it was all faded. There was one window, and it was wide open. Outside she could hear a whirring buzz, not crickets, but some other kind of bug. It was going to take time to get used to this new place—if they even got the chance.

"You just relax, doll. I'll go get us something to eat. I saw a little grocery a couple blocks back."

Ed wasn't gone long. He returned with a carton of milk, a loaf of Wonder Bread, and some liverwurst. He took out his jackknife and sliced the meat and made them a couple of sandwiches. Celia would have eaten just about anything then, and she gobbled down two sandwiches and drank a lot of milk, too. That food was like a shot in the arm. She started feeling better now that her belly was full.

After they finished eating, Ed said, "There's a police station about a block away. I saw it when I was coming back from the grocer."

She looked at Ed. "Why didn't you go in and invite them to our picnic?"

That was the first time since the robbery that either of them cracked a smile.

Scrambling Around
Jacksonville, April 5–10, 1924

For breakfast on Saturday, they ate some more liverwurst on Wonder Bread. Celia said to Ed, "I hate to think of having the baby in this dump."

Ed sat hunched over his knees. "What can we do? We don't have much money, and we have to eat."

She hated hearing him talk like he was giving up on them. "You got to go find some work. That's what."

"No sense going out looking for work on a Saturday."

"Will you go on Monday?"

Ed swiped a hand under his nose. "Yeah, I guess I'll have to. I wish I had some more clothes."

"I'll clean your shirt and undershirt so they'll be fresh for you."

One thing Celia knew was how to do laundry, even though all she had to work with was a chip of soap in a rust-stained sink down the hall. She scrubbed Ed's shirt and their underclothes and hung them to dry over the bed rail.

They lived on liverwurst, Wonder Bread, and water on Saturday and Sunday. Come Monday morning, Ed lolled around the room for a few hours, then put on his clean shirt and the same pants he'd been wearing every day since they left New York.

"Good luck," she said and gave him a peck on the lips.

While Ed was out Celia sat in the chair looking around the room. She didn't have anything she could clean the room with—no rags or Lysol. It was depressing being stuck in such a filthy, flea-bag joint. She wished they were back in their old room in Brooklyn. At least she could keep it clean, and they wouldn't be worrying about coppers chasing them down for robbery and murder. It wasn't much, but they'd been happy. But no, they weren't satisfied with that. And look where their bright ideas got them.

Ed came back after a couple of hours. He'd sweated out the armpits and chest of his shirt and looked deflated and downcast.

"I'm not used to this weather," he said.

The room they were in faced south, and the sun had been beating in through the window, which didn't have a curtain. Celia was hot, too, probably more than she would have been if she weren't as big as a whale.

She stood and walked up to Ed and took his hand. "Did you have any luck?"

"I asked at a few warehouses and stores, but they didn't have any openings. Or maybe they didn't like my looks. Or the way I talk."

"There's nothing wrong with your looks. And I think they talk awful funny around here."

Ed unbuttoned his shirt. "I'm going to splash some water on myself."

When he came back from the bathroom, she said, "I'm starting to get scared about the baby. We don't know a soul here. How am I going to have the baby and give it a good start? We don't even have any diapers or baby clothes."

Ed looked like he might start crying. She'd never seen him so shot down. He stood there hanging his head.

She took his hand and led him over to the bed. As they sat down side by side, the mattress sagged under their weight.

Ed stared at the grimy wood-slat floor. "I can't stop thinking about shooting that guy. They'll get me for murder, and then it'll be all over."

Celia felt awful sorry for him—maybe even sorrier for him than for herself. She couldn't do any kind of work with the baby coming. It was all on his shoulders. "I know. But we got to find a way to live. I know you'll find something if you keep trying."

"I'll go out again tomorrow. Now I just want to lie down and cool off. Is that okay?"

Ed went out the next three days, scrambling around Jacksonville. Every day it was the same: None of the places he checked with had any openings. He didn't try for a job as a chauffeur or driver because he'd have to show his driver's license. And he was afraid to check on a garage job in case the coppers had discovered that was his main business.

When he came back on Thursday, he told her, "I wish I'd never thought about coming to this two-bit town. If we were back in Brooklyn I could be going to the garage and working like I been doing for two years. Everybody there liked me."

"It's just lousy luck, Eddie. I know something'll come

up." She had to say that, but she was getting scared herself. Ed had only been going out a couple of hours each day, probably because he was so down in the dumps he could hardly drag himself out of bed in the morning. Whenever she thought things couldn't get any worse, they sank lower into the gutter.

"Maybe I should write to my mother and see if she'll send us some money."

"No, don't do that. I'd be awful ashamed to ask your mother for money."

The sky outside their window was turning purplish when Celia started having terrible stabbing pains in her belly—pain like she'd never known.

She howled and grabbed her stomach.

Ed looked at her with big eyes. "Is it the baby?"

"I don't know." She was gasping for air. "I thought… it'd be a few more weeks."

"What else could it be? Where does it hurt?"

All she could do was pant and crunch herself into a ball.

"I'm going to find a doctor for you."

"No. Maybe it'll pass." She knew the cops had probably figured out she was pregnant after their last job, and she was scared that if a doctor came the birth would be reported, and the cops would track them down.

She curled up on her side, grabbed his hand, and guided it to the bottom of her belly. "It hurts here."

Ed clapped his hand over her belly. The warmth of his touch soothed her. Then the pain stabbed at her again, and she couldn't keep from crying out and buckling into a tight ball.

Ed's mother had told her labor would start with contraction pains. It didn't seem right to have such piercing pain. She felt panicky—like something was going wrong—and worried she might die, like the pregnant girl in their tenement in Manhattan.

She told Ed, "I didn't think… it'd feel like this."

He looked down on her with worried eyes. His mouth was clamped shut like he didn't know what to say.

Then a strange kind of calm washed over her, like she was floating outside her body, looking down on herself and Ed from a soft, fluffy cloud. She had this crazy thought: What if I die? Eddie will be free. If I don't bring the cops down on us, he'll be able to go anywhere and get a job and start over.

Even though pain stabbed at her like a sharp knife, she felt peaceful. She didn't care if she lived or died. Whatever was going to happen would happen. But she hoped her baby would make it. Ed would be a good father, and having a baby to take care of would keep him busy and happy.

"Don't, Eddie," she said, "don't get anybody. Just stay with me."

Stories Lining Up
Brooklyn, April 10, 1924

Casey had been dragging himself all over Brooklyn and Manhattan, working with the precincts on raiding possible hideouts for the bob-haired bandit and her companion. McGowan had tracked down photos of Ed Cooney at both the driver's license bureau and Navy Recruiting Office, and Casey had circulated the picture to all the boroughs. But everybody was coming up empty. The twosome must have found a helluva good hiding place, and they probably had someone helping them out. They hadn't staged any more robberies lately, but that was most likely because of Celia's delicate condition.

Come Thursday, Casey phoned Nathan Mazo's doctor at Jewish Hospital. Mazo had turned it around and was making a good recovery. The biggest worry was infection, but the odds of that diminished every day. The doctor explained he'd decided not to extract the bullets. They were buried deep in his flesh, in his buttocks to be exact, and it'd be riskier to dig them out than leave them there. Casey figured Mazo was lucky he landed ass up when those bullets drilled the door. And, yes, the doctor said, he was certainly well enough for an interview. So Casey drove over to the hospital.

Casey knocked on the door frame to his room. "Hello, Mr. Mazo. I'm Captain Casey, from the Atlantic Avenue Precinct."

Mazo broke into a mile-wide smile. He was obviously enjoying his time in the limelight. The newspapers were full of his boasts about trying to take down the bandits one-handed.

"Hi there, Captain. Pull up a chair."

The counter held a good dozen cards and a few vases of flowers. "Nice room you got here."

"Yeah, they gave me a room of my own on account of all the reporters coming around and generally disturbing the peace."

"Well, I'm going to have to ask you to tell your story all over again."

"Haven't you been reading the papers?"

"Ha," Casey snorted. "Newspaper articles hardly qualify as reliable reports. Let alone eyewitness testimony. And there are conflicting reports about who fired the shots."

Mazo propped himself up on an elbow and twisted around to face Casey. "Yeah, probably because I can't say for sure. They both had guns, him two, her one. They were all aimed right at me, even while the dame was down on the ground. If I hadn't dived into that room, it would've been curtains for me."

"If you had to guess, who would you say fired the shots?"

"Probably the guy. He had a mean look about him."

A mean look? That wouldn't hold up under cross-examination. If these two got themselves a good attorney, they might beat an attempted murder rap. Who knows how many jurors would sympathize with this bob-haired bandit? He didn't understand why some people hailed these two hoodlums as modern-day Robin Hoods.

Casey had Mazo recount his story of the robbery from the top, mostly for the record.

"When do they set you free, Mr. Mazo?"

"I go home tomorrow. Wouldn't mind taking one of these swell nurses home with me."

Casey chuckled. "Well, I guess you'll be going home with a few other souvenirs of the event."

"Yeah, I'm sure I'll never live that down."

Casey took his time driving back to the precinct. He'd been eating, breathing, and sleeping nothing but this bob-haired case for weeks. Just when he nailed down the suspects' identities, they disappeared like a magician's helpers. The damn newspapers took every opportunity to humiliate him and the force for not catching these two. Even Fiona was getting in on the act, asking him: Why in the world did it take you this long to discover the bob-haired bandit is pregnant? And have you checked under your desk for those two?

Casey let himself in the back door of the precinct and strolled to his office. There was a note stuck on his door, "Bill, come by my office. Frank."

Casey hung up his coat and headed to Gray's office. "What you got for me, Frank?"

"Come on in, Bill."

Frank scooted forward in his wheeled chair and leaned

over his forearms. "Schwartz's Furniture sent a truck to the Cooney's apartment this morning and collected all the furniture. I got over to the store and talked to the owner. Seems a Mrs. Cooney phoned them a few days ago and told them to put all the furniture in storage."

"Mrs. Cooney? You mean the wife?"

"No, said she was Ed's mother."

"All right. It's time to talk to the mother. Let's get going."

Not surprisingly, the officers who'd been keeping the mother's home under surveillance hadn't reported any sightings of the twosome. Casey doubted the Cooneys would be brazen—or stupid—enough to show their faces there. He'd also put a tracer on all the mother's mail in case they tried to contact her.

Mrs. Cooney lived in a modest two-story house with a tidy front porch. They knocked on the door. A stout woman with salt-and-pepper hair greeted them. Her round face and blue eyes showed no sign of surprise when they introduced themselves as detectives.

"Would you like to come in?" she asked.

Casey took off his hat. "Yes, please. We have some questions for you."

Mrs. Cooney motioned them in. The kitchen was small but neat, with a small bouquet of daffodils on the table. "Would you like some coffee?"

"No, thank you." Casey was craving his afternoon coffee, but he didn't want to put this nice lady to any trouble. She was in for a big surprise about her son Ed.

She invited them to join her around the kitchen table.

Casey said, "I understand you telephoned Schwartz's Furniture store on Monday asking them to retrieve the furniture from your son's apartment."

"Yes, that was me."

"Were you asked to do that?"

"Yes, by my son Ed." She fingered a button on her dress. "Can you tell me why you're asking?"

There was no reason to sugarcoat this. She'd have to face the facts soon enough. "He and his wife are under suspicion for robbery and assault."

She clamped her lips together hard and gave a little nod like she was trying to absorb the news.

Casey gave her a minute. "When did you last talk to your son?"

"He came over to visit me about two weeks ago. That's when he asked me to telephone the furniture store."

"What exactly did he say?"

"That he and Celia were going away for a while, but they'd be back in a few months."

"Did he say where they were going?"

"I asked, but he didn't want to tell me."

"Has he done this before? Taken off for a while?"

"Well, he was in the Navy. But, except for that, no."

"Have you had any contact with him since that visit two weeks ago?"

"No, nothing. And I just have to say my Ed is not a trouble-maker. And he's a loving husband."

Casey had a few other questions, but it seemed clear she knew nothing about her son's criminal activities. Or whereabouts.

He pulled one of his cards out of his suit pocket and handed it to her. "If he gets in touch with you, let us know. It's in his best interest to contact us. And we know his wife is about to have a baby."

She looked at the card and scrunched up her nose like it stunk or something.

As they were walking to the car, Gray said, "I think we should pay another visit to the landlady."

"Yeah, I was thinking the same thing."

Mrs. Dougherty ushered them in, and before they could get a question in, she said, "Oh, Mr. Casey. I don't know what to think."

Casey stood clutching his hat over his stomach. "What do you mean, ma'am?"

She wrung her hands. "The Cooneys said they'd be back in a week, but I haven't heard from them and then the furniture store truck came to take away their furniture. I had to go to the grocer and get some cardboard boxes to put their clothes and bed coverings in so the men could take the bedroom set away."

"Well, Mrs. Dougherty," Casey said. "I think it's fair to say they won't be coming back anytime soon."

"They're in trouble, aren't they?"

"Yes, they're suspected of having committed a string of robberies."

She clapped a hand over her heart. "Oh, I would never in a million years have thought they were criminals. It just goes to show you can never tell about people."

"Have you heard from them since they left on March 29?"

"No, and they owed the rent for this month last Friday."

"They probably won't be paying you any more rent."

Mrs. Dougherty shook her head. "I guess I'll store their belongings in the basement."

"Yes, and if they should be in touch, please let us know."

On the drive back to headquarters Casey tapped his fingers on the steering wheel. "Finally, all the stories are starting to line up."

Gray asked, "You think they're hiding out somewhere in Manhattan?"

"My money says they've flown the coop. But to where?"

"Is it time to put out an all-nation bulletin?"

Casey nodded. "Probably, but let's wait until Monday. I'd hate to tip them off now that we've got good descriptions out to all the precincts. And they like Saturday nights. Let's see if there are any sightings around town this weekend."

Baby Katherine
Jacksonville, April 10–12, 1924

Even though Celia asked Ed to stay with her, he didn't. He ran out of the room, leaving the door open behind him. A lady with rouged cheeks and painted-on eyebrows came and sat down on the bed beside her. Celia was still in that weird floating place, looking down on the scene, with pain doubling her up and tears running down her cheeks. This lady stroked her shoulder and told her everything would be fine. But she didn't care anymore if she lived or died. She was panting like a dog and all scrunched up from feeling like a hot knife was slicing her belly. She wanted her Eddie by her side.

After what seemed like hours, he came and stood over her. "I got a doctor for you."

This doctor held her wrist and peered into her eyes, and she could hear him asking Ed questions and Ed mumbling to him. Then the doctor said, "She has to get to a hospital. I'm going to call an ambulance."

Celia was in such terrible pain she was rambling and raving, hardly aware of what was going on around her. She heard sirens blaring and coming closer and closer. Then two men were in the room, lifting her onto a stretcher. They bounced her down the stairs, and Ed must have been trailing them because she heard him saying, "It'll be all right, honey. Just hold on."

The men slid her into an ambulance. Ed held her hand and talked to her. She felt groggy from the pain, and all she could do was moan every now and then. That ambulance jostled her along the roads and around the corners, and by the time they got to the hospital she was nearly passed out.

The men rolled her into a room with white walls and bright lights. People bustled around her. She looked for Ed but didn't see him anywhere. A nurse's face closed in on her and said they were going to get her out of her clothes. A bunch of hands pawed at her. She felt woozy and weak from all the pain, like she was being dragged through a wringer. The nurse said she was going to feel a little poke. She didn't remember much after that.

She kept passing in and out of consciousness, and time shrank and swelled like it was some caterwauling accordion. After a while, the pain let go of her and she felt nothing but weak, sore, and limp. She was in a different room, one with a window and another bed, but it was empty. The sky was dark outside.

Ed was standing over her. "Celia, you did it. We have a baby girl."

She reached for his hand. "Is she okay?"

"Yeah. The nurses have her."

A nurse brought in a tray of food and propped her up. The food looked good—a square hunk of fish, peas and carrots, red jello, and a glass of milk. She ate half of it and made Ed finish the rest.

She slept after that, and when she woke up, it was still dark outside. Ed was sitting in a chair in the corner.

He stood up and came over to her. "They're going to bring the baby to you now."

"Okay," she said. She felt better after she'd had some food and a nap. She was limp as a wet noodle but relieved to be out from under that awful pain.

Ed bunched up her pillows so she could prop herself up.

A nurse came in with her baby and told her she should be fed. Celia looked at the baby and almost started crying. She was a spindly thing, not like babies she'd seen pictures of in advertisements. Her eyes were sunken and her face was narrow, not plump like you'd expect. She tried to get her to take her breast and eat, but she didn't seem interested. The baby just lolled in her arms and made whimpering noises. After a while, the nurse took the baby away, and she slept again.

When she woke up in the morning, the sky was orange-streaked and the nurse brought the baby back to her. This time she ate a little and then the nurse came and said she'd change her diaper. Another nurse brought her a tray of breakfast food. She didn't know where Ed was.

A few hours later, he came in, closed the door, and dragged the chair over to her bed. He took a hold of her hand. "How are you feeling?"

"Okay, I guess. Kind of sore."

"You have to leave the hospital. We can't pay the bill, so they said you have to check out."

She could hardly believe it. She felt so groggy and

weak she didn't know if she could even stand up. She heaved out a big breath. "Right now?"

"Yeah, I think so."

"My clothes are in that bag."

Ed helped Celia into her underclothes and maternity dress, and then she sat down on the bed to catch her breath.

"I got some more bad news," Ed said.

Celia looked up at him. His eyes were bloodshot, and he reeked of sour sweat.

"The manager at Ocean Avenue told me last night we couldn't come back without paying for next week. And we're broke except for a few bucks."

She wanted to collapse back onto that bed and shut out the whole world. Nothing was going right for them. Her baby was a puny thing that would hardly eat. They were broke, and she was a wreck, all wrung out from the birthing.

Ed took a hold of her hand. "I been walking around, and I found a boarding house that'll let us pay later. It's about a mile from here. Do you think you can walk a mile?"

"I guess I'll have to. Let me rest a minute." She could hardly believe all their hardships. Mrs. Cooney had told her she'd stay in the hospital two or three days after the baby was born, but here she was getting kicked out the next morning. And she'd be having to slog around this strange town where they couldn't even ask anybody for help.

A knock sounded at the door and a nurse let herself in. She had some papers and a pen. "I need to record some details. I'm sorry we have to discharge you," she said. "It's just the rules."

She was chubby and maybe about forty, and she seemed sad for them. She stood at the counter with her pen over her papers. "What name should I put down for the baby?"

Celia had already thought of what she wanted to name her so she spoke up. "I'd like to call her Katherine, with a K, after my husband's mother. Is that okay, Ed?"

Ed nodded. "Sure."

The nurse asked, "Any middle name?"

"Gosh, I don't know," she said, looking at Ed.

He asked her, "How about Mary?"

"Okay."

The nurse said, "I've got everything I need for the birth certificate. Let me get Katherine for you."

Celia said, "I don't have any baby clothes or diapers."

The nurse gave her a feeble smile. "I'll see what I can do."

She came back after a few minutes with the baby wrapped in a blanket. "I put an extra diaper in the blanket for you."

"Thank you," she said, taking baby Katherine.

Celia and Ed trudged out of the hospital, and Ed pointed the way. "Here, I can carry the baby."

She handed Katherine to him and then latched onto his arm. She felt weak and woozy, but she walked as steadily as she could. Holding onto Ed's arm helped.

Ed clutched the baby with both arms. "It couldn't get much worse for us, could it?"

There wasn't a thing Celia could say to that. She'd

wanted to give their new baby a nice home, and here they were in this strange place with a sickly baby that hardly had the gumption to cry. It was Friday and she was hoping Ed could go out looking for work again before the weekend, so she said, "Maybe if you tell people we just had a baby, they'd give you a job."

"The truth is, Celia, I've only asked at a few places about work. I been too scared since I got a price on my head."

She could hardly believe what he was telling her. "What have you been doing when you go out?"

"Mostly walking around. That room was awful depressing."

Her legs almost gave out under her. Here she'd been counting on her man to take care of them, and now he was telling her he'd been slacking off. "I know you're discouraged, but we got to eat. We got to feed the baby."

"I wrote a letter to my mother and asked her to send us a hundred dollars to keep us going."

"But we don't want anybody to know we're here."

"I asked her to keep Mum about our address. And I told the manager at Ocean Avenue to hang onto any mail and that I'd come around and check."

"Oh, Eddie. I don't think I've ever in my life been as miserable as I am right now." She was so low-spirited and wobbly she felt like her legs might buckle under her.

They came to a little park with a bench, and she asked Ed if they could sit and rest. There were some swings and a slide, but they looked lonely without any kids playing on them. Celia slumped against the bench and closed her eyes.

She thought about when she was a kid and played in the streets. She'd have never pictured herself in a strange city with a baby—and wanted for robbery and maybe murder. It was like a terrible nightmare, except it was true. And her poor Eddie, who was always so good to her, was too scared to track down a job.

After trudging along blocks of old beat-down houses, they made it to this place Ed had found for them on East Monroe Street. The house was two stories and had porches on both levels with columns holding them up. They walked up to the front door and went in. The hallway was narrow, and Ed pointed the way up the stairs to a room on the second floor at the back, with '#14' on the door. He pulled the key out of his pocket and opened the door.

The smell hit her like a sledgehammer—it was like a mouse or rat had died in the wall. She almost gagged. She walked over to the window and opened it as wide as she could. There wasn't any sense asking Ed if there was a different room since they didn't have any money to pay for it.

She took Katherine from Ed and said, "I'll see if her diaper needs to be changed."

She put Katherine on the bed and unfolded her blanket and unpinned her diaper. She had peed and made a little loose poop. Celia needed to clean her up before she put a new diaper on her. She saw that Ed had already brought their suitcase to the room. She opened it and dug through their belongings. She took out her clean underpants and went to the bathroom and dampened them. Then she used them to clean up Katherine and put on a fresh diaper. The baby moaned when she lifted her bottom to put the diaper under her. She was so puny and didn't seem to weigh much at all. How would she ever turn into a regular plump baby? Celia took her dirty diaper to the bathroom and cleaned it out as best she could and brought it to the room to hang and dry.

Ed was sitting on the bed beside Katherine looking at her kind of sad-like. He asked, "You think she'll be okay?"

"I don't know. I should see if she'll eat." She took her in her arms over to the one chair in the room, a stuffed chair with worn-down reddish upholstery, and got her to eat a little.

While she was feeding Katherine, she asked Ed, "Do we have any money at all?"

"I been holding onto a few bucks so we can eat."

"Will you buy us some bread and a hunk of cheese? I'm hungry for cheese." She wasn't really craving cheese, but she knew they shouldn't spend what little money they had on meat.

When Ed came back he sliced the cheese and they had it on bread. Celia was thinking they shouldn't pin all their hopes on getting money from his mother, but she didn't want to punch down Ed's hopes.

He chomped down on his sandwich. "The letter won't get there till late next week, but at least we'll know some money's coming."

"Sure, your mother will come through for us. I know she will."

They moped around that smelly room all day, not knowing what to do with themselves and fretting over baby Katherine. She seemed as sad as they were and hardly had the energy to move around.

When they went to bed that night, Celia put Katherine between them so she wouldn't roll off the bed. She fell asleep snuggling her little body against her belly.

Celia woke up in the morning and nestled Katherine close and kissed her cheek. She looked pale, and her eyes seemed sad and dull like she couldn't see or focus.

She poked Ed's back. "Hey, wake up."

Ed rolled over toward her. "Yeah?"

"Something's wrong with Katherine. What should we do?"

Ed looked at her and said in a shaky voice, "See if she'll eat. Maybe she's hungry."

Celia got out of bed with her and sat in the chair. But Katherine wouldn't eat. As Celia held her close, her scrawny arms and legs flopped about, like she didn't even have the energy to hold them up.

"Eddie, I'm scared. Look at her."

Ed came and stood beside her, looking down on Katherine. "Is she breathing?"

Celia held her close to her face to see if any breath was coming in or going out. "I don't think so."

"Give her to me."

Ed put Katherine on the bed, massaged her chest, and blew air into her mouth and nostrils. Celia sat beside her and cupped her hand over her sweet little head. But it didn't do any good. Her narrow chest seemed to cave in on itself, and her breath wouldn't come. Her skin turned waxy white, the white of church candles. Celia'd never seen a more pitiful creature. Her skinny face and sunken eyes made her look like an old woman, an old woman with a secret—that life is too precious to smudge with sin.

Little Katherine died with them looking down on her woebegone face. She hadn't even lived two days.

Celia and Ed slumped onto their knees beside the bed. They sobbed for their poor baby, holding onto each other and every now and then blubbering about how their poor little girl never had a chance and how sorry they were they couldn't get her taken care of and how she was nothing but sweetness and it wasn't right she'd suffered on account of them.

Ed got up and sat on the bed looking at Katherine. He swiped his sleeve over his face and wiped away his tears. "We didn't even have time to get her baptized."

Celia leaned over the bed on her knees and put her hands together. "Dear God, please don't hold that against our innocent baby. Please take her up to Heaven."

Ed stroked the wispy hair on Katherine's head. "We have to at least give her a decent burial."

"Do you think you can find a funeral home that will do that?"

"Yeah, I will. Even if I have to get down on my knees and beg."

Ed left to see if he could track down an undertaker. While he was gone Celia stretched out on the bed and wrapped her arm over Katherine, telling her they loved her and that she wished she could have stayed with them.

"I was going to bring you up right," she told her. "You wouldn't have had to walk the streets with dirty feet and beg and scrape for food."

Celia was all out of tears, and she could only think about the sadness and misfortune of losing the baby they'd been looking forward to welcoming. They were supposed to start a new life with their baby and instead they were all weighed down with loss and desperation.

She didn't know what was going to happen to them. And she hardly cared, being as sad and miserable as she was about losing their darling baby. Katherine was the reason they wanted to make a better life, and instead they'd let down this new life that had been growing in her. She'd failed their baby Katherine, and she would never be able to make it up no matter how long she lived.

When Ed came back, he said he'd found a man who would give them a coffin for Katherine and let them pay when their money came in. Celia had cleaned up Katherine and swaddled her in her blanket. She looked like an angel—her face white as snow and her nose and mouth and closed eyes so tiny and sweet.

They walked to the undertaker's house, and the man welcomed them to his parlor in a soft voice. He was gentle with baby Katherine, placing her in her miniature coffin and fluffing her blanket around her. He took down the details about Katherine for the death certificate, and then the three of them had a ceremony to say goodbye to baby Katherine. A big lump stuck in Celia's throat, and she couldn't swallow it down.

She hated walking out of that funeral house and leaving Katherine alone for all time and eternity. It was probably the saddest day of her life ever. She felt nothing but heartsick and dejected. Their poor baby never had a chance, and it was all their fault.

New York Times, Page 1
April 16, 1924

POLICE GET A CLUE TO BOB-HAIRED BANDIT
Circular Sent All Over Country
Describes Brooklyn Girl
and Tall Companion

The identity of the 'bob-haired bandit of Brooklyn,' as she is known in police annals, is no longer a mystery. She is, police say, Celia Cooney, nee Roth. So anxious are the detectives to get her that a circular has been broadcast throughout the nation, giving her name, her description, and a photograph of her tall companion.

The attempted holdup of the National Biscuit Company, 1000 Pacific Street, on April 1 by the bob-haired bandit and her male companion may prove to be the undoing of this notorious bandit couple, who have been terrorizing Brooklyn storekeepers for four months.

As a result of this affair, in which Nathan Mazo, cashier of the Biscuit Company, was shot, the police have made numerous inquiries and investigations, which have resulted in procuring what they believe to be accurate descriptions of the feminine Jesse James and her companion.

The couple, according to the police, have been married since May 18, 1923. The man's name is given as

Edward Cooney. Police offer, as one reason why there have not been any holdups since the National Biscuit Company affair, the theory that Mrs. Cooney, otherwise known as 'the bob-haired bandit,' is approaching motherhood.

Identity Learned

The identity of the couple was learned from employees of the Biscuit Company and other persons who either witnessed the holdup or saw the bandits leave the building after the shooting.

These persons, on being questioned by police, said they recognized in the man and woman a newly married couple who had been living in a Brooklyn apartment that is almost within a stone's throw of the Atlantic Avenue police station. They gave the couple's names and said that the man had served in the Navy during the war.

The man was employed in a garage and, according to witnesses, was an expert mechanic and a first-rate chauffeur. He might at present be employed in either of these capacities, and police accordingly are making a careful survey of men engaged in both professions. The authorities have the fingerprints and a photograph of Cooney. Copies of both have been broadcast. Not so long ago he applied for a New York State automobile license and at the time furnished a photograph of himself, which was an excellent duplicate of the one held by the U.S. Navy.

The detailed description of the notorious couple is contained in the directions broadcast to the police all over the country, which follows.

"Make inquiries at garages, automobile repair shops, welding shops for Edward Cooney, alias Parker, Lyons, Roth, or Smith. He is five feet eleven and a half inches in height, weighs 175 pounds, has blond hair, ruddy complexion, and when last seen wore a light tan overcoat with a belt on the back; may wear a brown or blue suit. He had a pearl-gray hat. He worked as a helper and automobile mechanic. May give reference as being a chauffeur. He has automobile and chauffeur's licenses issued to Edward Cooney. He is wanted for assault and robbery, and he is believed to have several revolvers in his possession.

"Make inquiry at doctors' offices, lying-in hospitals, sanitariums, and other places where a confinement case may be treated. The girl's name is Celia Cooney, and her maiden name is Roth. She may give the name of Parker, Lyons, or some other fictitious name. She is about twenty years old, five feet one inch in height, and 120 pounds. She has dark bobbed hair and when last seen she wore a three-quarter-length coat, a green dress, a pink turban hat, and a dark veil."

Cornered
Jacksonville, April 17, 1924

Celia and Ed felt nothing but dismal after Katherine died. They didn't know a soul in Jacksonville they could talk to about their baby. Celia missed everybody from Brooklyn—Ed's mother and brothers, her friends from Foster's Laundry, even their nice landlady. Their life was crumbling apart bit by bit, day after day. They were down to a few coins and getting by on what food Ed could scrounge from behind grocery stores—moldy baked goods and fruit and vegetables covered with dents and cracks and all the wrong colors. It was Thursday and, with the weekend coming, she thought she should ask Ed to go out job-hunting.

"Eddie, I know that money from your mother will be coming next week, but we won't be able to live on that forever. You got to find a job."

"How can I show my face when I'm wanted for murder?"

She hadn't hounded Ed much about looking for work on account of how broken-hearted they both felt about baby Katherine. But she was fed up with being at rock bottom. Even when she was a scraggly, hard-up kid she always found a way to tough it out. "If you don't go out and find some work, I will."

"All right," he said. "I'll go."

He trudged out, and she sat at the open window looking down on the beat-up garbage cans in the alley, thinking about poor Katherine all tiny and alone in her coffin.

A half hour later Ed barged in and slammed the door behind him. "Celia, they know who we are."

"What are you talking about?"

He had a newspaper, a day-old *New York Times*, and right there on the front page it said 'POLICE GET A CLUE TO BOB-HAIRED BANDIT.'

She grabbed the paper, and he stood over her shoulder while she read the article. It revealed their names and descriptions and reported that news of their identities had gone out all over the country.

The breath went right out of her. "Now what are we going to do?"

"Cops everywhere will be looking for us." Ed walked over to the dresser and took out their three guns and lined them up on top of it. "We might as well be ready when they come."

A nauseating feeling, like the flu on top of seasickness, washed over her. "You think they'll shoot us?"

"They've been gunning for us ever since we started." He plunked down on the bed and shook his clasped hands. "It'll be curtains for us."

She was so shocked she hardly knew what to say. She never thought they'd end up such big-time criminals. She read through the article again, trying to think what they should do. Then it hit her. "Hey, it doesn't say anything about murder. It just says we're wanted for robbery and assault. Maybe that Nathan guy is okay."

"Yeah, but I shot him all right. They'll get me for attempted murder."

Her wheels were turning fast now. "Listen, Eddie. Nobody saw which one of us fired the shots. Remember? That door was closed when you let those bullets fly."

"It's all over for us." Ed got up and grabbed the thirty-eight and sat back down on the bed.

"What are you doing?"

He didn't say a word, just bent over his knees and fingered the pistol.

She needed to figure out something—the cops were nipping at their heels. The hospital and undertaker knew about them and the baby. They couldn't afford to get on a train and go somewhere else. Cops everywhere would be on the lookout for them. They were cornered. Would the bulls hunt them down and slaughter them like animals?

Maybe when the money from Mrs. Cooney came they could take a bus or train to some other place where no one knew about them and the baby. Celia could dye her hair, and Ed could grow a mustache. Maybe the money would come before the cops found them.

She was terrified that they might get gunned down. Sure, they shouldn't have robbed all those stores, but they didn't deserve to die for it. She wanted Ed to snap out of his slump so they could figure out what to do. Here they were cornered in this room. But if they made a break for it, they risked being spotted. The bulls would probably expect them to cut and run. The way she saw it, they only had one good choice.

She walked over to the bed and put her hand on his shoulder. "Eddie, we can't just sit here and wait to get caught."

He didn't say a word, just kept smoothing his hand over that gun.

She asked him, "Do you think we should go to the police and turn ourselves in?"

"No," he mumbled. "I'm not going to prison."

"But they could shoot us. I don't want to die."

He snorted. "You got any idea what prison's like?"

"I sure don't want to get killed."

"Then you better think about what it'd be like spending your life behind bars."

His shoulder felt hard under her hand, like he was bracing himself against her words and touch. He sat there bent over and flat-footed, staring at the gun. Her Eddie was all out of hope. She had to figure out a way to lift him out of his gloom and doom. It chilled her blood to see him stroking that gun like it was his last friend in the world.

On The Hunt
Brooklyn and Jacksonville,
April 19–21, 1924

Casey didn't usually hit the office on Saturday. But with the bob-haired bandit and her companion still at large, he needed to pursue every single lead. Since the all-nation circular had gone out, sightings and tips about the bandit and her tall companion had poured in, not just from New York City, but across the country, too—so many that determining which ones to take seriously was like hunting for the proverbial needle in a haystack. Chasing down every sighting would have had him crisscrossing the country for months to come. So Casey, Gray, McGowan, and the other five detectives on the squad divided the tips among them and got to work sifting through them.

Casey had also been intercepting all Mrs. Cooney's mail. Most of it was mundane—bills and a chatty letter from a cousin who lived in Boston. He'd promptly resealed all those missives and sent them along to Mrs. Cooney. On that Saturday morning, the latest batch of her mail yielded a letter with a return address of Jacksonville, Florida. Casey steamed it open.

He could hardly believe his eyes. It was from Ed—asking his mother to send a hundred dollars to him in

Florida so he and Celia could get by a little longer before they returned. Cooney had obviously written the letter before his identity had been broadcast all over the country. Or maybe he still didn't know he and his wife had been fingered. In any case, Ed was holding to the line he'd fed his mother before they fled—that they'd be returning in a few months.

Casey trotted down the hall to Gray's office and thrust the letter under his nose. "Hey, Frank, look at this."

Gray scanned the letter. He snapped his head up. "Holy Toledo. We hit the jackpot."

Casey and Gray gathered the rest of the team in the bullpen and briefed them on the break and their next moves. They all sat on the edge of their chairs, mouths gaping open or voicing astonishment.

Casey stood before the group rapping his knuckles on the table. His thoughts were racing ahead, ticking off a to-do list. "Mac, contact the Jacksonville police and let them know Frank and I are on our way. We'll want their assistance once we arrive."

McGowan nodded. "Sure thing, Captain."

Casey scanned the expectant faces of his team. "I'm sure this goes without saying, but let's keep this out of the news for now."

Casey asked the dispatcher to check on trains that'd get him and Frank to Florida in a hurry. There was an express departing at eleven fifteen. He rushed home and had a quick bite to eat with Fiona, rattling off the news between bites of his sandwich. He telephoned Commissioner Enright to let him know he was fielding a solid tip from Jacksonville and headed down there to follow up. He threw his toiletries, a few clean shirts, and some undergarments in his suitcase and took a taxi to Grand Central Station.

Once on the train, Casey and Gray settled in for the long train ride. Casey hadn't thought to bring a book so he ended up reading newspapers set aside by other travelers, first a few New York papers, then *The Philadelphia Tribune*, and even a Washington, D.C., rag. He and Frank jawed about a bit of everything—their wives and kids, the start of baseball season, and whether they should tell Enright they'd broken the case by intercepting mail. It wasn't exactly by the books, Casey said. But, Gray responded, when did Enright give a damn about following rules?

By the time the train pulled into Jacksonville around eleven on Sunday morning, they'd had a good night's sleep and were raring to go. They took a cab to Police Headquarters on Newnan Street. The Jacksonville force had summoned three detectives to assist them with the case: Alex Wethington, Jim Hulbert, and Leo Harvey. After welcomes and handshakes all around—these fellas were as polite as southern belles—Casey whipped out the letter.

"Here's the address we've got, 125 Ocean Avenue." He handed the letter to Wethington. "They have three guns between them, and they're not afraid to use them. So the situation could be dangerous."

"We can handle them," Wethington said. "Jim, you stay here and work the phones."

After Wethington asked for back-up from another car, the four of them piled into a Ford police vehicle and drove over to Ocean Avenue. Wethington parked the car a block from the address. The other car, with two officers, snugged up behind them minutes later.

Wethington said to his sidekick, "Leo, you go around the back of the house in case they try to run for it." He told the two cops in the extra car to drive close enough to keep an eye on the front door once they went inside.

The house was a beat-up two-story. Casey, Gray, and Wethington let themselves in the front door. Just inside was a room with a 'Manager' sign on the door. Casey knocked.

A man's voice sounded. "Yeah, yeah, just a minute."

The door opened to reveal a whiskered guy in a dirty undershirt.

Casey asked, "Are you the manager?"

"Sure I am, what do you want?"

Casey pulled out his badge. "I'm Captain Casey from the New York police, and these are my colleagues. Mind if we come in and ask a few questions?"

"Okay," the guy said, stepping aside to let them enter.

The room was cluttered with odd pieces of furniture, and a radio in the corner aired the news.

"We're looking for a man and a woman we believe are at this address." Casey showed him Ed Cooney's picture. "Do you know this guy?"

The manager eyed the photo. "Yeah, they were here, but they couldn't pay anymore. I kicked them out over a week ago. The little lady had her baby though. An ambulance took her to Humphrey's Sanitarium."

"When exactly was that?"

The guy squinted like it pained him to think. "A little over a week ago. I think it was Thursday night."

"Did they leave any of their belongings behind?"

"No, they cleared out everything."

"Do you know where they are now?"

"Nope. The guy said he'd come around to check on any mail, but I haven't seen him since the day after they took his wife to the hospital."

"What name did they give you?"

"Sheehan, Mr. and Mrs. Sheehan. Ted and Sally."

Wethington stepped forward and handed over his card. "Please call me if he comes around or if you learn anything about their whereabouts."

Casey and his crew hurried back to the car.

"Let's get over to the sanitarium. What can you tell us about the place, Alex?"

"It's a run-of-the-mill lying-in hospital."

At Humphrey's Sanitarium, Casey and his team made their way to the admissions office. Yes, the clerk did have a record of Mrs. Sheehan, who gave her first name as Sally. Sally had had a rough labor. She'd delivered a baby girl, and they named her Katherine Mary. The father's name on the birth certificate was Theodore Sheehan. The baby weighed only five and a half pounds. The hospital had discharged the mother and baby on Friday, April 11, the morning after the birth. They gave their address as 125 Ocean Avenue.

Damn, Casey thought, *we've already been there*. Had

they hit a dead end? He hoped the Cooneys weren't on the run again.

Wethington suggested they go back to headquarters and see if Leo had uncovered anything. But, no, he hadn't. It was two in the afternoon.

"I tell you what, Captain," Wethington said in his homespun drawl. "Let's all get some food in our bellies and reconnoiter."

The broad-shouldered Wethington led the way to a diner a few blocks from headquarters. The Jacksonville fellas recommended Casey and Gray try the shrimp and grits, so that's what they ordered. Casey wasn't keen on sampling strange food, but he had to admit the shrimp tasted like they'd just jumped into the skillet, and the buttery grits were lip-smacking good.

After lunch, they fanned out to gather more details. Gray and Harvey went back to see the manager at Ocean Avenue. Casey and Wethington returned to the hospital to track down nurses and doctors who'd had any contact with the couple. Harvey stayed at the station to telephone hotels around town.

At the hospital, Casey and Wethington spoke to an on-duty nurse, Sue Marie Simon, who had gathered details for the birth certificate.

Sue Marie walked them to the nurse's station and invited them to sit down. Casey had spent more time in hospitals than jails lately. This one smelled like mold and baby poop.

Casey asked, "What can you tell us about the couple?"

"They seemed pretty down and out. They couldn't pay

the hospital bill so we had to discharge them. They didn't put up any fuss, though. The baby was in poor health. She wasn't eating much and was underweight. I felt awful having to discharge them."

"Do you know where they went?"

"I have no idea."

"Did you overhear any conversations between them?"

"Only about what they wanted to name the baby. Honestly, I'd be surprised if the baby lived long. I've seen a lot of newborns brought into this world, and this little girl was pretty feeble. She hardly had enough energy to hold her head up."

Casey and Wethington struck out on finding any more hospital employees with first-hand knowledge. They went back to the admissions office.

Wethington asked the clerk there, "Do you know who ordered the ambulance that brought Sally Sheehan to the hospital on April 10?"

The clerk flipped through a few pages of his ledger. "That was Dr. Gerald Sisson. He has an office over on Seminole Road."

Casey and Wethington hastened back to headquarters and telephoned Sisson's office. There was no answer, which wasn't surprising given it was Sunday. They telephoned his personal residence.

When Sisson answered, Casey explained his business and asked the doctor for his account of what led up to the ambulance call.

"The husband knocked on my door about seven in the evening and said his wife was in bad shape. I could tell by his accent that he was from out of town. He was pretty frantic, so we drove over to their room on Ocean Avenue, and I examined her. It was clear she was in labor, a distressed labor. I'm not an obstetrician, but I knew she was in danger. I went straight to the manager's office and called for an ambulance."

"Did you go to the hospital with them?"

"No, I bowed out after that."

"Have you had any contact with them since then?"

"No, but I was curious about what happened so I called a doctor I know at the hospital on Monday. He told me she delivered a baby girl late Thursday night and that the mother would be fine. He wasn't sanguine about the baby's chances though. She was underweight and not responsive to feeding attempts."

That's as much as they got out of the doctor. Nobody seemed to know where the Cooneys had gone after the hospital discharge.

Wethington suggested they get back to the station and see if any of the others had gathered anything useful. Hulbert hadn't located them at any hotels. Gray and Harvey's visit to the rooming house on Ocean Avenue had netted them a list of other rooming and boarding houses they could check.

Casey told the rest of the team, "We had a nurse and a doctor say that the baby was in poor health and might not live, so I think we should pursue that angle."

Wethington nodded. "I tell you what, Bill. Why don't we get you and Frank checked into a hotel so you can get some rest. We'll stay here and call around to doctors and hospitals to see if a baby's been brought in."

Casey didn't argue with Wethington. It made sense to let the local fellas scour the town. He and Gray took a room at Hotel Windsor, a lavish place facing a park with a fountain and tropical trees and plants. It was late, eight in the evening, and they were both hungry. They decided to eat in shifts so one of them could wait in the room in case Wethington telephoned.

By eleven, they'd both eaten and were stretched out on their beds. Thunder rumbled in the distance. Casey had tried to nap but his thoughts banged around like Coney Island bumper cars. He couldn't imagine hitting the sack with the Cooneys somewhere in Jacksonville. He'd never forgive himself if he let these two slip through his fingers when he'd gotten this close to capturing them.

Casey sat up and looked at Gray. "Let's grab a cab and get back to headquarters. See if they've come up with anything."

At the station, they headed for Wethington's office and knocked on the door.

Wethington called out, "Come in."

When Casey opened his door Wethington said, "I just phoned the hotel looking for you two. We located an undertaker who buried a baby last Saturday. Sounds like the Cooneys. We told him we were coming over."

The three of them hopped into a patrol car. It was Sunday, approaching midnight. A hard rain started to fall, and there was hardly anybody out on the windy streets. Rain bounced off the road, and the window wipers were working overtime. Wethington drove them to a house with a sign on the lawn, "Jenkins Burials and Funerals."

Wethington parked the car, and they all hustled up to the porch. A light shone from one of the front windows, and the undertaker must have been watching for them because he met them at the door.

"Mr. Jenkins?" Wethington asked.

"Yes, you must be Captain Wethington. Come in."

Casey and the other two detectives took off their wet hats and paraded into the house. The musty smells of fading perfume and dust hit his nostrils. The undertaker led them to a parlor with stuffed wingback chairs and a plush sofa.

Jenkins, a portly man with a rim of gray hair, motioned to the chairs and sofa. "Please, make yourselves comfortable."

Wethington introduced Casey and Gray, explaining they were detectives from New York.

Casey said, "We understand you presided over the burial of a baby girl last Saturday." He showed the photo of Ed Cooney to the undertaker. "Was this man the father?"

Jenkins took the photo and studied it a moment. "Yes, I believe this is the man."

"What can you tell us about their visit and business with you?"

Jenkins leaned back in his chair and crossed his legs. "The guy came around late Saturday morning and pleaded with me to bury the baby even though they couldn't pay for the coffin. He said he'd be getting some money in a week or so and would come back and pay me. I didn't have the heart to turn him away.

"Both of them came back an hour later carrying their dead baby in a blanket. The baby was a sorry-looking creature, obviously undernourished. They were dressed in nice clothes, but it looked like they'd been living in them a while. They were quite crestfallen about their loss. The woman did most of the talking. At one point, she said, 'Our poor baby is in heaven now, I just know it. We didn't have time to baptize her, but she's nothing but innocent.' I held a little ceremony with the three of us."

Wethington asked, "Did you get details for the death certificate?"

"Yes, but I confess I haven't sent it in yet. I was quite busy this past week."

Casey spoke up. "Can we see it?"

Jenkins left the room and returned with a piece of paper. Casey scanned it. Right there in black and white was an address—412 East Monroe Street, #14. Holy mackerel, he finally had the Cooneys in his crosshairs. He'd not waste a minute—in case these two were thinking of skipping town.

With a jerk of his head, he signaled to Gray and Wethington. "Let's get going."

Always and Forever
Jacksonville, April 20–21, 1924

On Sunday morning Celia woke to church bells ringing, and she could tell the church wasn't far away. She wanted to go to Mass and be around other people and feel like a regular person.

She rolled over in bed and clutched Ed's shoulder. "Let's go to Mass. We can say some prayers for Katherine."

"No, we can't show our faces. You know that."

They hadn't been out of the room for days, not even to scrounge for food. They'd eaten the last of their bread scraps and beat-up oranges, and her belly was too empty to even growl.

Her nerves were shot, and Ed was so down in the dumps he'd been getting up in the middle of the night and sitting in the chair. Sometimes having a smoke calmed him down, but he'd run out days ago, and they couldn't afford a pack.

By Sunday night they were drained and dreary from worrying and hardly sleeping. Ed wouldn't even talk to her. He was sitting in the chair and she was lying on the bed when the sky turned as black and blue as a fresh bruise. The wind picked up, and the air smelled like wet concrete.

While thunder rumbled in the distance, she stared at

the ceiling, racking her brain about how to get them out of this fix. No matter how many times she'd asked, Ed nixed going to the police and giving themselves up, and she couldn't think of anything else. She figured it was the end of the line for them.

Late that night a hard rain started falling, and Ed slammed their window closed like he was disgusted with the weather and God and everything else. The wind howled and rain pelted the glass. Celia took in short, shallow breaths because the room stunk like a dead rat without any fresh air.

Ed said, "Celia, there's nothing left for us."

Finally, he was talking to her. She sat up and looked at him. "I know. The cops are sure to find us sooner or later."

"We got no baby, we got no money. What reason do we have to keep living?"

Her heart hammered in her chest, and her skin turned clammy. "We got each other, don't we?"

He sat hunched over his clasped hands. "Once we're arrested they'll separate us. If they don't kill us first. It's all over. We ruined our lives."

She figured she should play along and see if he meant what she thought he did. "I know. We were fools. I wish we'd never got started on the robbery business."

"We can end it right now. Be out of our misery."

Oh God, she was afraid that's what he was getting at. "I know you're awful sad, but you can't mean that."

"I do. We got guns. Let's use 'em on ourselves."

Her mouth dried up. She had to talk some sense into

him. She wasn't ready to die. If he tried to use the guns she wouldn't be able to wrestle them away from him. He was a big strong guy. "Think about your mother. And your brothers. They wouldn't want you to do that."

"They don't have to live with what I've done. And I just can't take it anymore."

"Please don't talk like that. You're scaring me."

"I mean it, Celia. I could shoot you if you're too scared. And then shoot myself. It'd be over in no time. We'd be done suffering."

Her heart banged against her ribs, and her throat tightened up so it hurt to swallow. She tried to keep herself calm so she could think. The guns were on top of the dresser. If she could get Ed to sleep, maybe she could hide them under the bed.

She got up and walked over to him and nestled his head against her belly. She'd been thinking about what she'd say to keep the cops from killing them, but first she had to keep Ed from shooting them. "I know you're miserable, Eddie. But let's wait a little longer. Let me think some more. You always said I'm a smart cookie. Will you trust me?"

"I don't see how we get out of this fix. We did it, and the cops know it. I ruined everything."

"Don't be saying that. Sure, it looks like things couldn't get any worse, but we still have each other. And your mother will send us some money."

"If they nab us and throw us in prison we won't have each other. I don't want to live without you."

"We still have a chance. Once we get that money from

your mother we can go somewhere else and start fresh."

"Coppers everywhere are looking for us. It won't work."

"We can disguise ourselves. I know we can." She wasn't sure they could give the coppers the slip, what with every bull in the country looking for them, but she had to say it anyway.

He just wagged his head and studied the floor.

The way he was talking he seemed like a stranger to her. She wanted her old Eddie back. She cupped her hand under his chin and lifted his face so she could look him in the eyes. "You love me, don't you, Eddie?"

"Sure I do. Any joy I ever had was because of you. But I ruined it all."

"Listen now. We love each other and nothing can change that. I want to keep living and loving you. You can't leave me now. Tell me you'll stay with me."

Ed's shoulders started shaking. He dropped his head and sobbed in a muffled sort of way. Her big guy was crying like it was the end of the world.

She stroked his back and let him cry himself out. She bent over and kissed his forehead and eyes and cheeks. "Come on now. Get ready for bed. Let me hold you close."

She unbuttoned his shirt, helped him out of it and his trousers, and made him crawl under the dingy bed cover. She undressed and got in bed beside him. She nestled her face against his neck and put her arm over his chest. Her poor Eddie's spirits were as shot as they could get. And she was pretty miserable, too, what with losing their baby on account of bungling everything. They were at the end of their rope, and for all she knew the cops were tracking them down this very minute and loading their guns with lead. Maybe they'd gun them down before they got a chance to give themselves up.

But she knew she had to keep Ed from using the guns on them. She didn't want to die, and she was afraid to go to sleep with him thinking such dark and dangerous thoughts. She didn't even dare try to hide the guns because he might yank them away from her.

She held him close and whispered in his ear, "Sleep now, Eddie. I promise I'll take care of you. Always and forever."

The Raid
Jacksonville, April 21, 1924

It was after midnight when Casey and his crew headed back to the station after their visit with the undertaker. The rain had finally let up, and its remnants streamed down street channels and spilled into grates.

Casey told Wethington, "We'll want some firepower there for sure."

"Yeah," he said. "I'll order another car and the Black Maria to accompany us."

At the station, Wethington got to work, gathering a caravan of three machines. Casey, Gray, and Hulbert rode with Wethington. A car with two boys in blue followed, and behind them the Black Maria with two more officers. It was almost one in the morning, and the streets were dark and deserted.

They parked a full block from the address on East Monroe and quietly walked to the two-story house at 412. As they approached, a dog in the yard next door barked.

"Come on, Alex," Casey said to Wethington, "let's do a walk around.

They left the others to guard the front entrance. As they passed by the big brown dog, it growled and barked, lunging against the chain-link fence. Casey said, "Quiet, you," but the dog kept barking.

"Okay," Casey said after he and Wethington had surveyed the territory. "We need two men covering the fire escape in the back, two out front, and the rest inside with me."

Once all the men were at their stations, Casey nodded to his crew. "Let's go. Have your guns ready."

Casey's heart was thumping so hard it pounded against his eardrums. He'd been on raids before involving guns and desperadoes, but these two had put him and the force through sheer hell, feeding the public a diet of brazen robberies that humiliated him and the city's police force. He wanted to take this duo alive, but he was prepared to shoot if necessary. These criminals obviously weren't afraid to use their guns.

Wethington opened the front door and walked in. The hallway was completely dark. He turned on his flashlight and signaled the others. Casey followed next and stood close to Wethington, who crept down the hall and shone his light on the doors.

All the rooms on the first floor were numbered with single digits.

"Must be upstairs," Casey whispered.

Wethington nodded and headed for the stairwell near the front door. Casey and the others trailed behind. They reached the second floor, and Wethington scanned the doors with his flashlight. He headed down the hall and aimed his flashlight at a door on the right at the end of the hall. With a sweep of his arm, he summoned the others to join him.

Casey, his gun in hand, crept forward and stood beside Wethington at the door marked #14. He turned around to check if the other men had their guns ready. Satisfied they were all set, he took in a deep breath.

This was it—the showdown. He banged firmly on the door and called out, "Open up in the name of the law."

Nothing but quiet.

Casey hammered on the door. "Open up, I said."

A man's voice sounded from behind the door, "All right but wait till my wife gets her clothes on."

A feeble line of light sliced out at the bottom of the door. Casey could hear footsteps and whispering. He clucked his mouth. It was dry as cotton. It seemed like too much time was passing for them to get dressed.

"Open the door. Now," he said.

Still, nothing but quiet.

Casey stepped back, lowered his shoulder, and lunged at the door. It rattled but held. Stepping back again, he signaled Wethington to line up beside him.

"Now," said Casey. He and Wethington surged forward, thudding against the door at the same time. With a loud crash, it burst open.

The Showdown
Jacksonville, April 21, 1924

In the middle of the night, Celia woke to a dog barking like crazy. She figured the coppers were casing the joint: Who else would be out after midnight on a Sunday? Her heart started thumping. Their time was up. The coppers had found them, and she didn't know how Ed would react. She hoped he was still sleeping. She tried to listen to the rhythm of his breathing, but she couldn't hear over the beating of her heart.

Before long she heard whispers outside their door. A guy hollered for them to open up in the name of the law. She jumped out of bed. Ed jolted up to sitting.

"Get up," she whispered to him, grabbing her dress off the chair.

Ed called out, "All right but wait till my wife gets her clothes on."

She threw her dress over her head and squirmed into it while Ed stepped into his trousers and pulled on his shirt.

The coppers banged at the door. She was so scared she wanted to jump out of her skin. Ed grabbed a gun off the dresser.

She latched onto his arm. "What are you doing?"

"Let's end it right now."

"No. Don't. Please. Put your gun away." She grabbed the other two guns. She didn't want him holding them when the coppers came in. She was afraid he might kill himself or fire at the bulls.

The coppers thudded against the door. It burst open with a big crack. She lunged in front of Ed, holding her two guns by the barrels—pointed at herself.

"Don't shoot," she said. "We won't shoot if you don't."

A stocky guy in a blue suit barreled into the room, and three other suits barged in behind him.

The first guy stepped right up to her. "Let me have the guns."

"Yes, sir." She handed her guns over to him.

This cop gave the guns to the big-shouldered guy standing beside him.

Ed said, "Hiya, Bill."

She guessed Ed knew this guy, and the guy must've known Ed, because he said, "Hi, Ed. It's all over now. Let's be peaceful about this. Are you armed?"

"Yeah," Ed said. "I got a gun. You want me to hand it over?"

"No, put your hands up."

Ed raised his hands and stepped out from behind her.

This guy Bill came up and took Ed's gun. Then he patted Ed's pockets.

Ed said to Bill, "I guess you know the baby died."

"Yeah, I know. I'm sorry about that."

This Bill guy was being real decent. Celia was so relieved it was all over and they hadn't been shot that her legs started wobbling.

She asked, "Can I sit down?"

"Sure," Bill said. He turned around and said to the other guy, "Let's gather their effects in case there's evidence we need."

Bill told her he was Captain Casey from Brooklyn. He introduced her and Ed to his sidekick Frank Gray, who was also from Brooklyn, and the other two detectives, who were with the Jacksonville Police Force. It only took five minutes for the coppers to round up their little bit of clothes and suitcase. They handcuffed Ed's hands behind him.

Bill took her by the arm, and they all walked out front. Bill put her and Ed in a paddy wagon, and the car drove them to the Jacksonville police station. Bill Casey and Frank Gray marched them to a bare room with a table. Bill took off Ed's handcuffs. Frank brought them paper cups of water, and they gulped them down.

Plopping his forearms on the table, Bill eyed her and Ed. "All right, you two, it's time to sing."

"I know," she said. "We did it. We robbed a whole string of stores. And you know it already."

"Well, I need details. And it's in your best interest to come clean with us. Did you rob a Thomas Roulston Grocery Store on the first Saturday in January?"

She looked at Ed, who was slumped in his chair. He nodded.

"Yeah, we did. That was our first job."

Bill scrunched up a cheek and eyed her like she was a freak show at the circus. "Why? Did you honestly think you could get away with all those robberies?"

"Well, we almost did. You guys made it easy on us. We wanted to give our new baby a good start. We were going to quit once we got set."

"What vehicle did you get away in after that first robbery?"

They'd used different cars, but she remembered that first one pretty well. "It was black and had nice ribbed leather seats."

"What make was it, and where'd you get it?"

Ed said, "It was an Oldsmobile Six. From Horgan's Garage."

"Did Mr. Horgan know you used his car?"

Ed shook his head. "No, he didn't. Leave him out of this."

"All right, so next you robbed the Atlantic and Pacific Store on Ralph Avenue, right?"

"Yeah," Celia said, "that was the next Saturday night."

"You threatened not only the clerks, but a man and a woman who were shopping there, didn't you?"

He was acting like they were cold-blooded killers. "Look, I told them to keep quiet and follow orders, but I was never going to shoot them. The gun was just to shut 'em up."

"You did have guns on them, though, didn't you?"

"Sure we did. Just like you had guns on us tonight. Maybe you should be arrested for threatening us."

Bill looked like he wanted to smile but was stopping himself. "And then that same night you robbed one other place, H.C. Bohack Company, right?"

"Yeah." Here it was the middle of the night, and she was awful tired. And weak. And Ed was all downcast. "Look, do you have to give us the third degree right now? We'll come clean. We did it. Can't you let us sleep a little?"

"Yeah," Ed said. "Celia's not well. Can't you lay off her?"

Bill narrowed his eyes at them like he was showing them he meant business. "All right, tell me this first. That guy at the National Biscuit Company, the one you shot, he's going to be fine, so you don't have to worry about a murder rap. Which one of you fired those shots?"

Celia didn't hesitate. She'd already planned what to say. "I did."

Ed looked at her with big eyes. "You know that's not true. I did."

"No, mister," she said. "I shot that guy at the biscuit company."

Ed looked at Bill Casey. "She's just saying that to protect me."

She latched her eyes on Bill. "No, he's the one who's fibbing."

Bill shook his head and looked from Celia to Ed and back again. He blinked his blue eyes, like he was trying to bring them into focus. "Well, one of you is lying."

Frank thumped his palms on the table. "At least we know you both didn't shoot." He turned to Bill. "Let's call it a night. We could all use some shut-eye."

"Sure," Bill said. "One more thing. Do you intend to

contest extradition to New York?"

Celia wasn't sure what he meant by extradition; she gave Ed a puzzled look.

He said, "They want to know if we'll go back to New York to face the music."

She nodded. "Sure, let's go home."

Jubilant Congratulations
Jacksonville, April 21, 1924

This was the most publicized and controversial case Casey had ever worked, and he felt like a fish let off the hook to have it over. So far the Cooneys had made it easy on him. They'd freely admitted to the first few robberies and seemed inclined to level with him about their spree—if not about which one of them shot the cashier at the National Biscuit Company. Casey figured Ed was covering for Celia. Once they got to New York, he and Frank would get to the bottom of the matter. Since these two were broke and would likely have to settle for a public defender, prosecution ought to go forward in a timely fashion.

First thing Monday, he sent telegrams to Enright and Brooklyn headquarters reporting he had the Cooneys in custody. Commissioner Enright responded swiftly with jubilant congratulations.

He and Gray took a cab to the Jacksonville police station. A boisterous crowd milled out front, no doubt hoping for a glimpse of the bob-haired bandit. The press had obviously gotten wind of the story and put it out on the airwaves. Casey and Gray forced their way through the crowd and into the station and found Wethington in his office.

Casey asked Wethington to check the train schedule

and arrange for him, Gray, and the Cooneys to have a stateroom to themselves on the express train to New York. It was scheduled to depart at noon. Casey took care of the paperwork for waiving extradition.

"The reporters are clamoring for statements from us, Bill," Wethington said. "You want to join me out front?"

"Sure." Casey figured it wouldn't hurt for him to show up in the papers as the man who'd rounded up the bob-haired bandit and her pal. And wouldn't it be better if Fiona read about his heroics in the paper than heard it from him? Let the journalists do him a favor for once and play up his valiant efforts.

He and Wethington exited the police station and stood on the top step looking out over the crowd of onlookers and reporters wielding cameras. People in passing cars had stopped to gawk, slowing traffic to a crawl.

Camera bulbs flashed and reporters launched a volley of questions.

Wethington held up a hand. "Whoa, one at a time."

A reporter in the front row raised a hand. "Do you have a confession yet?"

"Yes," Casey said, "they have admitted to committing a series of robberies in Brooklyn. But there's more work to be done on confirming details."

"Did they commit any robberies in Jacksonville?"

Wethington said, "No, they've kept a low profile since arriving here."

"Why did they come to Jacksonville? Did they have any special ties to the city?"

"Not to our knowledge," Casey said.

"What happened to the baby? How'd it die?"

"According to the undertaker, the baby was in poor health and likely died of malnourishment."

"Which one planned the robberies—the wife or husband?"

"Those are details we have yet to establish," said Casey.

"How'd you break the case?"

Casey wasn't about to admit he'd intercepted a letter from Ed to his mother. He smiled and glanced at Wethington. "Good old-fashioned detective work, including excellent cooperation between Brooklyn and Jacksonville police departments. And the help of doctors and nurses here.

"And let me add," continued Casey, "they were apprehended at a boarding house by Captains Wethington and Hulbert of the Jacksonville force, myself, and my colleague Frank Gray. They resisted at first, and we were forced to break down the door. All four of us had our guns drawn, and the accused had their three guns in hand. It's a minor miracle and testament to police know-how that no one was hurt. They were taken peacefully and will be prosecuted for their crimes."

"Why'd they do it?"

Casey had no interest in giving out details that would endear these two to the public, like how they only wanted to give their baby a good start. "That hasn't been established."

"Will the suspects be made available for any interviews?"

Casey gave an emphatic no to that, and he and Wethington wrapped up the session after fielding a handful of questions about extradition and what was in store for these criminals. He was itching to get on the train and head for home.

A Long Ride
Jacksonville to New York City,
April 21–22, 1924

Celia and Ed had to sleep in different cells at the Jacksonville jail, the first time ever they'd slept apart. Celia figured she and Ed were facing a long string of days and nights on their own. Before the coppers separated them, she gave Ed a hug and a smooch.

He said, "Sleep well, kid."

And boy, did she ever. She didn't care that she was in a room with clammy gray walls and a metal toilet and sink. She had a clean bed and a warm blanket. They weren't going to the electric chair, and they were done worrying the bulls would shoot them on sight. She was still awful sad about baby Katherine, but she had to think about her and Ed now and how to keep his spirits up so they could face what was coming down the pike.

A guard woke her at seven sharp. He unlocked the sliding door and handed her a breakfast tray. It had a steaming cup of coffee, some scrambled eggs, toast, and even a slab of ham. She gobbled down every morsel. It was the best meal she'd had in weeks. Then she sat and waited, wishing she had her Eddie by her side.

After a couple of hours, Frank and Bill came to get

her. They had Ed with them, and when they took her out of the cell, they handcuffed them together.

Celia nestled up beside Ed. "How's my man?"

He looked down at his feet. "Okay, I guess."

"All right," Bill said. "We've got a train to catch. Let's go out the back door. There's too much commotion out front."

Bill and Frank herded them down the hallway of the jail and into the paddy wagon they'd ridden in the night before. The four of them sat in the back, and Captain Wethington got in the driver's seat.

When they drove around the side of the building, someone hollered, "It's them."

Celia swiveled around so she could see the crowd, which was difficult because she was handcuffed to Ed. Cameras flashed and people mobbed the wagon, their heads bobbing and weaving as they tried to get a look at them.

Bill leaned forward and asked Captain Wethington, "Can you ease through the crowd?"

"Sure thing." He drove slowly, nosing the car through the pack of gawkers.

Isn't this a kick, Celia thought, giving the crowd a smile and wave. They lost the mob after a block or two and pulled up to the train station in less than ten minutes. This town was sure small potatoes compared to New York City.

The coppers said goodbye to each other like they were bosom buddies, and Bill and Frank led them into the station. Celia was thinking it'd be a long train ride, so she asked, "Can I get something to read?"

Bill hunched a shoulder. "I suppose."

She made a beeline for the rack of books and magazines, dragging Ed along with her. What she really wanted was a detective story, but she couldn't find any so she grabbed an issue of *The American* with beauty tips inside.

Bill paid for the magazine and said, "Let's board before we create a scene."

Of course, people were staring at them, probably because of the handcuffs, nudging each other and talking like they were trading hush-hush secrets. The four of them piled onto the train and filed down the car to a private stateroom. It had two upholstered benches facing each other and a narrow table in between. There were even curtains on the windows and the door looking out on the corridor. It was a lot nicer than the windowless cabin they'd had on the ship.

Frank stood up and closed the curtains. "No need to encourage gawkers."

Celia asked, "When will we be home?" But then she thought, I'm not really going home, just to another jail.

Ed must've thought the same thing because he looked at her dismal-like and said, "Home, huh? I wish."

Bill tapped his watch. "We should arrive at Grand Central around three tomorrow afternoon."

Celia couldn't think of anything to say to cheer Ed up. He sat slouched over in his seat looking all sorry and shamefaced. She opened her magazine and started reading. Bill and Frank stuck their noses in newspapers. The train pulled out of the station and picked up speed.

After she read every word of the magazine, she didn't know what to do with herself. Ed had nestled into the corner of the seat and was snoozing. Still, he was hogging the window seat, and she couldn't trade places with him because they were handcuffed together.

"Hey, Bill," she said, "you think you could let me out of these cuffs so I can look out the window? It's not like I'm going to bust out of this train."

Bill looked at Frank, who swiped a hand through his black locks and said, "I don't see why not."

Bill reached into his pocket and pulled out a key.

"Wake up, Eddie," she said, giving him a little jab.

He blinked his eyes open.

Bill undid the handcuff on her wrist and latched it over Ed's other wrist. "Sorry, Ed, but I have to keep you cuffed."

Celia traded places with Ed and watched the scenery go by. It was a dreary day, and a light rain was falling, but she still liked seeing the fresh green countryside. They were traveling through a stretch with some farm fields and in the distance tall trees. The field was planted with rows and rows of little green plants, maybe lettuce or cabbage. Every now and then they went through a small town, and the train's whistle blasted at the road crossings.

But she got bored after a while and said, "Hey, fellas, what do you say we play some cards?"

"Okay," Bill said. "Let me see if I can scare up a pack." He came back with a deck, and they settled in and played hearts, except Ed didn't want to play. Celia figured she'd let him skulk. But her, she always said if you can't find something to smile about, you won't see nothing but grumpy in the mirror. Hard times always go down easier if you find a reason to smile or josh.

She won several hands of hearts because she was good at keeping track of cards. After a few more wins, she said, "Can't you boys play any better? How about you loan me a few quarters to bet and see if that helps."

"Oh, no," Bill said. "Your robbing days are over."

They had a good laugh at that and played some more hands. At dinner time, the steward brought them menus, and they ordered. Celia asked for the chicken with mashed potatoes and green beans, and Ed ordered the roast beef dinner, like the other fellas.

Dinner in their stateroom was swell. They all talked while they ate, even Ed. Bill asked him what baseball team he backed, and then the guys egged each other on about whose team would do better this season—the Brooklyn Robins or New York Giants.

After they finished dinner, Bill said, "I might as well tell you what to expect once we get back to Brooklyn."

"Sure," Celia said. "I never had no business with the law before."

Ed swiped a hand over his mouth. "You going to play it straight with us, Bill?"

"You know me. I'm an on-the-level guy."

Ed stuck out his chin and nodded for Bill to go ahead. Celia was glad to see him coming out of his shell, even if he was scoffing at what Bill said.

Bill pushed his plate out of the way and propped his elbows on the table. "We'll go from Penn Station directly to Brooklyn, to the District Attorney's office. He'll question you as to the crimes you are alleged to have committed. And you'll be expected to enter a plea."

Ed snorted. "Should I guess what you think that ought to be?"

Bill pretended Ed hadn't asked that question. "What happens after that depends on you two. If you plead guilty you won't need a lawyer. The whole process will play out with a minimum of disputation."

"Jeez," she said, "you make it sound like it'll be a cinch."

"That's right," Bill said. "Without all the labored testimony and need to call witnesses and make motions, you'll be spared a long drawn-out trial. And if you plead guilty, the judge'll go easier on you at sentencing."

Ed smirked. "And you get to be the big hero that caught us."

"That's my job, Ed. You ought to understand that."

Celia took a hold of Ed's hand. She didn't see any way around the hot water they were in. They robbed those joints, and all those clerks and customers saw them. Once the bulls found out their names, they knew the jig was up.

She said, "All right, Bill, if that's how it's going to go I guess we'll have to play along."

Ed asked, "And what about sentencing? What are we likely to get?"

"That's out of my hands. The DA can give you an idea of that."

Celia was glad Ed had said some words to Bill, but after dinner, he went back into his slump.

It grew dark outside, and she couldn't see much except when they went through towns with neon signs, streetlights, and lit-up house windows. She started nodding off and jerking awake because of her head lolling around. She said to Bill, "Can't you have the porter come in and make up the bed so I can sleep like a regular human being? You bruisers can sit up all night if you want."

Frank went out and fetched the porter, and he came and pulled down one of the beds. Celia crawled up onto it and stretched out. The click-clacking of the train soon lulled her into a deep sleep.

When she woke up, it was morning and the train had stopped. The steward was telling the guys that they'd need to go to the dining car to get breakfast.

"No, we're not going to the dining car," Bill said. "We need to be served here."

"I'm sorry, sir, but we don't have enough workers to serve all the staterooms."

"Then I'll just talk to the conductor."

Bill got up and opened the door. Celia saw a bunch of guys in suits standing outside like they'd been waiting there. They all angled for a look into the compartment, and one of them said to Bill, "Can we have a few words with your passengers?"

"No, no interviews. Make way." Bill pushed his way out and slammed the door behind him.

By the time Bill came back, a half hour later, the train had started up again. He was shaking his head with disgust. "The damn steward took a bribe from a reporter who wanted to snap some pictures of us. I told him to bring breakfast to our room on the double."

That was the beginning of the press trying to get a peek at her and Ed. Every stop they came to was the same—reporters flooding the train and banging on their door. And crowds gathered at the stations and ogled the train windows, too. The conductor came around after they left the station in Richmond, Virginia, and apologized.

"Can't you keep them off the train?" Bill asked.

"Between helping passengers with luggage and such, we can't guard every single compartment. I expect it'll be like this the rest of the way."

When the train pulled into Philadelphia, she heard the same shuffling and talking outside their door, and the conductor came around again. He squeezed in and said to Bill, "I've never seen anything like this. You sure you don't want to say a few words to the press?"

"Why not?" Celia said, looking at Bill and showing a palm. She thought it might be fun to feed those reporters a few choice lines.

Bill heaved out a big sigh. "Well, Ed, are you up for being interviewed?"

Ed thumped his hands on the table. "I don't want to talk about the robberies. Or anything else. Celia can talk if she wants. Except about the jobs."

"Well," Bill said, "if I were your attorney, that's what I'd advise."

Celia sat up straight and folded her hands on her lap. "What if we just see what kind of questions they have?"

Bill looked up at the conductor and nodded.

The conductor said, "There's a lady reporter out here

says she's shorter than Celia."

"Ha," Celia said, "that I'd like to see."

The conductor eased out of the stateroom and returned in a minute, opening the door and motioning in a little lady in a green dress and matching hat with a big bow on it. She was probably about thirty and had a heart-shaped face with a pert nose.

"Hello," she said, "I'm Mary Mallon."

Celia stood up and held out her hand, "Hello, Mary, I'm Celia. Now, why don't you take that hat off, and we'll see who's shorter."

"Oh, I'm sure I'll win. Bets anyone?" She chuckled and lifted her hat off with both hands.

The guys looked at them like the cat had their tongues.

Celia stood up beside her. "Well, fellas, who's shorter? And prettier?"

Bill said, "I believe, Miss Mallon, you have bested Celia here by a good two inches."

Celia flared her hand and said to this lady, "Show me your hand."

She placed her hand up to Celia's, lining up their palms. "Even my hands are smaller."

"All right," Celia said. "You win. Are you going to put that in your paper?"

"No, I'd really like to hear what happened to your baby."

"You might as well sit down if we're going to talk." Celia motioned to Ed to scoot over, and she and this lady reporter sat down side by side. "That's one sad story. We both loved that little girl, but our baby never had a chance.

Katherine's with the angels now. That's all I'm going to say."

"How long did she live?"

Celia's eyes turned watery and a lump pressed at her throat. She held back tears. She didn't want to blubber in front of the coppers and this reporter. "Just two days, but can't we talk about something else?"

"What did you do all the time you were in Florida?"

"We didn't go swimming and sunning, I'll tell you that much. We stayed shut away in lousy rooms. It was no picnic, that's for sure."

"Are you looking forward to being back in New York?"

"I'm glad it's over with. But I don't expect an easy time of it if that's what you're getting at."

"Are you frightened about what's to come?"

"No, I'm not afraid of nothing. We'll wait and see what happens. I guess we'll take our medicine." Celia knew once the coppers figured out who they were that they'd have to pay for robbing all those places. Nothing in life is free, and she was a fool to think they could steal all that money and get away with it.

The lady reporter looked at her coat hanging up in the compartment. "Is that the famous sealskin coat you wore when you pulled off the robberies?"

"It's swell, isn't it? It was a present from my husband."

"How many robberies did you commit?"

"I'm not saying anything about that. So you can quit asking."

The reporter asked a few more questions, and then Bill said, "Miss Mallon, I think it's time for you to leave so we can get ready for our arrival."

"Thank you for the conversation, Celia."

"Be sure you get the story right. I'll be reading the papers."

After Mary left, Celia snugged up against Ed and took a hold of his arm. Bill said they'd be at Penn Station in less than a half hour. It was three in the afternoon, and they'd been on that train for around twenty-seven hours. She figured there'd be a crowd at the station, like at all the other stops they'd made that day. She wanted to be ready for them.

As the train approached the station, she stood up and checked herself in the mirror. She didn't look her best. "Oh, my, I am a sight."

Bill said, "You're not going to a beauty contest."

"Yeah?" she said, pretending to give him the stink-eye. "What do you know about where I'm going?"

Bill and Frank chuckled at that.

She was still wearing her gray dress, and it looked awful rumpled, but it was all she had. She took her powder and lipstick out of her purse and did up her face. She ran a comb through her hair and arranged it as best she could into its bob style. Then she sat down beside Ed and waited, wondering what the law had in store for them.

When the train pulled into the station, she looked out the window at the platform. It was mobbed with people. Cameras went off with a whiz, bang, flash.

"Holy cow," Bill said. "It looks like you have a few

admirers, Celia."

"Just like you said, I'm going to a beauty contest."

One Helluva Muddle
New York City, April 22, 1924

Casey looked out the train window, angling for views up and down the crowded platform. How the hell were they supposed to fight their way through this pandemonium? The peculiar thing was, most of the assembled were dames. Fiona had said it was primarily young women holding the bob-haired bandit up as some kind of heroine. Why in the world were they lionizing a criminal? Since winning the vote, women had gotten punch drunk on power—cutting off their hair, swigging gin, and dancing the Charleston in flapper outfits.

He slung one leg over the other. "Let's wait a while and see if the crowd dies down."

Looking out the window, Celia said, "Gosh, you'd think the president was in town or something. Did you ever see anything like this?"

Casey hadn't minded joshing with Celia during the train ride. She was being a good sport about the arrest. And playing cards and jawing passed the time, but he had a job to do. He'd told them if they pled guilty they wouldn't need a lawyer, and they'd get off lighter. They seemed to buy it, so he figured conviction and sentencing would be swift. All he had to do now was get them to the DA's office.

Casey watched a bevy of police officers, including special officers of the Pennsylvania Railroad, struggle to control the crowd so exiting passengers could make their way to the stairs. Little by little, they created an aisle and kept the passengers flowing. Casey spotted Chief Inspector John Coughlin on the platform, making his way toward their car with a phalanx of police.

"All right," he said. "Let's get going. Grab your coats."

He handcuffed Ed and Celia together and led the way down the empty corridor. When he reached the exit, he scanned the crowd and waved to Coughlin, who was closing in on them.

"Clear the way," the lanky Coughlin ordered, and the police around him pushed the crowd back.

Casey glanced behind him. Ed and Celia froze at the top of the steps, gawking at the crowd. Frank Gray brought up the rear.

"Okay," he said, "let's go." He stepped down and shoved his way through the mob. The police beside Coughlin surrounded him, and he and his party squeezed along, elbowing their way toward the stairs.

Someone hollered, "It's her, the bob-haired bandit," and cameras shot up high over the bobbing sea of heads and flashed in their direction.

The party slowly wended its way toward the stairs. Ahead of them the police ordered people obstructing the stairs to back out of the way. Casey and his entourage slowly mounted the iron stairs. On the main floor, the crowd thinned, and Casey led the party toward the exit.

Coughlin turned back and caught Casey's eye. "We've got cars waiting outside. This way."

Taking Celia's arm, Casey followed close behind Coughlin. He pushed through the door, pulling Celia and Ed along. When he spotted three police cars lined up at the curb, he made a beeline for them.

From beside the police cars, a short fellow in a pricey brown suit approached. He walked right up to Casey, who still had Celia by the arm, and said, "Hold everything, I have writs of habeas corpus here."

Casey stopped in his tracks. "Who the hell are you?"

This wiry little guy sported glasses so thick they made his eyes look as big as silver dollars. He waved his papers in Casey's face. "I'm Sam Leibowitz, and you know it's the law. I've got a judge's order here for you to produce the suspects forthwith."

Damn it, Casey thought, *I have to see that.*

Leibowitz handed him the papers. Casey glanced at them. He didn't have time to study whatever orders this interloper had finagled: They'd been spotted on the sidewalk, and a clot of reporters converged on them.

"Into the cars," Casey said. He opened the rear door of one of the police cars and ordered Celia and Ed in. Leibowitz maneuvered around and scooted in beside them.

"Hey, not you," Casey hollered at Leibowitz.

"Sorry, pal, you've got the signed writs. Look for yourself."

Casey opened the front door of the car and ordered the officer in the passenger seat to get out. Then he slid in, keeping his door open. He signaled Frank to come over.

Casey skimmed the documents. Sure enough, this damn lawyer had gotten some judge to approve these writs. Leibowitz contended the Cooneys had been arrested without a warrant and, thus, were being detained in violation of their constitutional rights. He looked up at Frank and handed him the papers. He scratched at the day-old growth on his cheek and shook his head. He was tired—and fed up with this whole business. Just when he thought he'd sewn up this damn case, some publicity-hungry attorney swooped in and tried to steal the show.

Casey stepped out of the car and stood beside Gray, whose gaze was raking over the papers. He motioned for Coughlin to join them.

Frank snapped his head up. "What the hell? He's taking over the suspects?"

Coughlin trotted up to them. "What's going on?"

Frank shoved the papers at Coughlin. "Here, read for yourself."

Casey gave the chief inspector a minute to scan the writs. When he looked up, Casey said, "Looks like we can't take these two to the Brooklyn DA."

Frank snorted. "I'm about as disgusted as I've ever been."

Casey whirled around and faced Leibowitz, who was keeping tabs on the conversation. His feet were planted on the sidewalk, and his rear end on the car seat. After all the work Casey had put in, this damn attorney was throwing a wrench in the works.

Leibowitz reached his hand out. "My papers, if you please."

Coughlin stepped forward and shoved the papers at Leibowitz. "Where do you propose taking the suspects?"

Leibowitz said, "To a court here in Manhattan. So a judge can consider whether they should be released."

Coughlin bounced a hand at Leibowitz. "They ought to go to Brooklyn. That's where the arresting detectives are from."

Leibowitz didn't budge from his seat in back of the police car. "No dice," he said. "We stay right here in Manhattan."

Coughlin turned his back on Leibowitz and said to Casey, "Okay, let's get over to the court on Chambers Street. Before this crowd suffocates us."

Casey got in the front seat of the car. He wasn't about to give this conniving lawyer time alone with the Cooneys, not after he'd primed them to think they didn't need a lawyer. This guy would sure as eggs try to convince them they needed his representation—and also get them to plead not guilty. This case was turning into one helluva muddle.

Courts, Reporters, and Jails
New York City and Brooklyn,
April 22, 1924

This little fella with thick glasses and a slick suit scooted in the back seat of the cop car beside Celia and said, "I'll handle the police."

She scooted to the middle of the seat and asked Ed, "What does the brown suit want with us?"

Ed wagged his head like he didn't care. "I don't know, Celia. I don't know anything anymore."

"Don't be like that. They're probably going to separate us, and we'll be all alone in our jail cells."

"My poor mother. She's been nothing but good to us and look what we went and did. She'll know I lied to her."

"I know, Eddie. I'm awful sorry. I wish we could go back to before all this started."

He slouched against the door and hung his head. Celia leaned forward and looked around the brown suit. Bill and Frank stood on the sidewalk reading the papers this guy had given them. She couldn't hear what they were saying, but she could tell they were grousing.

Bill had kicked the cop who was in the front seat out of the car, and he hopped in and told the copper behind the wheel, "Let's get over to the court on Chambers Street.

And quick."

The sidewalk and street were crawling with gawkers and reporters, but finally the driver inched out and tailed the police car in front of them.

This fella sitting beside her said, "I'm Sam Leibowitz, attorney at law. I filed some papers on your behalf since you were arrested without a warrant. Now we'll go before a judge and determine your disposition."

She didn't understand what Sam was talking about, which made her feel like a sap. She was trying to think of how to ask him what he meant when Frank swiveled around and eyed the guy.

"Yeah, that's right, Leibowitz. You're not the one calling the shots. It's up to the judge."

She could tell Frank thought this guy stunk like rotten eggs. And Ed didn't seem to care if he lived or died. She figured she'd better get wise since they were about to meet some big-time judge.

She asked Sam, "What do you mean—our disposition?"

"Whether you should be held. Since you were arrested without a warrant. I'll handle it."

Their driver wove his way through Manhattan's crowded streets, and the cop car ahead of them pulled over in front of a building with tall round columns. Their car nuzzled in behind it. Bill popped out and opened the back door. Sam got out, and she and Ed followed. Grabbing her arm, Bill pulled her along like he owned her or something.

"Hey," Sam said. "Take it easy on her, will you?"

Bill ignored him and made for the door pell mell,

dragging her and Ed through it. About twenty people milled around inside, and Celia could tell some of them were reporters because they had big cameras hanging around their necks.

One of the reporters turned to them and shot off his camera and then all the others joined the show. Frank wedged himself between her and the reporters and shooed them away while Bill kept them moving. The other suit who'd met them at the train, this lanky guy with a big schnoz, came up beside Bill and told him to take her and Ed to Courtroom 3. He pointed up the stairs. Bill and Frank moved them along, and Sam brought up the rear.

At the top of the stairs, Bill herded her and Ed into a room with rows of seats behind a wooden railing. Right in front of the railing there were two long tables and facing these tables was a desk on a platform. Bill brought them to one of the tables and sat them down. She and Ed were still handcuffed together. She scooted her chair close to his and whispered, "Do you know what this is about?"

He swiveled his hung head toward her. "No. Ask Bill."

Bill huddled with Frank and some other suits a little way from the table, and Sam was horning his way in on them. Celia couldn't hear what they were saying, but they were jabbing their fingers at each other and yapping like riled-up dogs. After a few minutes, a judge in a long black robe waltzed in and plopped down at the desk at the head of the room. Frank and the other guys shut up and shuffled to their seats. Another fella said some mumbo-jumbo about this judge being honorable, and the hearing being in session.

Sam stepped up and started jawing. "Your honor, I have here two writs of habeas corpus for your review and consideration. You will see they're signed by the Honorable Aaron J. Levy."

Sam walked up to the judge and handed over his papers.

The judge pushed his glasses up on his nose. After he checked the papers, he said, "Very well, you may proceed."

"Your honor, these two were arrested without a warrant, and it is my contention they should be released pending proper procedures for arresting and charging them."

One of the suits shot up and said, "Your honor, it has not been established that this man is their attorney. I appeal to the court to determine the matter of representation before proceeding further."

Next thing Celia knew all these fellas crowded around the judge's desk and started arguing. The judge put a quick end to their squabbling. "Let's hear from the suspects. All of you, take a seat."

The guys pulled back and sat down at the long table on each side of her and Ed.

The judge looked at Ed and said, "Mr. Cooney, is Samuel Leibowitz your attorney?"

Ed studied the judge with big eyes. "No, he's not."

The judge asked, "Would you like to have him represent you?"

"I don't think so."

Leibowitz stood up. "Your honor, I have here a letter from Mr. Cooney's brother. May I show it to him?"

The judge said yes, and Leibowitz pulled a paper out of his folder and eased it in front of Ed. Celia leaned in close so she could read it, too.

Ed, we have retained Counselor Leibowitz to represent you and Celia. Do whatever he tells you. Don't worry. We will do all we can to help you. Brother Tom.

Celia had only met Ed's oldest brother Tom once, at their wedding. All she knew was that he was funny enough to make a cat laugh and liked to tell stories about his garbage collecting job in Queens. When Ed finished reading, he looked at her, and she could tell he didn't know what to say.

The judge asked, "Mr. Cooney, does this communication clarify the matter of representation?"

Ed nibbled at his bottom lip. He looked so miserable she thought he might start to cry. "I don't know."

"Would you or would you not like to accept representation from Counselor Leibowitz?"

"I can't decide."

Ed gave her a questioning look. He was about as beat down as a washed-up boxer. Celia figured he was so ashamed he couldn't do anything but shillyshally. She whispered to him, "Do you trust Tom? Or should we do like Bill said?"

Ed's face filled up with gloominess, like after they'd shot that guy at the biscuit company. Her poor Eddie was on the skids. She was going to have to step up for them.

She swallowed and looked up at the judge. She

thought she ought to talk to him like Sam had. "Your honor, we don't want an attorney."

The judge snapped his head back like someone had just said boo to him. "You understand that you are declining to be represented by Counselor Leibowitz?"

"Yeah, ain't that what I said?"

Sam slapped a hand over his forehead like he couldn't believe his ears. Bill leaned back in his chair, and a smug look spread over his face. Her Eddie didn't budge.

"I hereby dismiss these writs." The judge rapped his wooden hammer. "Captain Casey, you may take custody of the suspects."

Leibowitz hustled over to them and whispered to her and Ed, "I hope you'll reconsider my offer. I can help you. I'll see you at the hearing."

Bill shooed Leibowitz away and whisked them out of the courtroom. The crowd on the first floor and outside had swelled, and they had to push and shove their way back to the cop car. Celia figured there'd be plenty of pictures of them in the papers, what with these reporters hounding them every step of the way.

They sped across the Brooklyn Bridge and landed at a white stone building with a mob out front. She imagined it was going to be courts, reporters, and jails for them from here on out. She only wanted to have Ed by her side through it all.

Bill and Frank steered them through the crowd and into this building and slammed the door on the reporters and everybody else.

"Jeez," she said, "finally, I can breathe."

"You can say that again," Bill said. "Come on. Let's go see the DA."

They got in an elevator and went up until it dinged. Bill walked them to a room with a sign on the door that said 'Assistant District Attorney Thomas C. Hughes.'

They were herded into chairs in front of a big desk facing this Mr. Hughes. There were two other suits in the room and three sour-puss ladies who looked like teachers who'd sat on tacks. The guys and these ladies shook hands like they'd all earned gold stars or something. She and Ed sat there like simps, jerking their heads this way and that.

Celia said, "Hey, Bill, do you think we could get out of these handcuffs? I'd like to freshen up."

"Sure," Bill said. He uncuffed her and Ed, and all three of these dames sidled along with her to the toilet. They wouldn't even let her close the stall door.

"Jeez," she said, "you think I'm Houdini's sister?"

When they were back in front of Mr. Hughes, he tapped some papers on his desk and said he had a lot of questions for them and hoped they would cooperate and yammer, yammer. First, he tried to pin the robbery of a milk wagon on them. Ed seemed stunned like he'd been blinded by a hundred camera flashes.

Celia looked this guy in the eye and said, "We didn't rob any milk wagon. We only robbed stores. And I'll tell you which ones if you shut up a minute."

Hughes looked at her like a kid whose mother surprised him with a birthday cake.

She rattled off all ten robberies they'd committed. It was easy to keep track of them because she'd collected all the news articles about them. She didn't always remember the exact dates, but Mr. Hughes helped her out on that. Every now and then she checked with Ed. He gave her a wobbly smile and let her keep talking.

She thought she should explain why they did it, so she said, "When I went into those jobs, I wasn't thinking about diamonds or gin and jazz. I was seeing cute baby booties and hoping our baby wouldn't have a rough time of it like I did. Our last job was the National Biscuit Company. That one was my idea, and it was supposed to be the last job we did. We wanted to get enough money to quit for good and raise our baby in a decent home."

Ed perked up and said, "No, that one was my idea. I knew they'd have a lot of money on hand, and I wanted to get us set up in Florida. See, I was in Jacksonville during the Navy."

She didn't like Ed saying it was his idea, even though it was. She wanted to take the blame so they'd go easier on him. And, seeing as she was a girl, maybe they wouldn't be too hard on her. She said, "No, I planned that robbery. And I was the one who shot that fella."

"Aw, you know that's not true, Celia. You were on the floor then. I fired the shots to keep that guy from hurting you."

"No, Eddie. I did it."

"You stop right now, Celia. I mean it." Ed stared her down, and she could tell he meant business.

He looked at Mr. Hughes. "Celia is trying to protect me. She promised me she'd never fire a single shot the whole time, and she kept her promise. And we agreed we'd never take any money from the clerks or customers, just the till. And that's the truth."

Mr. Hughes narrowed his eyes at her. "Is that true, Mrs. Cooney?"

She figured Ed had her licked about claiming she shot the cashier. He wasn't going to stand for her taking the rap. "Yeah, that's the truth. But I egged him on. It wasn't just Eddie cooking up all those robberies."

Brooklyn Citizen, Pages 1, 2
April 23, 1924

COONEYS PLEAD GUILTY
WHEN ARRAIGNED FOR
FIRST-DEGREE ROBBERY

Celia Cooney, Brooklyn's bob-haired bandit, pleaded guilty to robbery in the first degree when arraigned today.

Her husband, Edward, who accompanied the girl robber in all her exploits, entered the same plea.

Two other indictments are still pending against both the woman and her husband, and an additional indictment was found charging Cooney with first-degree assault for the shooting of Nathan Mazo.

The arraignment followed speedily after identification of the pair by twelve of their holdup victims.

Gun Girl Smilingly Faces Thirteen Witnesses at Brooklyn Headquarters, Revels in Notoriety, Husband More Nervous

The couple were led into the 'guest room' of the Poplar Street Station, where they were placed with their backs to the wall and facing more than fifty detectives and thirteen witnesses brought in to identify them. Mrs. Cooney appeared refreshed and smiled as if she was enjoying the situation thoroughly. She is a diminutive woman and inspired pity as she was surrounded by all the heavily-built detectives who were prepared to 'sweat' her if she denied the charges made against her. Twelve persons made positive identification of the couple, four of these being women.

There is something strange about this twenty-year-old girl, something fascinatingly unusual about her manner. It was not defiance. It was poise. Where does she get her strength? It is something which comes from her mind, untrained as it is. In the ready and bright smiles of the girl bandit, there was little token of a broken and weakened constitution. She was apparently in very good health, despite her recent motherhood. Her slight frame appears strong as steel.

Cooney smiled indulgently as he saw that his wife was enjoying the attention. He is a big man and towers over his wife. He has curly hair and blue eyes, with a profile marred only by unusually thick lips. His wife's face, on the other hand, is rather pretty. It is small with high cheek bones and a short, stubbed nose.

Pass Night at Poplar
Street Police Station

Mrs. Cooney had awakened after a sound sleep in a cell at the Poplar Street Station and, with a cheerful smile, asked the matron for a comb. Edward Cooney, her husband, spent the night in a cell at the same station but far removed from that which lodged his wife.

"How's Ed?" was the woman's first query when the warden awakened her.

"How's the kid?" asked Cooney when he was roused after a fitful sleep, broken by periods of wakefulness during which he smoked numerous cigarettes.

Sam Bobs Up Again

Samuel Leibowitz, the attorney who attempted to inject himself into the case when the Cooneys arrived yesterday from Florida, attempted to appear as their attorney again today in the County Court. When the Cooneys were charged with their offense he rose and announced that he would waive the reading of the indictments and plead not guilty.

"Are you sure you know what you are doing?" Judge Martin demanded of the aspiring attorney. "Just a minute," said the judge, and he turned to the Cooneys to ask them if they wanted to take such mercy as they could get by pleading guilty.

"Do you want a lawyer?" he asked, and they said they did not.

"Gentleman," said the judge to Leibowitz, "you may retire."

"This woman," said the would-be counselor for the girl bandit, "has a meritorious defense. Her fate should be placed in the hands of twelve trial jurors. There is a man in Jacksonville, Fla., who should be showed to tell what he knows of her career."

"Your counsel is not needed. You may retire," said Judge Martin, and Leibowitz perforce did so.

Judge Martin Praises Police

"I want to take this opportunity to commend Captain Casey and his staff for their excellent work on this case," said the judge, "and to speak of the efficient manner in which the District Attorney and his staff have secured these indictments and pleas. It is a splendid example of the cooperation that exists here between the District Attorney, the courts, and the police."

Not in the history of Brooklyn has the rounding up of any crook caused so much congratulations between the local forces of law and order. Celia Cooney, as a matter of fact, had 'got the goat' of all the cops, the detectives, and the District Attorney. With this mere slip of a girl at large, it was impossible for these public servants to maintain any sort of dignity, flouted as they were on so many occasions by the bob-haired flapper.

All the police at headquarters wore broad smiles today—for the little twenty-year-old street gamin who has literally had her finger to her nose in characteristic gesture at them for months. Her daring, impudence, and nerve have had the police on edge. Her letters of derision, the jeers of the public at her constant onslaughts are over now. Celia faces ten to twenty years in prison, and so does her husband, Edward.

Life in the Clink
Brooklyn, April 24, 1924

After being dragged around like dogs on leashes—to a lineup with clerks and customers at the stores they'd robbed, through the messy finger-printing business, to another round in the ring with Sam Leibowitz, and to meetings with so many suits, Celia couldn't keep track of who was who—the bulls herded her and Ed to the Raymond Street jail. Warden Harry Honeck was a friendly guy, a real straight shooter. He promised her she and Ed could see each other regular-like. That was about the best they could hope for, being locked up and all.

Celia's first day in the Raymond Street jail was so miserable she cried herself to sleep. But when she woke up she thought, enough of that: You better get used to steel bars and concrete walls because that's how it's going to be for you. Did she wish they'd never started robbing? Did she want another chance to be a good mother? You bet. But it was time to face the music. What else could she do?

But life in the clink was no party. There are all kinds of characters, and the worst kind is the drunk. When drunks get hauled in they will holler and curse their head off and wake you up in the middle of the night with their fracas. They've got no respect for anybody, and all they care about is where their next drink is coming from. Celia learned when she was a little tyke that you can't ever trust a drunk.

Being in jail is about as miserable as you'd imagine—a cramped cell and nothing to look forward to. She used to go to the zoo in Prospect Park when she was a kid and look at the animals and wonder what it was like for them to be behind bars. And now she knew. At least the warden let her read newspapers so she could keep up on what they were saying about her and Ed. That's how she learned they could get ten to twenty years. Staring down all that time will sure enough make you think hard about what they say: Crime doesn't pay. That is the God-awful truth.

Being behind bars didn't stop the newspapermen from trying to get to her. They came around every day asking for pictures and stories. She wasn't in the mood to talk to them anymore. They were a bunch of bloodsuckers who wanted to get famous telling her story. One pudgy fella with a camera offered her twenty-five dollars to take her picture through the bars.

"You piker," she said, "that's nothing but cigarette money."

Then Celia got to thinking. If these reporters were willing to offer her money, maybe she ought to make it worth her while. She and Ed would need some dough so they could start fresh after doing their time.

So when the reporters came around she said, "If you want to get a peep out of me, you better show me the color of your money." And, sure enough, on Thursday this serious, square-faced fella with a mustache offered her a thousand dollars if she'd tell her story to him and nobody else. Buehler Seabrook was from William Randolph Hearst's newspaper, and he said Hearst was one of the richest men in the world and that's why his newspaper could pay top dollar. All she had to do was tell the story of her life and let them take a bunch of pictures to run with the pieces.

Celia asked him, "Can you get me some decent clothes and make-up for the pictures?"

"Of course," he said.

They shook on it. He told her he'd be back on Monday with a cameraman to take the pictures and then the two of them would have some long sit-down talks over the whole week.

"Say," she said, "I never heard that name Buehler. I'll be calling you Boo."

"Well, Celia," he said, "that's all right with me. We'll be spending lots of time together."

The warden let her and Ed visit that afternoon, and she was excited to tell him about this big deal with Mr. Hearst's newspaper, *New York American*.

"Boo told me Mr. Hearst is filthy rich. Sounds like the kind of guy who sneezes big bills."

They met in a regular cell with a bed. The guard locked them in together and kept an eye on them. But at least they got to sit next to each other, hold hands, and talk the whole half hour.

"That's swell news, doll," Ed said. "You be careful about what you tell him, okay? Don't say nothing that'll peeve the judge. We still got to be sentenced."

"I know. Maybe this can even help us, if you know

what I mean."

"Sure, I know. You got to be the brains for both of us now because I got some news, too."

"What kind of news can you get from in here?"

"Mr. Hughes told me this morning that Judge Martin ordered some tests and interviews for me. To see if I'm sane or not."

"Why would he do that?"

"Well, I never told you, but my father died in an insane asylum, and now this judge wants me tested to see if I'm insane, too."

"That's the most cockamamie thing I ever heard."

"He said they'll probably test you, too. Because some guy who's an expert on criminals says it's not normal for a girl to go around with a gun and rob people."

"Well, isn't that some harebrained idea? Of course, I'm a girl, and of course I robbed. And maybe that wasn't the smartest thing I ever did, but that doesn't make me insane. If you ask me, it's that hot-shot expert who's got the nutty ideas."

"I don't want either one of us to go to the loony bin. It's full of people screaming and cursing and beating their heads against the wall. Once they put you in there, you never get out."

"Then we just got to show them we're no loonies. How hard can that be?"

"Yeah, and I'm telling you one more thing, Celia. I'm going to send the judge a letter telling him I was the ringleader. I don't want him to go too hard on you."

"That ain't right. I was there every step of the way.

And I don't want the judge giving you the max."

Ed swiveled around toward her, took her by the shoulders, and looked her in the eye. "No, I'm telling him I was the ringleader. That's all there is to it. And don't you go mucking that up because I won't stand for it."

She clamped her lips shut. She didn't like this plan one bit.

Ed stared her down and gave her shoulders a little shake. "You hear me?"

"Okay, Eddie, whatever you say."

Read All About It
Brooklyn, April 28–May 1, 1924

Come Monday morning, Warden Honeck showed up at her cell with Boo Seabrook. He was toting a suitcase full of clothes for her, and a skinny, happy-go-lucky guy trotted along behind him with a camera. The warden was all smiles, like maybe Boo greased his palm, and he was making out pretty good on this deal, too.

The matron unlocked her cell and shooed away the fellas while she made up her face and put on a blue dress with a lace collar. The girls in the cells around hers giggled and whistled like it was a party. When she was all pretty, Boo and the guy with the camera, Marvin, came back and took picture after picture of her. The warden even brought around a miniature desk, which he set up in her cell. She sat down at it, and Marvin got some pictures of her signing her name with a fancy fountain pen. Boo said her signature would be at the top of every single story in the paper for all twelve days, just to show she was the certified author. She wrote it in neat cursive over a dozen times until she was happy with it.

She and Boo spent almost the whole morning taking those pictures, some with her wearing a sealskin coat and a classy turban. Boo even brought along a pistol, and for one of the pictures she pointed the piece straight at the camera. Marvin hammed it up, hollering, "Don't shoot!" when he flashed his camera.

The rest of the girls got a kick out of all the excitement, hooting and joking that they wanted their pictures in the paper, too. Everybody took a break to have some lunch, and she and the girls ate the usual jailhouse chow. Boo and Marvin were probably going to some fancy restaurant.

"Hey, Boo," she called after him, "bring us some cookies for dessert."

Boo laughed and said he'd see what he could do. Sure enough, after lunch, he came back with a box of molasses cookies from a bakery and handed them out. All the girls thanked Boo, and a few asked if he was looking for a wife.

The warden locked Boo in her cell with her, and they started in on the business of her story.

"Let's pretend I've been living in some foreign country and just came to New York City," Boo said, "and I don't know a thing about you. Now tell me about you and Ed and the robberies."

Celia folded her hands on her lap. "I'm the famous bob-haired bandit, the one that scared the life out of Brooklyn and made monkeys out of the cops for four months. I did it. I'm the gun girl, and you should have seen those boobs behind counters jump and do just like I said when I pointed my gun at them. Toting a pistol and giving orders like you mean it will get you lots of respect.

"The big joke is half the time that gun wasn't loaded. Eddie made me promise to not ever fire it, and I never did."

"Yeah?" Boo said. "How'd you get started?"

"The honest-to-God truth is I wanted to give our baby the right kind of start in life—like I never had. But when I saw those articles about us in the newspapers, it went to my head. It was a great ride, and I guess I was proud of being the bob-haired bandit. But every once in a while I thought about getting caught and knew I was a fool. But it was too late. We'd started in on the robbing business, and we needed the money, so I smiled and kept going.

"A couple of months ago, I thought it was a romp, but it's not so funny now. Here I am locked up in a cage. My baby's dead. The fancy furniture and nice apartment we got with our loot are gone. My Eddie and me are going to be torn apart, and the judge is trying to prove he's crazy so they can send him to the insane asylum.

"On Friday, these two guys with doctor's cases and a pile of papers came around and asked me a bunch of questions to find out if I was crazy, too—silly questions like who is the president, what did I have for breakfast, and did voices tell me to commit robberies. They watched how I walked and tapped a rubber hammer on my knees.

"I got awful tired of their foolishness and finally said, 'You know darn well I'm not crazy, so what's the use of all this poppycock?' I could have told them right off the bat that they didn't need to waste their time testing me because I'm as normal as they come. Except for the robbing. Anybody who does that is a fool.

"So, yeah, I'm ashamed of myself now—ashamed of what I did. But I'm not ashamed of why I did it. There's been a lot of bunk written about me, like saying I'm a dope fiend and wondering what kind of lousy family I came from. And I never wanted to spill my guts to coppers or judges about my family. I've got some pride, and I ain't looking for sympathy. But you said people would want to know about that, so I'm ready to tell a little about what it was like for me growing up."

All this time, Boo was writing like crazy on his pad of paper. She stopped to let him catch up.

He scribbled some more and looked up at her, his eyes as eager as a puppy looking for a pat. "Okay, so tell me about your family, and what it was like for you as a kid."

The fact was, her upbringing was plenty shabby, and there wasn't much good she could say about her parents. But she wasn't about to tell Boo every miserable detail. She'd got on with her life, and nobody needed to know about her pathetic past. "There's nothing wrong with my family, except that we were too poor, and there were too many of us to have a decent chance in life. I was born in a three-family tenement in Manhattan. My father was a truck driver, and he worked hard for poor pay. My mother couldn't work regular-like because she had eight kids. I was the youngest, so nobody had much time for me.

"My mother slaved over piles of laundry and didn't want me in the way. She'd tell me, 'Go outside and play,' and that's what I'd do—get out of her hair. I didn't want my baby to grow up in a house where she had to play in the streets.

"I don't really remember my brothers. They were older and got out when they were young. But my three sisters I remember. When I was around nine, my father got too sick to work, and my mother had to take care of him.

My three sisters and me went to our aunt's apartment in Brooklyn. My sisters got jobs in factories and brought their pay home. I stuck around the house doing washing and helping in the kitchen.

"I did get to go to parochial school then and kept going until I was fourteen, and I'm glad because I learned to read, and I like reading stories and magazines. And I went to Church. I'm a good Catholic, and Eddie and me were married by a priest at St. Augustine's Church.

"I'm telling you, outside of robbing, I'm a good girl. I'm no drug addict. I don't like swearing. I never had a drink or smoked in my life. I leave that stuff to the swell dames that can get away with it and still be ladies.

"But that doesn't work for poor kids like me. I kept my nose clean and went to confession every Saturday. Except once I started robbing. But I went to the chapel here in jail on Saturday, and I confessed to every single robbery, so I am in the clear with God. He knows and I know that what I did was wrong."

"But you only went to school until you were fourteen. What happened then?"

"I started working when I was fourteen. And I will tell you that working nothing but laundry jobs you learn a few tricks, like how to eat on three or four dollars a week. Here's how you do it: You buy a loaf of bread and a half dozen eggs and have one egg and a slice of bread for breakfast every morning until Sunday, when you lie in bed late. You have coffee with condensed milk, not the evaporated kind because the condensed is sweet and it saves on sugar. A can costs a nickel, and it lasts all week.

So you have coffee, bread, and an egg for breakfast. It's the best meal of the day, and if you start working at eight in the morning, it's when you need it most.

"You take four slices of bread to work with two cents worth of bologna for lunch. At night, you have some more bread with a can of beans or something like that. You might not think it from looking at grocery shelves, but canned stuff is the cheapest for a girl living alone.

"And I will tell you that the food in jail isn't that bad, and you know you're getting to eat three times a day. I'm not complaining about that. Except we don't get fresh-baked cookies like you brought us."

That made Boo smile.

After asking her a few more questions, Boo said that was good for their first day. He came back the next three days after that. On Tuesday, she told him about when she and Ed met at the Fulton Theatre and she knew right away he was the guy for her. He was tall and handsome, had the sweetest smile, and he'd been in the Navy. All the sailors she'd known always kept themselves neat and clean. She played hard to get with Ed, and it worked because they got married four months later.

The next two days, she told Boo all about the robberies and their time in Florida, which was even worse than being in jail. Then he said he had everything he needed for all twelve newspaper stories and that he could just hear the newsboys hawking the issue—"Read all about it—the bob-haired bandit tells her story."

When they said goodbye, she shook his hand, and he promised her he'd deposit her certified check in an account for Celia and Edward Cooney so it'd be waiting for them when they needed it.

New York American started running her story that week, and she read every single installment. Gosh, who'd have thought little old Celia Cooney would be on the front page of a big New York newspaper for twelve days straight?

No Maudlin Sentiment
Brooklyn, May 1, 1924

"I wouldn't miss it for the world," Bill Casey told his wife. The judge on the Cooneys' case had scheduled a hearing with the grand jury for that morning. "Judge Martin is not fooling around with these two."

Fiona reached across the corner of their dining room table and patted her husband's hand. "I never doubted you'd bring those two to justice."

"I heard Celia sent a letter to the judge begging that she and her husband be sentenced to the same prison. But if they're hoping for leniency, they've picked the wrong time and the wrong judge."

"They ought to be made an example of," said Fiona.

The Brooklyn newspapers that had trumpeted stories about the daring gun girl were singing a different tune now: The courts were making quick work of sentencing, and the Cooneys were a case in point. They'd been apprehended a mere ten days ago, and they were slated for sentencing in less than a week. *Sure enough,* Casey thought, *that's how justice ought to be meted out.*

Casey went directly from home to King's County Court Building on Schermerhorn Street. He stood outside the door of the courtroom greeting men he knew from the court offices and accepting their congratulations.

When he spotted Frank Gray heading down the hall, he waved. "Hiya, Frank."

"Hey, Bill, did you hear about the lunacy board rulings? Just came down this morning."

"No, what'd they say?"

"Both Ed and Celia were found legally sane and responsible for their actions."

"Good, they ought to be treated like the common criminals they are."

Casey and Gray grabbed seats halfway back in the chamber. The room was packed with reporters, and Casey figured Judge Martin wouldn't miss this opportunity to show the newspapers he knew how to crack down on the tide of crime and gun violence the papers claimed was running rampant.

Before long Judge Martin marched in, took his post at the head of the room, and addressed the grand jury. "Gentlemen of the jury, I commend you for your work during this past month. You have acted with dispatch in both the consideration of testimony and the execution of your duty to hand down indictments."

Casey couldn't help but recall the testimony of the victims of the Cooneys' robberies: They had minced no words. The manager of the Bohack store said of Celia, "She's no heroine. The fact that she was an expectant mother does not excuse her. She and her husband deserve severe punishment." Although the clerk at Weinstein's drugstore said he pitied her, he wanted to be protected from another such harrowing experience. And Abraham Fishbein, the grocer robbed in January pleaded with the court to show 'no mercy for these dangerous hoodlums.'

Judge Martin turned his attention to the matter of the Cooneys. "You gentlemen will be remembered as the grand jury which returned the indictments against the famous bob-haired bandit and her husband. They are both bold individuals, but their boldness ceased when they were bereft of revolvers. All criminals become cringing and fearful when brought within the toils of the law. Your indictment against them was well-founded, and you can rest assured this judge will see to it that your judgment is upheld by the imposition of a proper and well-deserved sentence. This disposition will be made despite the maudlin sentimentality and misplaced sympathy certain individuals have attached to this case. Were such persons' views given free rein, the streets would soon be rendered a paradise for robbers, thieves, and other criminals—and a place of terror for law-abiding citizens."

Ah, yes, Casey thought, *this judge would not be taken in by the sentimentality that so many reporters had succumbed to.* No, Judge Martin had cut the legs off the bleeding-heart melodrama attendant to this case.

The judge continued. "The intelligent and conscientious manner in which you have carried out your duties as grand jurors merits the highest commendation and should serve as a pattern worthy of imitation. You have remembered that you were grand jurors appointed for a particular service, and you have carried out that service.

"I must also include in my commendations the many excellent men of Brooklyn's police force who have so ably executed their duties, including Detectives William J.

Casey and Frank S. Gray of the Eighty-eighth Precinct. The public appreciates all you fine civic servants."

Casey gave Frank a nod of congratulations, and Frank returned the gesture. Yes, Casey thought, this was what made his job worthwhile. And Commissioner Enright was pleased that this twosome had finally been brought to justice. Maybe Casey could take that vacation Fiona'd been hoping for after all.

The Brooklyn Daily Eagle, Page 3
May 6, 1924

MATRON'S REPORT ON CELIA'S
LIFE BARES GIRL BANDIT'S
HISTORY FROM COAL-PILE BED

Life for Celia Cooney, Brooklyn's two-gun girl, has been a series of hard knocks. From the time of her birth in a basement in the lower East Side of Manhattan to years ago she has been batted from pillar to post. Denied any home life, she spent many nights sleeping on coal piles in cellars and was brought up amid the most undesirable surroundings.

Upon Celia Cooney's arrest, Judge George W. Martin ordered an investigation into the girl's upbringing and history. Probation officer Mrs. Cristina Mahon sought out and interviewed several persons familiar with the family.

Following is the complete report submitted to Judge Martin today:

"The defendant was born at 38 E. Fourth Street, New York City, twenty years ago in a basement. The parents had eight children, and Celia was the youngest. Her father's name is Michael Roth, and the mother's name is Evelyn Roth. The parents were born in New York City. The mother can neither write nor read and never went to school. The father has had very little education and has been a habitual drunkard all his life. He has never worked steadily and never supported his family. What little support came into the family came through the mother. The children were sadly neglected, and were sent out to beg; they had been known as little children to sleep all night on the coal pile in the cellar and in the early morning aroused and sent out on the street. Half the time the children were scantily clad and had very little to eat."

Sent Children to Beg

"The father's record is as follows: Oct. 28, 1899, summoned to the Third District Court, Manhattan, and ordered to keep sober and send the children to school. None of the children had been attending school but had been sent begging. Lived in one furnished room, 169 Allen St., Manhattan. The house was visited by disreputable people. When neighbors took pity on the children and gave them clothing it disappeared, and any money realized on it was used by the father for drink. They were finally put out of this room, the children and the parents, and they moved to 171 Essex St.

"On Nov. 21, 1899, the Charities Department recommended that the children be committed to an institution.

"On Jan. 16, 1900, the father was sent to the penitentiary for three months. He pleaded guilty to violation of Section 288 of the Penal Code. It has been alleged that the father was arrested several times for illegal voting and fighting in saloons. It is said that he has also been beaten up on several occasions and taken to the hospital.

"On Jan. 22, 1900, three children—May, Maggie, and Annie Roth—were committed to St. Agatha's Home because of improper guardianship. They had been found deserted by their parents. These three girls remained in the home until they were fourteen years of age when they were taken away by an aunt, Miss Margaret Roth, and Mrs. Shorlein, another aunt of the children, residing at 2014 Grove St. These two aunts have both stated that the children were sadly and painfully neglected. The children never had a home; the parents had absolutely no love or affection for them; and the aunts were not surprised at the actions of Celia. They also stated that the father of Celia, their brother, was a habitual drunkard and had never worked.

"The mother had an illegitimate child before she was married to Roth. This child, when he was thirteen years of age, was adopted into a family in the country, through Pastor Leonhard of the Oliver Chapel, 20th St."

Mother Was Heartless

"The mother always was heartless and most unnatural to the children, seldom visiting or seeing the children when they were with the aunts, and not seeing them for years at a stretch. Although at times she worked and made a little money, her attention was turned always toward her husband, and the children were totally abandoned and uncared for by her. She has worked at different times in different hotels, the last place being the Ritz-Carlton, where she worked from June 1923 to Feb. 22, 1924, as a scrub woman. She left this place on a telephone call from her husband and never returned.

"The defendant, Celia Cooney, about June 25, 1908, then about four years of age, was in the charge of the Children's Society of New York. On Dec. 17, 1908, Celia was given to her mother through the Children's Bureau of the Department of Public Charity. Shortly after Celia was found by neighbors deserted for three days in a furnished room. Miss Roth, the aunt, took Celia to live with her in Brooklyn. She sent Celia to a Catholic parochial school. From the time Celia was first taken by the aunt until she was fourteen years old, the mother came on several occasions, had Celia all dressed up by her aunt, and took her to New York with her. She kept her in a furnished room and later deserted her after she had taken the child's clothes from her. When Celia would be found by neighbors she would be dirty and ragged and would be returned to her aunt. This happened on several occasions. Meanwhile, two of the older sisters had grown up and gone to work and had established a home in Brooklyn, asking the mother to take care of the home and little Celia. The mother came there with Celia, but it wasn't long before she brought the father in, too, meeting and feeding him during the day at the home at the expense of the two girls, neglecting Celia and failing to properly provide dinner for the girls when they returned in the evening, and finally leaving them altogether, going away with her husband."

Left Brooklyn When Fourteen

"At about the age of fourteen years, Celia left her home in Brooklyn, going to live with her mother. There she remained for a very short period and came back to Brooklyn to live with a married sister at 97 Prospect Pl.

She remained there about one year. During that time she worked steadily in a brush factory. This sister states that Celia left her home because she disapproved of her remaining out at night and associating with and bringing sailors into the home. Although Celia was ambitious and always worked, the sister states she would steal little things. Celia left her sister's home and went to live with her mother in a furnished room in New York. Celia was then about sixteen years of age and the sisters heard nothing more of her until the present case came up.

"The employers of Celia were: New York Hospital (laundry), Feb. 25, 1919, to June 30, 1919. Stated they had nothing against her.

"St. Luke's Hospital (laundry), Aug. 18, 1919, to Sept. 1, 1919, then returned June 5, 1920, and left Dec. 17, 1920. Authorities say she was very noisy, troublesome, and very impertinent and, finally, they had to discharge her.

"Lincoln Hospital (laundry), Jan. 21, 1921, to April 13, 1921, a good worker, steady, jolly disposition, no trouble at all.

"Women's Hospital (laundry) worked there about four years ago from April to June and returned twice afterwards. There she was discharged. She was considered a ringleader, upsetting the place. She was very bold: She would take the good girls away from the place, taking them to out-of-town places, and, when questioned about their movements, she would lie. She also worked for Sheldon Foster, 572 DeKalb Ave., in the laundry. There she was considered a good worker, steady and no fault could be found with her, in fact, they would give her a recommendation."

Rents Room for 'Husband'

"About March 1922, she rented a furnished room for 'me and my husband,' at 4139 Franklin Ave., for which she paid $30 a month from a Mrs. Vatilli. She lived there until April 18, 1923, with a man named Cherison. She went to work steadily and so did the man who was known in the house as her husband. This man was positively not Cooney. She never took anything in the house, and the house was always left open.

"From May to Sept. 1923, she lived at 461 Franklin Ave., where she had a room for $8 a week. Mrs. Gallagher was the owner. There she lived with Cooney, having married him in May of 1923. Mrs. Gallagher states that she stole $20 out of her pocketbook and a picture worth $40. Mrs. Gallagher states she used vile language, fought with all the roomers, and they were all afraid of her. Mrs. Gallagher had finally dispossessed her.

"Next, at 52 Madison St., she rented a $7 furnished room from a Mrs. Ford who says the girl was a good tenant, and she was sorry when she left.

"The investigator located two aunts, two sisters, an uncle in New York, and the parents of Celia Cooney. The sisters, the aunts, and the uncle all stated that the environment of the house while these children were small was the worst that could possibly exist."

<h1 style="text-align:center">The Sentencing
Brooklyn, May 6, 1924</h1>

The day rolled around pretty quickly—the day the judge would sentence them. Celia was sorry to be leaving Raymond Street jail. Warden Honeck had allowed her and Ed to visit every few days and let her read his day-old newspapers. She figured she and Ed wouldn't get that kind of consideration at the next place.

The guards fetched her after breakfast, and Ed was waiting for her in the bright red paddy wagon. She stepped into the back of the wagon and sat down beside him. They were both in handcuffs, and the guard slammed the door on them. The two guards sat in the front of the wagon, so they had some time alone together on the way to court.

Ed gave her a peck on the lips. "Hi, sweets, how you feeling?"

As she reached over and took his hand, their handcuffs clinked. "I figure we might as well start doing our time so we can get it over with."

"I'll probably get a longer sentence. You going to wait for me?"

"You think I want to be free when you're still behind bars? Besides, there's no reason you should get a longer sentence. I was right there beside you."

"Yeah, but like I already told the judge, I was the

ringleader."

"If I get out first, I'll try to get you out. Maybe go talk to that Sam Leibowitz."

"Maybe we should've listened to him from day one."

"No sense crying over spilled milk," she said. "And Bill told us the judge would go easier on us if we just said we're guilty."

"The fellas on my block said we were fools to believe that—that the coppers will always want you to plead guilty because it makes their life easier. And they get to notch a win."

Celia figured those fellas probably knew better than they did. When she and Ed started the stick-up business they were babes in the woods and didn't know diddly about coppers and the law. "Maybe we were simps, but what's done is done."

"I just hope we end up at the same place and can see each other sometimes."

"Yeah, I told the judge we want to go to the same joint. I'm hoping he will show us some mercy. And maybe not give us the maximum either."

Ed gave her a tight-lipped smile and squeezed her hand. The paddy wagon rolled out onto the street, and when they got close to the County Court Building, Celia saw a big crowd milling around. The paddy wagon had to slow down because people and reporters were mobbing the car, taking pictures and gawking at them like they were a circus attraction.

She wasn't surprised by the crowd because she'd been getting lots of letters from people she didn't know from

Adam. A few told her she deserved to burn in hell, but most of them were from girls who said things like, "You are the bravest girl in Brooklyn and don't let the coppers and judges beat you down." She couldn't possibly respond to them all, but it was swell of so many girls to write her. She didn't tell Ed about all those letters because she knew he wasn't getting any and she didn't want him to feel like a heel.

Once the paddy wagon squeezed through the crowd, it pulled over to the curb in front of the court building. Two rows of cops cleared an aisle for her and Ed, and the guards hustled them up the stairs and into the courtroom. They sat them down in a little room and told them they had to wait for their turn on the docket.

About an hour after they got there, the guards marched them into the packed courtroom. As they took their place in front of Judge Martin, cameras popped from every which way. They'd had so many pictures taken of them since they'd gotten back to New York that every single person who read a newspaper could have picked them out on the street.

While they stood there looking at the judge this guy off to his side said, "Edward and Celia Cooney, have you anything to say why this judgment should not be passed on you?"

Ed studied his feet and shook his head. Celia looked the judge in the eye and said, "No, nothing."

Everybody in the courtroom started jabbering then, and Judge Martin called out, "Silence, this is a court of law."

Everybody shut their yaps, and all Celia could hear was shuffling feet.

Judge Martin spoke up, and because it was so quiet in the courtroom his voice boomed like some street hawker. "I have talked to you before, both of you, about the crimes you have confessed. I have given you every opportunity to tell the police and to tell me in my chambers about the crimes. I have had you examined as to your sanity, and you have been found sane. I am going to give you a lesson that you cannot carry on as you have been doing around Brooklyn.

"You are sentenced, both of you, to the maximum for your crime, ten to twenty years. You, Edward Cooney, will serve your sentence at Sing Sing. You, Celia Cooney, will be housed at Auburn Prison."

Celia's knees went wobbly. The maximum—they were getting the maximum sentence. And going to different places. She wouldn't see her Eddie for all those years. Her heart sank in her chest. But she wasn't going to cry, not in front of a roomful of rubberneckers.

She twisted around and looked at the crowd, holding her head up high to show she still had an ounce of pride left and that she was taking her medicine like a man. There, right in the front row, sat her parents. She hadn't seen them in at least four years. They looked awful haggard. Her mother had a bruise on her face, and Celia knew who she got it from. No way was she going to say a word to them, not after how they'd treated her all those years when she was nothing but a scraggly little squirt. And she didn't like how the lady who wrote a report on her smeared her private affairs all over the papers. Jeez, just because the judge asked this woman to dig around in her business didn't mean she had to hand the dirt over to every newspaper in the city.

Anyway, Celia wondered what in the world her parents were doing in the courtroom. Did they think someone might pay them to take their picture or say a few words about her? Fine, let them do whatever they wanted. She'd finished with them years ago. Just like her brothers and sisters.

She braced herself and marched out of that courtroom like she was a soldier doing her duty. When they got back to that little room and the door closed behind them she dropped her cuffed-together hands in front of her and gave Ed an armless hug.

"You okay?" She turned her head sideways and nestled against his chest.

"I ain't happy. We didn't get any kind of leniency by pleading guilty. We been duped."

"Yeah, I guess that's the truth. We shouldn't have trusted Bill so much. But there's nothing to do now but face the music."

"Come on, you two," the burly guard said. "We need to get you back to Raymond Street."

The paddy wagon was waiting for them outside the courthouse. When Celia got to her cell, it all came crashing down on her—how she'd be locked up like an animal, never see her Eddie, and be treated like the hoodlum she was. She couldn't help herself. She started balling. The tears rolled down her cheeks. How was she going to manage all those years without her Eddie?

The gal in the cell next to hers said, "Hey, sugar, what are you crying about?"

She sniffled and wiped her tears. "I just got ten to twenty in Auburn."

This girl had been at Auburn and told Celia what to expect, and she knew it was going to be bad. She'd have to wear scratchy clothes, get up at six every morning, and work, work, work. Celia asked this girl what kind of work she'd have to do, and the girl asked her what she'd done before she got picked up. When Celia told her she'd worked in a laundry, she said that she'd probably draw laundry duty.

Celia started cackling. Wouldn't you know—she was going back to what she hated most, back to aching feet and wet steam and the mangle. It was so pitiful to think about she couldn't do anything but laugh. Life was taking her around in one big, hard-hearted circle.

Warden Honick came by later that day and asked her how she was doing. She told him she couldn't complain, that the judge was all business, and she supposed she was owed the sentence he gave her. And she asked the warden if she could see Ed again before they got shipped out. He said he'd think about it. He didn't sound too sure, so the next day, she wrote him a note asking again. She said she wanted to give her Eddie one more smile before they said goodbye for all those years.

When Friday came, the warden visited and told her to get ready for the train trip to Auburn. He said he'd bring Ed around so they could say goodbye. A few minutes later, Ed came to her cell and they sat down on her bed together.

She started crying, which was exactly what she didn't want to do.

Ed cried, too. "I'm so sorry, Celia. I did you wrong, and now we're both paying for it."

She stopped her blubbering so they could have some final words. "Don't say that. We're in this together. I love you, and when we get out we're going to start a new life together. And keep clean. We got some money to get us going."

Ed swiped his hands over his cheeks to dry his tears. "Yeah, I'll start a welding business, and we'll go straight. I won't ever do you wrong again. I promise."

"I know, Eddie. I know I can trust you. I'll write you letters. Will you write to me?"

"Sure I will. And we both got to keep our noses clean in prison. Maybe we can get out early for good behavior. I heard they do that sometimes."

"I won't be a troublemaker. I just want to start over again with you."

They nestled up against each other and hugged each other tight. Tears pressed at her eyes, but she managed to stifle them.

The warden unlocked the cell. "Okay, Ed, it's time for me to take Celia to the train station."

They stood up, and she looked into Ed's face. His eyes looked so sad. She gave him a smile and a poke in the chest.

"So long, kid," he said, turning and walking away.

She called after him, "Hey, tall guy, I'll see you in my dreams."

Afterword

About six weeks after Celia and Ed began their prison sentences, Ed was transferred to Auburn, and he and Celia were allowed half-hour visits once a month. They wrote letters between visits. Celia became a model prisoner. She worked in the laundry for three years but took courses in shorthand and typing and worked her way up to a clerical position in the warden's office. She went on to teach typing and stenography to other inmates. She took full advantage of the prison library, borrowing the maximum allowable books and magazines, and also took courses in practical nursing and cooking.

Ed was not so fortunate. A few months after he was transferred to Auburn, his hand was mangled in a license-plate machine. There were complications, followed by a series of surgeries, and Ed's arm was amputated just below the elbow. He contracted tuberculosis and was sent to a TB hospital at another prison. He and Celia had had only two years together at Auburn, but they continued to write regularly.

Ed was released from prison after seven years, in October of 1931, and Celia joined him in November. Ed, with the help of the law offices of Sam Leibowitz, filed suit against the state for loss of his arm and contraction of tuberculosis. The decision was handed down in December

1931, and Ed was awarded a cash settlement of $12,000, half of which went to his attorneys.

Ed and Celia bought a house and settled on Long Island, where their two sons Patrick and Ed Jr. were born. But Ed never fully recovered his health, and he died at age thirty-seven in 1936. Celia moved to an apartment in Queens, which burned down in 1939, leaving her homeless. To get money for a new start, she sold her story to the magazine *Modern Romances*. The series, "What the World Didn't Know: The True Story of the Bobbed-Haired Bandit," ran for four months in 1940.

Once her sons started school, Celia worked at a variety of jobs and, during the war, she took a position at a war plant. She married a bus driver in 1943. They separated after only a few years, but she kept his name. Celia's sons said she was a devoted and hard-working mother who charmed all who met her.

Her youngest son, Ed Jr., looked after her in her late years when they both moved to Florida. Celia was diagnosed with Alzheimer's there, and around 1989 was placed in a nursing home. Her memory may have been failing, but her fetching personality still shone through. She became the darling of the nursing staff and residents. She died in 1992 at age eighty-eight.

At one point during her nursing home stay, she mentioned she didn't want to be taken back to New York (after being retrieved from one of her many wanders) because they'd find out she was the bob-haired bandit. Ed Jr. thought she was spouting nonsense. But after Celia died, Ed Jr. and Patrick did some digging and uncovered

the story of the bob-haired bandit, which was a shock to
them: How had their mother covered up such a big secret
all those years? In the end, Celia had kept her promise to
build a new life.

Notes, Acknowledgments,
and Resources

The story of Celia and Ed Cooney captured the attention of not just New York City but the whole nation for much of 1924. The novelty of a girl bandit and the police force's inability to round up the gun girl and her tall companion led to a journalistic feeding frenzy. Newspapers angled to report the most alluring details and competed for the public's attention with ever more eye-catching headlines and exaggerations. The story had it all—a bold and pretty young girl toting a pint-sized pistol, her handsome but seemingly reticent tall companion, police ineptitude, and Robin Hood daring.

This account is based on the true story of the bob-haired bandit and faithfully adheres to most of the details, including the actual robberies and tactics police employed in efforts to apprehend her. Many Brooklyn detectives figured in the search, too many to accurately portray in a work of straightforward fiction. Thus, portraits of some of the detectives are composites. Also, some characters' names have been modified to avoid confusion among similarly named characters. A few dates have been shifted around in the interest of clarity and narrative pacing, and some of the newspaper reports have been tweaked or blended for the sake of simplicity or parsimony. Still, all the newspaper text is taken from actual articles of the day. My aim was to accurately capture the story that gripped the country for much of 1924.

I consulted many sources in bringing this story to the page, and I am especially grateful to Stephen Duncombe and Andrew Mattson for their excellent analysis of this story and its cultural, political, and economic context in their nonfiction book, *The Bobbed Haired Bandit: A True Story of Crime and Celebrity in 1920s New York*. I highly recommend their book to anyone who wants to take a deep dive into the story and times. I'd also like to thank Elizabeth K. Mahon for bringing the bobbed-haired bandit to my attention in her fascinating book *Pretty Evil: True Stories of Mobster Molls, Violent Vixens, and Murderous Matriarchs*. Thanks are due to my wonderful beta readers Tonya Mitchell and Kerry Cathers and to editor extraordinaire Andra Miller.

Below are some of the many sources utilized or quoted in the novel.

Bibliography and Resources

"2-Gun, Bob-Haired Bandit Holds up 6 in Boro Store," *The Brooklyn Daily Eagle*, February 24, 1924, p. 1.

"2 Stores Held Up By Armed Woman and Confederate," *The Brooklyn Daily Eagle*, January 13, 1924, pp. 1, 5.

"A Word for the Yeggs," *The Brooklyn Eagle*, April 3, 1924, p. 6.

"Bobbed-Haired Bandit and Husband Plead Guilty—Are Jailed," *The Brooklyn Daily Eagle*, April 23, 1924, p. 1.

"Bobbed-Haired Bandit May Be a Boy: Cusses Like Sailor But Has Feminine Feet," *The Brooklyn Eagle*, February 3, 1924, p. 4a.

"Bobbed-Haired Bandit's Own Story," *New York American*, Twelve installments running from April 28 to May 10, 1924.

"Bobbed-Haired Girl Bandit Keeps the Town Guessing," *The Brooklyn Standard Union*, February 11, 1924, p. 1.

"Bobbed-Haired Girl Captured as Store Bandit," *New York Herald*, January 15, 1924, p. 1.

"Bob-Hair Bandit Robs 2 More Shops," *New York Telegram and Evening Mail*, January 13, 1924, p. 1.

"Bob-Haired Bandit Fully Identified by 12 of Victims," *The Brooklyn Daily Eagle*, April 23, 1924, p. 1.

"Bob-Haired Bandit Known to Police: Wide Alarm Out," *The Brooklyn Daily Eagle*, April 15, 1924, p. 1.

"Cooneys Plead Guilty When Arraigned For First Degree Robbery," *The Brooklyn Citizen,* April 23, 1924, p. 1.

"Court Intimates Girl Bandit Will Get Limit Sentence," *The Brooklyn Daily Eagle*, May 1, 1924, p. 3.

"Demotion of Fourteen Sleuths of Old School and Promotion of New Men Startles Police," *The Brooklyn Citizen*, February 3, 1924, p. 1.

"Detectives Here Organize Bobbed-Haired Bandit Squad." *The Brooklyn Standard Union*, February 28, 1924, p. 1.

Duncombe, Stephen, and Mattson, Andrew. *The Bobbed Haired Bandit: A True Story of Crime and Celebrity in 1920s New York*. New York: New York University Press, 2006.

"Enright Takes Charge of Girl Bandit Hunt," *The Brooklyn Citizen,* February 8, 1924, pp. 1, 5.

"Ex-Chorus Girl Arrested as Chain Store Bandit," *The Brooklyn Standard Union*, January 15, 1924, pp. 1, 18.

"Gang of Bobbed-Haired Bandits Here; 2-Gun Blond Cultured, Brunette Nervy." *The Brooklyn Daily Eagle*, March 7, 1924, p. 3.

"Girl Bandit Adds Another to Long List of Hold Ups," *The Brooklyn Standard Union*, January 23, 1924, pp. 1, 18.

"Girl Bandit and her Aide Back at Work," *The Brooklyn Citizen*, February 3, 1924, p. 1.

"Girl Bandit Believed Known; Wed and Lived Near Police," *The Brooklyn Standard Union*, April 15, 1924, pp. 1, 18.

"Girl Bandit Leaves Note Saying Police Made False Arrest," *The Brooklyn Citizen,* January 16, 1924, p. 1-2.

"Girl Bandit Ubiquitous," *The Brooklyn Citizen,* March 8, 1924, p. 4.

Kolisch, Mitzi. "Celia Cooney Calm While Mate Wilts," *The Brooklyn Citizen*, April 23, 1924, p. 1.

Mahon, Elizabeth K. "Celia Cooney: The Bobbed Haired Bandit." In *Pretty Evil: True Stories of Mobster Molls, Violent Vixens, and Murderous Matriarchs*. Guilford, CT: Globe Pequot, 2021, pp. 157-174.

"Matron's Report on Celia's Life Bares Girl Bandit's History From Coal Pile Bed," *The Brooklyn Daily Eagle*, May 6, 1924, p. 3.

"Mob Greets Bobbed Gun Girl," *New York Daily News*, April 23, 1924, pp. 1, 3, 12.

"Police Get a Clue to Bob-Hair Bandit," *The New York Times*, April 16, 1924, p. 24.

"Salesgirl is Held as New Girl Bandit With Two Youths," *The Brooklyn Citizen*, January 18, 1924, p. 1.

"Shakeup Seen for Detectives of Brooklyn," *The Brooklyn Citizen,* February 9, 1924, p. 1.

"Shoot to Kill Edict Fails; Girl Bandit Strikes Again," *The Brooklyn Standard Union*, February 10, 1924, pp. 1, 22.

"Two Stores Robbed by New Hold Up Gang, Bob-Hair Girl Busy," *The Brooklyn Standard Union*, February 11, 1924, p. 16.

"Woman With Gun Holds Up Six Men as Pal Robs Store," *The Brooklyn Daily Eagle*, January 6, 1924, p. 1.

www.ingramcontent.com/pod-product-compliance
Lightning Source LLC
Chambersburg PA
CBHW030528190726
48283CB00006B/1820